Fifty Tales of Toronto

Donald Jones' walking tours of Toronto have drawn crowds of up to 5000 at a time. His 'Historic Toronto' column in the *Star* has proved one of the city's most widely read newspaper features. Now for the first time he has gathered together some of his personal favourites · stories of triumph and treachery, the celebrated and the notorious. The result is a richly entertaining collage of amazing and amusing tales o the city and its people.

Here we learn that the first airmail plane in Canada landed in Toronto so loaded with liquor it could barely fly. We find out how a forgery by John Strachan brought tens of thousands of immigrants to the city. Jones recounts the visits to Toronto by great writers, including Oscar Wilde and Charles Dickens, and tells of Torontonians who made international names for themselves, like Bea Lillie and Elizabeth Arden.

Old mysteries still unsolved are reconsidered: Was the founder of Upper Canada College the real hero of the battle of Waterloo? How did Prince George, remembered in the name of the Princes' Gates, really die? Did Toronto's Captain Roy Brown in fact kill the Red Baron during 'the most controversial 60 seconds in the history of aerial warfare'?

At the heart of his stories are people. Some of their names have been forgotten and deserve to be remembered: Dr Anderson Abbott, Canada's first black doctor, who was greatly admired by Lincoln; Margaret Saunders, whose book *Beautiful Joe* has sold 7 million copies to date; and Ernest Jones, who helped Freud escape from Austria and the Gestapo.

Old Toronto comes vividly to life in these tales. For the hundreds of thousands of *Star* readers who love Donald Jones' columns, here is a collection of the best. And for those who have yet to discover the delights of his perspective on the city, *Fifty Tales of Toronto* provides a marvellous introduction to its history.

Donald Jones was born and educated in Toronto and has published nearly 1000 stories of Toronto in the *Star* over the years. For his articles and his walking tours he has received a Toronto Historical Board Award of Merit and a Heritage Canada award.

DONALD JONES

FIFTY TALES OF TORONTO

UNIVERSITY OF TORONTO PRESS

Toronto Buffalo London

Printed in Canada

ISBN 0-8020-2761-X (cloth)
ISBN 0-8020-7697-1 (paper)

Printed on acid-free paper

Cover illustration: *View of King Street, Toronto, 1844/45* by John Gillespie. Oil on paper. Courtesy: Royal Ontario Museum. Gift of Miss Isabel Howarth. Accession Number 955.175

This view of the original centre of Toronto, looking west from the corner of King and Jarvis Streets, shows the spire of an earlier St James' Cathedral, the Market building at the far left (on the site of today's St Lawrence Market) and the long line of shops that impressed Charles Dickens during his visit in 1842. Almost every building in this picture, including St James', was destroyed in the great fire of 1849.

Canadian Cataloguing in Publication Data

Jones, Donald, 1924-
Fifty tales of toronto

ISBN 0-8020-2761-X (bound) ISBN 0-8020-7697-1 (pbk.)

1. Toronto (Ont.) — History. I. Title.

FC3097.4.J65 1992   971.3'54   C92-094815-4
F1059.5.T685J65 1992

This book has been published with the assistance from the Canada Council and Ontario Arts Council under their block grant programs.

Contents

Preface

Toronto and Torontonians hold a unique place in the literary history of this country.

In 1883, in spite of objections from some of the wealthiest and most powerful figures in the city, Torontonians voted in overwhelming numbers to establish a public library supported entirely with public money. With a proper sense of the importance of what had taken place, the city announced that this library would be opened on one of the single most historic days in Toronto's history. On March 6, 1884, on the 50th anniversary of the day when the little town of York became the new City of Toronto, the first free public library in all Canada was opened in a building on Church Street in downtown Toronto.

From its first planning stage, it was agreed it would be no ordinary library. In addition to building a large collection of works of fiction and books on the sciences, one of the library's principal goals would be the fostering of pride and the spreading of knowledge about all things Canadian, especially the history of Toronto. As a result, more than a century ago, Toronto was one of the few cities in North America that began to preserve records of its heritage before they were lost.

Today, the world's single most important collection of books, manuscripts, photographs, paintings, and ephemera about Toronto and its people is in the history department of the Metropolitan Toronto Reference Library. A daily record of the city's life and growth was also to be preserved. As a result the world's most complete collection of nearly one hundred newspapers published in Toronto since the 1790s – some lasting for only a few months and others enduring more than a century – is now in the library's newspaper department.

Since the end of the 19th century, the library's collection has been a principal source of material for everyone who has written about this city, and has been the main source for the stories I have written over the past eighteen years. Since the founding of that library, and particularly during the decades since the 1950s, close to a hundred archives as well have been established in the greater Toronto region to preserve records of individual societies and organizations. A large number of my stories dealing with very specialized fields would never have been possible without their resources.

My debt is to a greater number of these archives than I can possibly list here, but as an indication of the range of these special centres, the following are some I have used most frequently over the years: the City of Toronto Archives; the Archives of Ontario; the University of Toronto Archives and the archives of its many colleges; the Archives of the Roman Catholic Archdiocese of Toronto; the Academy of Medicine Archives; the Toronto Board of Education Archives; the Art Gallery of Ontario Archives; and the Royal Ontario Museum Archives. For those who have recently started to research the history of Torontto, a complete list of archives in the Toronto area can be found in any of the city's major archives.

Other major institutions such as the Toronto Historical Board and the Ontario Heritage Foundation have also been invaluable in my research.

But, most especially, it is to a host of reference librarians and archivists and their staffs to whom I am most beholden. I doubt if my career would have survived beyond the 1970s without their support and encouragement, nor would I have been able to meet my weekly deadlines at the *Toronto Star* with all the pressures such deadlines entail. Any and all errors that have resulted and that may appear in this book are, of course, entirely my own.

The list of individuals I would like to thank could fill pages of this book. By right, it should include every member of every staff of all the libraries and archives where I have spent the greater part of my life during these past eighteen years. Since space prohibits such an undertaking, I must limit myself to those who were there at the crucial beginning and who have borne with me the longest, together with a few notable new supporters.

First, and beyond all question, the one person who has helped and guided my research more than any other is Christine Mosser, senior collections librarian of the history department at the Metropolitan Toronto Reference Library. I will never be able to express properly my great debt to her. Four other specialists at that library have also saved my stories (and my sanity) on more occasions than I can possibly tally. All of them were there at the beginning so it is impossible to list them chronologically, but alphabetically they are Keith Alcock of the newspaper department and three members of the history department's Baldwin Room: John Crosthwait, recently retired head of its picture collection, William Parker, curator of Ephemera, and Alan Walker. I would also like to single out my special thanks to Harold Averill of the University of Toronto Archives.

There are so many others: Marion Addison, Mary Allodi, Fern Bayer, Nancy Biehl, Robert Cupido, Marcia Cuthbert, Norma Dainard, Edith Firth, Rachel Grover, Ethlyn Harlow, Jeanne Hopkins, Luba Hussel, Gwen Ing, Scott James, Joan Kinsella, David Kotin, Mary McTavish, Kenneth MacPhearson, Linda Moon, Katharine Martyn, Julia Matthews, Philip Ower, Marjorie Pearson, Larry Pfaff, Henri Pilon, Elizabeth Price, Patricia Rogle, Victor Russell, Father R.J. Scollard, David Smith, Randall Speller, Alan Sudden, Anne Sutherland, Sheila Swanson, Faye Van Horne, Iqbal Wagle, and Leon Warmski – but no list will ever be complete. I am, in particular, deeply indebted to the entire staff of the Baldwin Room and the history department of the Metropolitan Toronto Reference Library; the reference librarians and staff of the Robarts Library, the Thomas Fisher Rare Book Library and the microtext department of the University of Toronto Library; Donna O'Gorman and everyone in the Metro Urban Affairs Library (formerly the Municipal Reference Library); and the entire staff of the Gladys Allison Canadiana Room of North York's Central Library.

My thanks also to the many photographers and photographic departments who have contributed so significantly to whatever success my articles have achieved. Specifically, I would like to express appreciation and my great indebtedness to Sarah Peters and Dona Acheson of the Metropolitan Toronto Reference Library, James Ingram of the University of Toronto Library, Steve MacKinnon of the City of Toronto Archives, the photographers and staff of the photo department of the *Toronto Star* and the staff of the *Toronto Star*'s photo library, especially Sonja Noble and Ann Pritchard. In hundreds of cases over the years, the illustrations I have used were taken from 19th century material that was frequently faded, discoloured, even torn. The small miracles that were wrought by an untold number of artists and technicians have been a constant source of wonder to me.

For many of the illustrations in this book, a number of individuals and organizations took special photographs or secured rare archival photographs, and I would like to express my thanks to Richard Warren of the Toronto Symphony Orchestra Archives, Net Watson of the Toronto Mendelssohn Choir Archives, Marjorie Rebanie and Robert Leonard of the Legislative Assembly of Ontario, Carol Putt of the Canadian National Institute for the Blind, Betty St Jean of the Royal Canadian Mint, Vernon Mould of Upper Canada College, Thomas MacDonald of the Royal Canadian Legion (Earlscourt Branch), Rick Walsh of the Confederation Life Gallery of Canadian History, Elizabeth Arden Limited, and the Canadian Red Cross Society.

In the 1970s, I received a grant that enabled me to spend a summer exploring the possibility of producing a book like this, but it was too early in my career to complete the book I wanted. However, that initial research provided me with the concept for this one and I am most grateful to the Ontario Arts Council for that opportunity.

In 1973, at the beginning of my research into this city's past, it was Donna Baker who first persuaded me that I could become a teacher of its history, and it was Tim Kotcheff who first convinced me I could find a career in this field by hiring me as a regular contributor to the CBC-TV 6 o'clock news program.

My greatest debt is, of course, to the editors of the *Toronto Star* who, in 1973, had sufficient faith in my proposals to commission me to write a series of weekly articles about some forgotten but important places and people of Toronto. In the spring of 1991, when I was approaching my 1,000th weekly article for the *Saturday Star*, the editors allowed me an extended leave of absence to write this book. My deepest thanks are due to the late *Toronto Star* editor, James Rennie, who first gambled on me and commissioned the first articles, and to a succession of *Saturday Star* editors, most notably Geoff Stevenson and Vian Ewart, with special thanks to Stratton Holland who for most of the past 18 years edited my articles – all the artistry in their layouts was entirely due to him.

My thanks, also, to Ian Montagnes, editor of this book, who many, many years ago was one of the first to say that my stories about Toronto could one day be compiled into a worthwhile book.

My most heartfelt thanks go to those members of the crowds who have joined me on my tours of Toronto – who occasionally had to survive unexpected heatwaves and thunderstorms, but who stayed with me to the end, not because I may tell a good story, but because they cared about this city and its heritage. You made me even prouder of this city. This book, in large part, is thanks to you.

To everyone who has begun to discover what a fascinating city this is, I hope you will find that I have, in these pages, done some justice to a few of its lesser known romances.

Donald Jones
June 1992

Fifty Tales of Toronto

1

Monumental murals recall the pageantry of Canada

As a memorial to student soldiers, gigantic murals fill the auditorium walls of Jarvis Collegiate with some of the greatest moments in Canada's past.

It is one of the least known of all the major war memorials in Toronto, and fills the walls of a great room in the most historic school in the city.

In the years following World War I, schools in every part of Canada raised memorials to former students who died in that war. In Toronto, few schools lost more than Jarvis Collegiate Institute. Almost 100 of its former students were killed in the trenches of France.

When the war ended in 1918, all the teachers at Jarvis and a new generation of students began plans to raise a series of memorials to the fallen. The first would be a plaque with the names of those who had served and died in the war. The second would be an eternal flame. The third would be a painting that would hang in a place of honour on the wall of the school's auditorium.

When a Toronto artist learned of the plans for a painting, he offered to donate his time freely to the school. But, he said, the painting should not be a small work. He offered to fill the auditorium with a series of enormous murals that would serve not only as a memorial to those who had died; they would be a lasting reminder to all future generations of students of the glory and the history of the country those men had died for. By 1928, when the murals were formally unveiled, the hall had become a spectacular setting for scenes of the greatest moments in Canada's past.

The artist who volunteered to paint the murals was G.A. Reid, then at the height of his fame. He had been the founder of the Ontario College of Art and was a former president of the Royal Canadian Academy. He had been painting historical scenes of Canada for more than a quarter century and probably knew more about the subject than most history teachers of that time. He was in his sixties and the murals became one of the crowning works of his career.

On the wall to the far left of the stage Reid painted Alexander Mackenzie at the moment he became the first European to cross the North American continent and stand on the shore of the Pacific Ocean. Beside that mural he painted a fleet of ships bringing thousands of the first United Empire Loyalists to Upper Canada. On the other walls he painted scenes from the lives of the early explorers – Jacques Cartier and John Cabot and Samuel de Champlain – and high above the balcony he painted a gigantic frieze that included more than forty more of the greatest figures in the early history of Canada.

The setting for these great murals is ideal, for Jarvis is not only the oldest collegiate in the city, it is the most historic. It was founded in 1807 when Toronto (then known as York) was a small town of a few hundred people. Its first main building, the little blue schoolhouse, stood behind today's St James' Cathedral on King Street. In the century that followed, the school moved to increasingly larger buildings, and under a variety of names – the Toronto Grammar School, the Toronto High School – until it finally moved to its present site at the corner of Jarvis and Wellesley Streets and received its present name.

In the 1920s, when Reid filled its assembly halls with murals, he was one of the most respected of Canada's painters. He was born in Wingham, Ontario, in 1860. From the time he was ten, he knew he wanted to spend the rest of his life as a painter.

Few artists were ever more proud of their country's history and its heritage. When as a youth he finally saved enough money to

G.A. Reid's murals of 'The Pageantry of Canada' dominated the auditorium of Jarvis Collegiate Institute soon after their unveiling.

study in Europe, he may have been the only Canadian art student in Paris who continued to use Canadian scenes as subjects for his paintings. He would pose Parisian workmen on the banks of the Seine, but he would paint them as if they were labourers on the banks of a Canadian river. It was in Paris that he first became fascinated by the idea of painting wall murals.

In the 1890s, while he was there, the city of Paris commissioned 96 artists to portray the history of their city on the walls of its new city hall. When Reid returned to Canada and settled in Toronto, he offered to paint scenes of Canada's history in Toronto's then-new (now the old) city hall. The officials refused to pay for such extravagances, so Reid painted them for nothing, and his murals can still be seen there.

He was determined that Canada should have a proper art school to train its young artists and in 1912 was the principal figure behind the founding of the Ontario College of Art in Toronto. He also donated more than 400 of his own works to the province for distribution to its schools in the hope that they might inspire young students to become painters.

By the 1920s he had also become one of Canada's most vocal

champions in the cause of murals in all public buildings. As he constantly reminded officials, murals were the oldest of all the branches of pictorial art.

In 1926, when he began his plans for the murals in Jarvis Collegiate, Reid knew that the final design for this vast war memorial would have to be more than simply a panoramic view of Canada's past. The focal point must be the two great murals that would be placed on either side of the stage.

For the mural on the left, he painted a majestic female figure, symbolizing Canada. In one hand she holds a scroll to signify freedom. In her other she holds a wreath as a token of merit recognized. On either side of her, Reid placed figures that would represent all the various people of Canada, and he titled the mural 'Patriotism.'

To the right of the stage Reid painted a single tall cenotaph, with a young girl laying a wreath at its base, and titled the mural 'Sacrifice.' On either side of the cenotaph, filling the rest of the painting, he placed educators, artisans, students, and representatives of all the other nation-builders of Canada. At the centre of both murals stand two young school cadets, holding high the flags of Great Britain and Canada.

In the summer of 1929, this Pageantry of Canada was formally unveiled before a proud assembly. Many years later, when a new generation of students enlisted in a second world war and reports of casualties started to reach Toronto, Reid was in his eighties; but he immediately began plans to fill the few remaining spaces on the walls of the auditorium at Jarvis Collegiate with a series of new war memorials. He never lived to complete them. On August 23, 1947, at the age of 87, he died at his home in Wychwood Park.

2

The royal opening of a 'royal' museum

In 1914 Queen Victoria's favourite son (not the Prince of Wales) opened the Royal Ontario Museum, and some of the first gifts included suits of armour from the owner of Casa Loma.

It was decided it should be an appropriately royal occasion. And so, in 1914, Queen Victoria's favourite son was invited to Toronto to open one of the most important structures to be built in the city in this century: the Royal Ontario Museum.

He was the first son of a reigning monarch to be appointed governor-general of Canada, and few royal figures in modern history were ever more universally popular. For years, the press called him 'the Soldier Prince,' and he was also called 'the ideal example of the royal type.' His official title was Duke of Connaught and Strathearn but he was popularly known as Prince Arthur. Today, his name is more familiar to millions of Canadians than any of the stories of his life. One of the principal ports on the Great Lakes was named after him and called Port Arthur (now part of Thunder Bay).

The Connaught Laboratories, also named after him, were opened in 1914 and, after the discovery of insulin in Toronto, were the first to produce that early 'miracle drug' against diabetes. One of the most famous regiments in Canada was named after his daughter and called The Princess Patricia's (the Princess Pat's) Canadian Light Infantry. In Toronto, a street just north of the ROM was named Prince Arthur Avenue.

When his appointment as governor-general in 1911 first was announced, the Canadian press carried countless stories about his military career and his earlier life as a young officer in Canada. At the time, however, only a few people were aware just how eagerly he was looking forward to his return to Canada.

The Soldier Prince was the seventh child and third son of Queen Victoria, born at Buckingham Palace on May 1, 1850. He was christened Arthur William Patrick Albert, and everyone in England knew why the Queen had named him Arthur. He had been born on the birthday of Britain's greatest living hero, Arthur Wellesley, Duke of Wellington, the victorious commander at the Battle of Waterloo. It was Wellington whom Victoria chose to be the god-father of her new son, and there has never been any question in the minds of historians of the royal family that Prince Arthur very quickly became Victoria's favourite son. In her diary she wrote, 'We adored our little Arthur from the day of his birth ... and he was ever like a ray of sunshine in the house.'

From his earliest years, his favourite toys were military figures. At the age of fifteen he entered the Royal Military Academy at Woolwich and three years later wrote a long letter to his mother about his pride in becoming an officer. In 1869, when he was 19, he was posted to Canada to join the 1st Battalion of the Rifle Brigade, then stationed in Montreal. He travelled extensively across the country and saw action as a member of the Red River expedition at the time of the Riel Rebellion of 1870. In a letter to his mother he wrote, 'The more I visit Canada, the more I like and admire the people.'

When his term of duty in Canada was over, he returned to England and was given the title Duke of Connaught and Strathearn by the Queen. Victoria was always concerned about whom he might marry. After he paid a visit to Prussia she was delighted to hear he had fallen in love with the beautiful and talented Princess Louise, daughter of that state's 'Red Prince,' Frederick. On March 13, 1879, the two were married at Windsor Castle. Victoria was enchanted by Louise, and a close and lifelong friendship developed between the two women. For the next 22 years the principal home of the Duke and Duchess was a suite of

The original building of the Royal Ontario Museum, opened in 1914,
had its front door on Bloor Street. When the ROM expanded
in the 1930s, this became its west wing.

rooms beside the Queen's own at Buckingham Palace.

In 1901, upon the death of Queen Victoria, her oldest son
became King Edward VII. Arthur assumed a number of major
military roles, including that of commander-in-chief of the Med-
iterranean force, constantly distinguishing himself.

From the moment he returned to Canada as governor-general,
he grew increasingly popular. He insisted that no series of programs or public engagements was too heavy for him, and anti-
royalists and even the most cynical newspaper reporters were soon
referring to him as a great gentleman.

In 1914, he warmly welcomed an invitation to come to Toronto
to open the city's most important new landmark, the Royal Ontario
Museum. The museum had been a gigantic undertaking, and had
become possible only when the University of Toronto offered to

provide a site on its campus at the corner of Bloor Street and Queen's Park Road and agreed to provide the expert ability necessary to mount the displays. The university also proposed to pay 50 per cent of the cost of the building; the other half would be paid by the provincial government.

Its first home was an elegant and imposing building 300 feet long and 60 feet wide, covering two and a half acres, with its main entrance on Bloor Street. Later buildings would fill most of the land to the east, with a new entrance facing Queen's Park Road; but that 1914 building, with its Renaissance-style balconies above the original main entrance, is still clearly visible from Bloor Street and now serves as the museum's west wing. On the opening day, March 19, more than a thousand officials and friends of the museum crowded into rooms on the top floor of the building to witness the ceremonies.

Many of Toronto's wealthiest families had donated gifts to ensure the immediate success of the museum. Sir Henry Pellatt, the owner of Casa Loma, gave an extensive collection of armour. The Massey family donated items from the time of Christ. Sir Edmund Osler donated an important collection of paintings of Canada's native people by the Toronto artist Paul Kane. Mrs H.D. Warren, who became such a generous benefactor of the museum over the years that she was known affectionately as its fairy godmother, donated a superb collection of Chinese porcelain. The head of a famous piano manufacturing company in Toronto in those days, R.S. Williams, donated a collection of more than 500 musical instruments and other musical items, dating back to Elizabethan times and earlier. The museum had also acquired collections from the fields of zoology, mineralogy, geology, and palaeontology.

After a personal tour of the museum, the Duke of Connaught expressed his great delight with both the variety and style of all the exhibits. 'I know of certain museums,' he said, 'which, although they possess many things of high value, appeal almost entirely to the experts. To my mind, this is a mistake. One of the most important functions of a museum is to share its treasures in a way that appeals to the ordinary mortal.'

He remained a highly popular figure throughout the five years of his term as governor-general. The only controversy that marred his time in office was his fury over not being allowed to serve as a military leader or, at least, an adviser when Canada entered World War I. These were roles the constitution of the country denied to all governors-general.

Soon after his return to England, in 1916, the sudden death of the Duchess of Connaught cast a shadow over the remainder of his life. It had been a long and happy marriage and, by the 1920s, the Duke gradually began to retire more and more from public life. When his eyesight began to fail, he withdrew entirely from all public duties. During those final years his daughter, Patricia, was his almost constant companion.

On January 16, 1942, aged 91, the last surviving son of Queen Victoria died at his country home at Bagshot Park in Surrey.

3

Two bronze cannon in Queen's Park recall Canada's greatest military heroes

Two cannon presented to the people of Toronto in 1859 have become lasting memorials to Canadians who received the British Empire's highest award for bravery.

Throughout this century, two of the most historic cannon in Canada have stood, largely unnoticed, in front of the main Parliament Buildings in Queen's Park. They are not the oldest or the most elaborately mounted of cannon, but they are among the most prized, for within their history are the stories of many of the greatest heroes in Canadian history.

Queen Victoria presented these cannon to the people of the City of Toronto in 1859. They were paraded through the streets with a full military escort and placed on two stone pedestals in Queen's Park. When the new Parliament Buildings were opened there in 1892, they were moved to a place of honour directly in front of the main entrance.

The inscriptions in Russian, Latin, and English tell part of their history. They state that the cannon were originally used by the Russians against British forces at the battle of Sebastopol during the Crimean War of 1853–6.

When wounded and dying British soldiers returned to England during that war, Queen Victoria regularly visited them in military hospitals. Told of the heroism that had been displayed by many of them under enemy fire, she ordered a special medal to be struck for those who had displayed extraordinary courage. It would be the highest award for bravery that could be bestowed upon anyone in the British Empire. And by royal command it would bear only two simple words on its face: 'For Valour.' It would be presented personally by the Queen herself, and would be called the Victoria Cross.

The bronze used to form the cross would be taken from Russian cannon captured during the war in the Crimea. Pairs of captured Russian cannon would also be sent to principal cities throughout the empire.

The first Canadian to receive the Victoria Cross was a soldier from Toronto, Lieutenant Alexander Dunn, for heroism during the charge of the Light Brigade at Balaclava in 1854. Five years later, Queen Victoria sent two of the captured Russian guns to his native city, and for almost 150 years they have commanded their place of honour in Queen's Park.

Bronze cannon in Queen's Park commemorate the heroism of Canada's Victoria Cross winners.

During that time, Canadians have been awarded the Victoria Cross for their courage in every war fought by the British Empire and Commonwealth. One of the most prominent was a young man from Deseronto, Ontario. George Fraser Kerr had recently turned twenty when World War I broke out in the summer of 1914. He went immediately to Toronto and enlisted as a private with the city's 3rd Battalion. He was with the first contingent of the Canadian Expeditionary Force that sailed for England, and from the time of his first experiences under fire became known to the men of his company as someone without fear.

In 1916, he was awarded the Military Medal for his courage at Sanctuary Wood. In 1917, he received the Military Cross for his actions at Amiens. He had been promoted to the rank of lieutenant, but his military career appeared to be over. He had been seriously wounded at Amiens. One of his arms was so badly shattered he could barely move it and he was officially listed as unfit for service.

In September 1918, while still in a convalescent ward in an army hospital, he learned that his regiment was to take part in a major advance. He immediately asked to be allowed to speak to the local military authorities and wangled his way out of the hospital. By the 27th he was back with his men of the 1st Central Ontario regiment, and ready to participate in one of the last great battles of the war.

As the Canadians advanced up the Arras-Cambrai Road and approached the German lines they were strafed by machine gun fire from a German machine gun nest. Kerr raced ahead of his men. According to *The Times' History of the War*, he rushed the strong point singlehanded and with such overwhelming impetuosity that he captured four machine guns and no fewer than 31 prisoners. Another soldier later recorded the final incident in that encounter, and it became one of the legends of the regiment. Before marching his prisoners back to the Canadian line, Kerr stooped and picked up a piece of chalk and wrote on each of the four guns, 'Captured by the 3rd Battalion.'

Kerr refused to believe he had acted particularly courageously, and didn't talk about what he had done. Several days later, Colonel 'Bart' Rogers was determined that he would discover the name of the young officer who had done such a great job. He paraded all his officers and went down the line asking each in turn, 'Did you do it?' Every officer denied being part of the operation. It was only when he reached Kerr that Kerr reluctantly admitted that he had been 'the young officer.' A few weeks later he was told he would be awarded the Victoria Cross.

In the years that followed the end of World War I, people wanted to forget the horror. There was little official recognition of the plight of thousands of badly wounded veterans. In 1929, the Prince of Wales (the future Edward VIII), who had served as an officer in the war, learned of the conditions faced by many of these men and their families and launched a fund-raising drive to help them.

To draw worldwide publicity and support, he invited every Victoria Cross winner to come to London. When word of the prince's campaign reached Ontario, the provincial government offered to pay the expenses for the ten men from Ontario who would attend. Kerr acted as their spokesman.

On November 9, more than 300 Victoria Cross winners – the greatest such assembly in history – were guests of honour at a dinner given by the Prince of Wales in the Royal Gallery of the House of Lords. Two days later, all the men paraded as a single unit to the Cenotaph in Whitehall for the Remembrance Day service.

The drive for funds was successfully launched, and back in Toronto George Kerr returned to his peacetime career, as manager of a metal supply house. On the morning of December 8, five days after his return, he was due to leave by train on a business trip to New York. It was a bitterly cold day and, after packing his bags, he went into the garage at the back of his home at 38 Cheltenham Avenue in Lawrence Park in North Toronto, to warm up his car.

While the motor idled, he apparently reached into the glove compartment for a magazine. A short time later he was found dead, slumped over the wheel, an open magazine in his hands. He had failed to realize that both garage doors had closed behind him. He had slipped into unconsciousness and been killed by carbon monoxide fumes from his exhaust.

There was no autopsy, no inquest. There was never any question that his death had been accidental. The funeral service was held at the Church of the Messiah, and he was accorded full military honours as one of Canada's gallant heroes of the recent war. When his coffin left the church, draped with a Union Jack, it was placed on a gun carriage. Seven Victoria Cross winners marched with the mourners in the long procession to his grave in Mount Pleasant Cemetery.

4

The 'loaded' story of Canada's first airmail flight

During Prohibition, Canada's first airmail letters arrived in Toronto in a plane so loaded down with cases of liquor it could barely fly.

In the summer of 1918, a small two-seater plane landed at the Leaside airport carrying the first letters ever sent by airmail in Canada. The story of that flight was front-page news and the Ontario government later erected one of its historical plaques to mark the site where the plane touched down.

One story about that flight was not told at the time – or for almost a half century afterwards. Along with the letters, the plane was smuggling a cargo of illegal liquor into dry Ontario. It had so many cases of scotch stashed on board that it could barely fly.

The events surrounding that flight are now recorded in all the major books about Canadian aviation but the flight itself was so unexpected that, even as the plane was approaching the airfield near Toronto, not even the mayor knew anything about it.

The man responsible was a young Canadian pilot named Brian Peck. Before World War I he had already flown his own aircraft at Calgary and become one of the Early Birds of America. In 1919, he would again make history by becoming the first Canadian to parachute successfully from a plane in Canada. During the early years of World War I he served overseas, but in the summer of 1918 he was posted to the Royal Air Force aerodrome at what

17

Canada's first air mail flight arrives at the Leaside airport in 1918.

was then the Toronto suburb of Leaside as an instructor with the 89th Training Squadron. He was a Montrealer and had not seen his family or friends for months. As soon as he arrived at Leaside he began trying to find a way to get to Montreal.

The personal story of how he engineered a flight, and the details of the smuggled cases of scotch, remained a secret for years. They were finally revealed when another of Canada's pioneer pilots, Frank H. Ellis, published a history of aviation in this country called *Canada's Flying Heritage.*

As Ellis told the story, Peck wangled the flight by convincing the authorities at Leaside airport that he could become a valuable part of their recruiting program. It was the closing months of the war and the number of recruits had fallen to almost zero. Peck offered to perform aerobatics over the centre of Montreal and end his performance by dropping thousands of recruiting leaflets. The commanding officer accepted the idea and on the morning of June 20, with a Corporal Mathers as passenger, Peck flew out of Leaside in a two-seater biplane, a Curtis JN4.

The flight to Montreal was uneventful. Peck's plane landed safely at the Bois Franc polo grounds outside Montreal and he immediately left the airfield to see his family. The next day, plans for the air show over Montreal had to be postponed because of a torrential rainstorm. While Peck happily celebrated his extra day, two Montrealers who had learned about his plans conceived an idea for a second promotional stunt. They began making plans to include a package of mail as cargo on his return flight to Toronto and thus inaugurate airmail delivery in Canada.

The two men were George Lighthall and Edmund Greenwood, both staunch executives of the Aerial League of the British Empire. They soon discovered where Peck was staying and won his consent. Then they got in touch with the postmaster-general at Ottawa and the grand plan for a historic first was enthusiastically approved.

Greenwood was made a temporary local postmaster. One hundred and twenty letters were selected at random from all the ordinary mail bound for Toronto and a small extra bundle of mail was addressed to local officials in Toronto. A rubber stamp was hastily made and the envelopes were stamped with the words 'Inaugural Service Via Aerial Mail – Montreal 23.6.18.'

As stamp collectors now know, the date proved wrong. Heavy rain struck again on June 23, but on the following day the skies finally cleared. That morning Peck raced his aircraft across the polo fields and pointed its nose into the sky, but the little plane was barely able to get off the ground.

Corporal Mathers, in the passenger seat, was not just holding the bag of airmail letters on his lap. He was also sitting on top of as many cases of Old Mull scotch as could be crammed into the narrow space. The extra cargo was part of an elaborate plot Peck had arranged in secret before leaving Toronto.

One of his friends at the Leaside airport, a lieutenant in charge of stores, was about to be married and had asked Peck to bring back 'something suitable' for the wedding celebrations. Ontario had introduced prohibition during World War I but Quebec had remained 'wet' and Ontario's thirsty drinkers were then resorting to every nefarious scheme possible to smuggle illicit liquor across the provincial border.

The Curtis JN4 had never been built to carry cargo. When Peck finally got his plane into the air he was able to keep it only 40 feet above the ground and had to fly underneath telegraph wires. Because of a strong west wind his ground speed was less than half what he expected and he was soon running out of fuel.

He had to make an unscheduled landing at Kingston but the only gasoline available was the ordinary kind – not designed for airplanes. He had no choice and filled his tank with several gallons, but once back in the air the engine began spluttering and missing so badly he had to make another stop at Deseronto. There he drained the tanks and filled them with proper aviation fuel and was soon on his way again.

In Toronto, news of the history-making flight had leaked to the press. Newspaper reporters were besieging Mayor Thomas Church's office for details, but the mayor knew nothing about the flight. Everything had happened so quickly that even the Toronto postmaster, William Lemon, knew nothing about it until the plane landed at Leaside. There, Peck requisitioned a car, drove into the city, and personally delivered the mailbag to the somewhat astonished postmaster, who gave the empty mailbag back to him as a souvenir.

The flight had taken slightly more than six hours. Peck had left Montreal at 10.30 a.m. and landed at Leaside at 4.55 p.m. All the letters he carried with him on that flight are now highly valued by stamp collectors. A single letter in fine condition sells for several thousand dollars; with a signature of Peck on the envelope the price is considerably higher. One of the letters was purchased for King George V and is now in the royal collection.

Captain Brian Peck, the pilot

The full story of all the events of that day has been recorded by J.I. Rempel in his *Town of Leaside*, for the flight made the little airport at Leaside one of the historic landmarks of Canada. And on September 6, 1958, in celebration of the 40th anniversary, the Ontario government placed one of its blue and gold historical plaques in front of the house at 970 Eglinton Avenue East. It marks the site where Canada's first airmail flight landed.

5

Roger Sheaffe and 'the most dramatic day in Toronto's history'

In 1813, as American troops attacked, Toronto experienced 'the nearest thing to an atomic blast in that age.' British troops abandoned the town; that night the Stars and Stripes flew from every flagpole.

On the morning of April 27, 1813, an overwhelming force of American troops landed on the shores of Toronto. British troops who attempted to defend the town were slaughtered on the beaches. At the height of the battle an explosion on an unprecedented scale totally destroyed the town's only fort. Moments later word spread through the streets that the British general, Sir Roger Sheaffe, had ordered the immediate retreat of all British regiments.

By nightfall, the town had surrendered and American troops began looting private homes. The occupation lasted for more than a week. Before the Americans pulled out they set fire to the town's parliament buildings.

Generations of Toronto families never forgave the British commander for abandoning the town. Sheaffe was branded a coward and a traitor, for the centre he had left to the enemy was no minor outpost of empire. It was the capital of the province.

To this day, writers and historians continue to argue over Sheaffe's decision. It is almost the only incident in his life anyone remembers. Yet, only a few months earlier, he had been the true victor of the celebrated battle at Queenston Heights.

Sir Isaac Brock, whose heroic monument overlooks Queenston Heights, had been killed in the opening moments of the battle. The man who assumed command and won what every military authority has always described as an unqualified victory was the 50-year-old Sheaffe.

In the aftermath of the loss of Toronto, he became one of the truly tragic figures in Canada's history. The full study of his life reads more like the tale of one of the brave but ill-fated heroes in a Robert Louis Stevenson novel. That story is told in the *Dictionary of Canadian Biography* by Carol M. Whitfield and Wesley B. Turner.

Sheaffe was born in Boston, Massachusetts on July 15, 1763, shortly before the outbreak of the American Revolutionary War. His father was a deputy collector of customs in the colony. When he died, Roger's mother had to turn the family home into a boarding house to support herself and her children.

In the face of an overwhelming American force, the munitions storeroom at Fort York was blown up before British soldiers abandoned Toronto during the War of 1812. It was the closest thing to an atomic blast in that age. The drawing is by a contemporary American artist.

With the revolution, the Duke of Northumberland moved his headquarters to Boston, and the city soon became overrun with British troops. Northumberland became acquainted with Mrs Sheaffe and her children, and decided to adopt the young Roger as his protégé. He arranged for him to be accepted into the British navy, and paid for his tuition at the famous Locke's Military Academy in London. There Sheaffe met the classmate, George Prevost, who, many years later, would destroy his career in Canada.

Northumberland remained Sheaffe's patron for many years, buying him a commission in the 5th Foot regiment, and seeing him well launched on a military career. In 1787, at the age of 24, Sheaffe came with his regiment to Canada, where he would spend most of the next 25 years of his life.

In 1794 he served as an emissary for the province's first lieutenant-governor, John Graves Simcoe, who was impressed and described him as 'a gentleman of great discretion, incapable of any intemperate or uncivil conduct.' It was not until sometime later that serious doubts began to arise from almost every quarter about his abilities as a military leader. He was proving to be a decidedly unpopular officer. General Brock, under whom he served, felt he was disciplining his men 'too harshly for small lapses' and had 'little knowledge of mankind.' Nonetheless, when war broke out with the United States in 1812, Sheaffe's former classmate, George Prevost, now governor-in-chief of Canada, appointed him to the senior army staff in Upper Canada.

Brock proved to be the first great British hero of that war when he successfully repelled an American invasion near Detroit. On October 13, 1812, when the Americans attempted another invasion and crossed the Niagara River, Brock was killed leading his men against the Americans, who had reached the top of Queenston Heights.

Sheaffe was Brock's second in command and quickly organized what Whitfield and Turner call a 'brilliant' manoeuvre, routing the enemy and capturing almost 1,000 American troops with almost no losses on the British side. A grateful British government conferred a baronetcy upon him and he became Sir Roger Sheaffe. He was also made chief military commander of Upper Canada and president of the province's government. Before long he moved his headquarters to Toronto (then known as York).

That first winter of the war passed uneventfully, but on April 27, 1813, a fleet of 14 American warships, carrying over 1,700 troops, sailed across the lake and attacked Toronto. In *The Battle of Little York* Canada's leading military historian, C.P. Stacey, described the events that followed as 'the most dramatic day in Toronto's history.'

Sheaffe had fewer than 700 British regulars to defend the town, and totally inadequate gunfire to repel any major invasion. In Stacey's words, 'Sheaffe decided that York must be given up, but he had no intention of surrendering his little force of regulars, for a line of retreat on Kingston was open.'

Before giving the command for a general retreat, Sheaffe ordered the Grand Magazine at Fort York to be blown up. Some said it contained as much as 500 barrels of gun powder. The explosion, wrote Stacey, 'was the nearest thing to an atomic blast in that age.' For miles around the town, people reported seeing a giant mushroom-shaped cloud rising over the site of the explosion.

The blast killed and wounded hundreds of Americans who had just reached the fort. Angered by these unexpectedly high losses, American troops stormed the town, looting and burning many of its buildings.

From the moment Sheaffe ordered a retreat, there was controversy over whether he had acted correctly in abandoning the town. He was well aware that Prevost wanted to wage a purely defensive war, based on holding Montreal and Quebec at all costs. But many of the leading figures in Toronto, including the Reverend John Strachan, then the minister at St James', openly started accusing Sheaffe of cowardice. When these accusations reached Prevost, he informed Lord Bathurst, the British secretary for war and the colonies, that Sheaffe had 'lost the confidence of the province.' Prevost then asked that Sheaffe be recalled. In November Sheaffe was ordered to leave his post and return to England.

He was in his fifties and had been seriously ill for many months, but, while other old soldiers may 'simply fade away,' Sheaffe was nowhere near the end of his career. To many influential people in Britain, he had proved a highly capable commander during his long tenure in Canada. He would continue to serve in the British army for more than another quarter century. In 1829 he was made colonel of the 36th Foot, and in 1838 at the age of 75 was promoted to the rank of general.

At the end of a long and, some would say, distinguished military career, he retired to Edinburgh where, on July 17, 1851, he died two days after his 88th birthday. His name, however, would be engraved on few Canadians memorials. Even today, Brock continues to be honoured for the battle Sir Roger Sheaffe won.

6

Anne Powell's fatal love affair

*A terrifying infatuation, involving two
of the town's most prominent families, led to a
notorious scandal in the early
history of Toronto.*

It is a story that would have fascinated the Brontë sisters or Jane
Austen.

In the early 1800s, when Toronto was a small town of fewer
than 2,000 people, the daughter of a socially ambitious family fell
fatally in love with a young lawyer who would become one of
the most powerful men in that province. Anne Powell, the re-
bellious daughter of Chief Justice William Dummer Powell, had
become hopelessly infatuated with John Beverley Robinson, one
of the heroes of the recent War of 1812. There is no question that
Robinson was initially attracted by her. But, on a visit to Britain,
he married an English girl and brought her back to Toronto as his
bride.

Anne had followed him and when she returned she was a
changed woman. To the alarm of her family, she announced that
she was still in love with him. When she called at his home, his
wife refused to let her see him. When the Robinsons sailed for
England, Anne pursued them across the ocean and died in her
last attempt to be with him.

All the details of that strange affair became common gossip in
the town for years afterwards, for it involved two of the most

important families in the early history of the city.

The Powells had long been leading figures in the history of New England. One member of the family had been lieutenant-governor of Massachusetts. In 1776, when war broke out between the thirteen American colonies and the British government, most of the Powells fled to England. William Dummer Powell soon returned to North America, however, and settled in Montreal, where he became a successful lawyer. When John Graves Simcoe arrived to become the first lieutenant-governor of Upper Canada in 1792, he appointed Powell as one of the province's first judges. In 1816 Powell became chief justice of the young province.

Both Powell and his wife were always concerned about their children and whom they might marry, especially their daughter, Anne. She had been born on March 10, 1787, while the family was still living in Montreal. After the end of the Revolutionary War, she spent most of her early years at the home of her mother's family in New York.

By the time she returned to Canada to live permanently with her parents, she had become a very independent young woman. In the words of one of the family's biographers, W.R. Riddell, 'she had developed a hearty contempt for mere conventionality.' She had little interest in being supported by her family and, for a while, thought of becoming a school teacher. When she was in her late twenties, she became attracted to a young lawyer in the town, John Beverley Robinson.

The Robinsons had been even more prominent than the Powells in the early history of the American colonies, and continued so when they moved to Canada following the American Revolution. Of them all, wrote Julia Jarvis in *Three Centuries of the Robinson Family*, John Beverley Robinson would prove to be 'one of the most brilliant and honoured statesmen that Canada has known.'

He was born in the village of Berthier, Lower Canada, on July 26, 1791. His parents had left America with little of their possessions and, when John's father died, the family was virtually penniless. John became the protégé of a minister, John Strachan, who had founded the Cornwall Grammar School, then the most famous school in the province. In later years, Strachan moved to Toronto, where he was appointed the first Anglican bishop of Toronto. In

Anne Powell

1827, he founded the college that became the University of Toronto. Robinson, meanwhile, had served with distinction as a militia officer during the War of 1812. He then had settled in Toronto, and eventually became chief justice of the province. These two life-long friends would become the two most powerful men in Upper Canada.

Robinson was only 24 years old when he was appointed solicitor-general of the province. It was shortly afterwards that be became involved in the affair with Anne Powell. He must have been flattered by the attentions of the daughter of the chief justice. But, for Anne, it was more than a flirtation.

John Beverley Robinson

In 1816, when Robinson decided to spend some time in England to further his experience in law at one of the Inns of Court, Anne vowed to follow him. Her father was due to sail to England on business, and she easily persuaded him to let her accompany him. Once in London, she sought out Robinson. He gallantly agreed to become her escort around the city. Unknown to Anne, however, Robinson had already fallen in love with Emma Walker, whom he had met in England.

Patrick Brode records the consequences in the *Dictionary of Canadian Biography*. As soon as Emma became aware of Anne's infatuation she issued an ultimatum. If Robinson wished to continue his courtship of her, he had to inform Anne and at once that he had no intention of marrying her.

The news came as a shock not only to Anne but to most people in Toronto. Everyone there had assumed that John and Anne were in love and would soon marry. Instead, it was Emma whom John brought back as his bride. The house where the two of them would live was a cottage built in 1812 that Robinson had enlarged and named Beverley House. It stood just west of Osgoode Hall at the northeast corner of John and Richmond Streets.

Almost two years passed before Anne returned to Toronto. She was now 32 and had become a very bitter woman. Her parents were repeatedly upset by her constant quarrelling. To their even greater alarm they discovered that she was once again shamelessly pursuing Robinson. She began writing him long and impassioned letters. One of these was later described by one of Robinson's brothers as 'the damnedest letter you ever saw.' The affair quickly became the greatest scandal in the town.

In 1822, Anne learned that Robinson and his wife were arranging to sail for England. She managed to reach him and begged him to allow her to sail with him. Robinson, of course, refused.

Beverley House still stood at the northeast corner of Richmond and John Streets in 1911.

When Anne's family learned she was still determined to follow him, they locked her in her bedroom until the Robinsons had safely left town.

Anne managed to escape and in a chartered sleigh started after them. Emma had become ill and Robinson had to make frequent stops on their way to New York. Anne quickly caught up with them and began booking rooms in the very hotels where the Robinsons were staying. Robinson immediately spoke to the captain of the ship that would be taking him and Emma to England, and made him solemnly promise not to let Anne on board under any circumstances. Instead, Anne booked passage on one of the next ships bound for England, the 600-ton *Albion*, and sailed after them.

On the night of April 22, 1822, off the southern coast of Ireland at the Head of Kinsale, *Albion* struck a gale. Her mast broke in two and the ship began drifting helplessly. The winds and tide began carrying her towards the shore. In the early hours of the morning she crashed against the rocks and sank almost at once. Of the 56 passengers and crew on board, 45 perished. Most of the bodies that were swept ashore were too disfigured to be identified.

Chief Justice Powell, who was in England at the time, left for Ireland as soon as he learned what had happened. He was taken to the sheds where the bodies had been placed, and it was only through a piece of jewellery on one of the corpses that he was able to identify the body of his daughter Anne. The next morning, he arranged for her funeral. She was buried in the graveyard of a nearby church at Garrettstown.

The tragic ending of the affair, in Brode's words, became a story that was reported throughout the province, 'from Government House to Forests Stable.' It played a considerable part in ruining the Powell's social standing, but had no effect on Robinson's career. To his friends and supporters, it was considered nothing more than 'an embarrassing and awkward incident.' In 1829, at the age of 38, John Beverley Robinson was appointed chief justice of Upper Canada, and, as a judge, would have few equals in the history of Canadian jurisprudence. In recognition of his service to Canada, he was awarded a knighthood.

On January 30, 1863, at the age of 73, he died at Beverley House. Seventeen years later his son, another John Beverley Robinson, was appointed lieutenant-governor of Ontario.

7

Kit Coleman: the world's first woman war correspondent

At the outbreak of the Spanish-American War, a Toronto reporter talked her way onto a freighter bound for Cuba and scooped every male war correspondent with her first datelined story.

In the spring of 1898, an American battleship, the *Maine*, was sunk off the coast of Havana. Word soon reached Toronto that in reprisal a force of American troops was planning to invade Cuba. One of the columnists of the Toronto *Mail and Empire*, a tall, striking redhead, immediately caught the night train for Washington. She forced her way into the office of the secretary of state and asked to be allowed to sail with the American troops.

General Alger Russell told her no newspaperwoman was going to be allowed on any American troop ship. She then talked her way onto a freighter bound for Havana. When she cabled back her first story from Cuba, Toronto's 'Kit' Coleman became the first accredited woman war correspondent in the history of newspapers.

Overnight she became one of the few internationally known newspaper women. For years, however, Kit, as she was always known, had already been one of the best known columnists in Canada. She wrote for the women's page, but the prime minister of Canada often boasted he was one of her most faithful readers. She was admired by most of the press world and in the early

1900s she became one of the first campaigners for the rights of women in the newspaper field.

In 1904, when she was told that no woman reporters were going to be given press passes to cover the world's fair at St Louis because 'there weren't 12 professional women writers in Canada,' Kit instantly produced 13 names and got press passes for all of them. On her way back to Toronto, still angry about the way they had been treated, she proposed that they band together and form a Canadian Women's Press Club. Her plan was instantly adopted and Kit was unanimously elected first president.

In 1911, she angrily quit the *Mail and Empire* over a matter of principle. So many other newspapers asked to carry her column

Kit Coleman

that within a year she had become Canada's first syndicated columnist. To those who have heard some of the legends newspaper people still tell, there was simply never anyone like Kit.

She was born Kathleen Blake and grew up in the west of Ireland on her father's estate. In 1880, when she was 16, her father arranged for her to be married to a wealthy friend of the family, George Willis.

As soon as she was married, her husband suggested she attend finishing schools on the continent to prepare her for social life with his family. But within four years Willis died, leaving almost everything to his mother. Virtually penniless, Kathleen decided to emigrate to Canada. In 1884 she arrived in Toronto and became a secretary. Within a year her boss, Edward Watkins, had proposed and as soon as they were married they moved to Winnipeg. Five years later, her second husband died. Broke again, Kathleen returned to Toronto, this time with two small children to support.

Her father had been a literary man and the Blake home in Ireland was always filled with writers. She had often thought of becoming a writer, and as soon as she found rooms in a downtown boarding house she began sending articles and stories to all the local editors. E.E. Shepherd, editor of *Saturday Night*, was so impressed by one of her stories about the Bohemian world of Paris she had seen on a holiday that he asked her for more and published most of them. Charles Banting, the editor of the Toronto *Mail*, liked the style of her writing and hired her to help him start a women's page in his newspaper.

She had arrived in Toronto at the start of the era of the 'New Woman.' For the first time in history, women were becoming students at Canadian universities and entering professions that had always been exclusively male. To the astonishment of most men, women were now being overheard discussing politics and golf!

Banting was certain he could boost his newspaper's circulation if he could appeal to these 'new' women. He promised Kit she could have a half page of his Saturday edition if she could fill it with subjects that would interest them. He fully expected her to fill it with fashion reports and gossip but Kit had other ideas.

She began devoting most of her space to interviews, theatre

reviews, and articles about the arts as well as political comments. Within a few months, her half page had become a full page and was spilling onto the next page. She called her new section 'Woman's Kingdom.'

When women wrote asking for personal advice, Kit printed her answers in the paper and became Canada's first 'Advice to the Lovelorn' columnist. Her answers were invariably frank: 'If you want a successful marriage, always have time for your husband – but not too much.' Some of her suggestions were so frank many readers cancelled their subscriptions, saying they would not let their teenage daughters read what she recommended. But men as well as women became regular readers, and some of the best of her columns have been reprinted in *Kit Coleman: Queen of Hearts*, an affectionate tribute from a fellow journalist, Ted Ferguson.

The prime minister of Canada, Sir Wilfrid Laurier, became one of her staunchest admirers. When she went to London to cover Queen Victoria's Diamond Jubilee, Laurier insisted she be his guest when he attended a reception at Buckingham Palace. As usual, her paper had given her barely enough money to cover her expenses; when Laurier arrived in his resplendent carriage at her London address, he found himself in front of a cheap boarding house in the east end of London, beside the docks.

But Kit put up with all the battles with her editors over money because she was now being allowed to cover major international stories that had previously been covered only by men. In 1898, when the sinking of the *Maine* led to the outbreak of the Spanish-American War, Kit announced she was going to cover the story from Cuba.

She hounded the officials in Washington until they finally gave her an official press pass. In Florida the men in charge of the press boat refused to let any woman reporter on board: Kit talked her way onto a freighter bound for Havana. On the day of her arrival, her newspaper triumphantly carried the headline: '"Kit" Reaches Cuba's Shores.' Thereafter she cabled a steady series of graphic reports about the horrors of that war. She scooped all her 134 male colleagues with a story about a shipment of American arms being smuggled to Cuban rebels.

PRICE TWO CENTS.

"KIT" REACHES CUBA'S SHORES.

Describes the Voyage, Undertaken After
So Many Difficulties Had
Been Surmounted.

HER EXPERIENCES ON A WARSHIP

Special to The Mail and Empire.   then silence would fall, and the ship,
On Board the Government Supply   lonely, sombre, an almost sentient

---

On her return to Toronto, one of her suitors, a Toronto doctor, Theobald Coleman, finally persuaded her to marry him. For both, it became a perfect marriage. Kit totally adored him, although there were always money problems, for he insisted that he would never charge his poorer patients for his services. Kit also soon discovered he was a heavy drinker. She forgave him that, too; and if friends ever mentioned his drinking her only comment was an Irish one: 'He's a cautious man. He's been drinking to ward off a bad cold.'

In 1901 they moved to Hamilton, and Kit had to send her columns to her paper by messenger or mail. Despite Banting's efforts, the *Mail* had not survived and had merged with the *Empire* to become the *Mail and Empire*. In 1911, a new managing editor told her to write an additional column for the paper's front page, but said he would not pay her any more money. Kit resigned on a matter of principle. She became a syndicated columnist, and no matter how much money she was offered the only paper that was never allowed to carry her columns was the *Mail and Empire*.

She continued to write until she was in her fifties. When she became ill, she wrote from her bed. In 1915, a cold turned into pneumonia and on May 16, the 'Kit' of legends was dead.

8

The mysterious visitor who truly founded the ROM's Chinese collection

One of Toronto's greatest treasures was built on a partnership that began with a postcard in the King Edward Hotel.

Between two world wars, the Royal Ontario Museum built one of the most important collections of Chinese art to be found anywhere outside China. The story of how it came to be is one of the more incredible legends still told about this city. It all began with the discovery of a postcard in a cigar shop at the King Edward Hotel on King Street.

It was no ordinary postcard and should never have been on sale at the hotel. It had been left behind by one of the hotel's departing guests and had been found by a chambermaid.

The picture on the card was not the usual view of the city but a full-colour photograph of a sculptured Chinese figure dressed in monastic robes. The maid took the postcard to a friend who ran the cigar stand, who offered to sell it for her for five cents.

A few moments later, it was noticed by another hotel guest who had arrived at the counter to buy a cigar. He was startled by the picture. When he turned the card over he discovered that the statue was in a museum in Toronto that he had scarcely heard of, the Royal Ontario Museum.

The year was 1918 and the ROM had been open for only four years. The card had been printed by the museum for sale at its information booth in the hope of publicizing the new institution and some of its rarest and most valuable pieces. By an extraordinary coincidence the man who discovered the postcard at the King Edward Hotel was the same man who had discovered that very piece of sculpture in China.

George Crofts had been working as a fur trader in China for a number of years and at the turn of the century had become fascinated by early Chinese art. He began sending some fine pieces to a dealer in London, England, and one of his major finds was an 11th-century Luohan of the Liao dynasty that he now found reproduced on a postcard in Toronto.

Although he had already packed and would be leaving later that day, he ordered a carriage and a few minutes later arrived at the ROM. He gave his card to the receptionist, saying he had just arrived from New York, and asked to speak to the curator in charge of the museum's Chinese art.

The director of the museum of archaeology, Charles Currelly, appeared, but said he was busy with another visitor and could spare only a few moments. He quickly solved the mystery that had been puzzling Crofts: one of the museum's benefactors, Mrs H.D. Warren, had bought the Luohan while in London and had presented it to the museum. Currelly then excused himself, and Crofts left.

In his biography, *I Brought the Ages Home*, Currelly wrote that it was not until he returned to his office that he realized he had made one of the biggest mistakes of his life. His conversation with the unexpected visitor had been brief, but Currelly now remembered a remark Crofts had made about another Chinese object he had noticed in the galleries, and realized that the man he had just met was no 'visitor' from New York. He was the mysterious figure whose name was unknown to most of the world's curators, but who had been responsible for sending some of the most important art treasures out of China.

Currelly quickly made a number of telephone calls and discovered that Crofts was staying at the King Edward. He hurried to the hotel and arrived at Crofts' room full of apologies, saying it was Crofts' comment that he had just arrived from New York that

George Crofts

had thrown him. As the two men talked, Crofts realized that Currelly had been one of the principal figures in founding the museum; he had also almost single-handedly created its department of archaeology that included a small Chinese collection. Crofts took an immediate liking to Currelly, and the friendship born between these two men at their first meeting would last for the rest of their lives.

At that initial meeting, Currelly explained that although the museum has been founded by the provincial government and the University of Toronto, there were no public funds available for acquisitions. Everything that the museum wanted to add to its collections would have to be paid for by 'friends' of the museum and other wealthy benefactors. Crofts decided to help and showed Currelly photographs of some of the Chinese objects he was currently planning to sell. Currelly was astounded by their quality but was convinced he could never raise enough money to buy even one of them. When he finally dared to ask about prices, Crofts named figures that were only a small fraction of what Currelly had expected. Currelly's immediate reply was, 'I will tear the money out of Toronto in 10-cent pieces before I let such a chance slip.'

Crofts left the city that night. Within a few days, Currelly wired him saying he had raised all the money that would be needed to buy all the pieces. Crofts sent word back that he would be happy to become the ROM's unofficial 'agent' in China and, in the years that followed, literally hundreds of crates of the most incredible treasures began arriving in Toronto from Crofts' offices.

Crofts frequently waved aside all questions about commissions for many of the shipments. On those occasions when Currelly was unable to find a donor for some particularly fine piece that Crofts believed the museum should have, he told Currelly to add it to his collection as a gift 'from an anonymous benefactor.'

In the 1920s China was beset with revolution and wars. Crofts was convinced that if most of the items he planned to buy were not immediately shipped out of the country they would be burned or destroyed by looters and invading armies, and the volume of crates arriving in Toronto rapidly increased. When the palaces of the emperor were seized by troops, Crofts was offered a considerable portion of the Imperial Wardrobe of rare and historic costumes, and added them to the collections he was sending to Currelly.

The most massive set of pieces Crofts acquired was a group of Chinese tomb sculptures complete with stone arches and several of the stone figures that once lined the avenue leading to the burial spot. It became one of the early great wonders of the museum, and now almost fills the enormous new glassed-in gallery facing Bloor Street.

For more than half a century the ROM's Chinese collection filled the entire top floor of one wing. Today, one of the most spectacular sights in the newly renovated museum is a group of large, richly carved figures sent by Crofts that dominate a major room named the Bishop White Gallery in honour of the first Keeper of the Chinese collection. They are known as *bodhisattvas*, the most important and approachable saints of the Buddhist faith, and these larger-than-life-size wooden figures are particularly fine and rare examples. Such figures would have been placed in pairs in Chinese temples, one on each side of the Buddha, 'The Enlightened One.' One of the fundamental principles of Buddhism is a belief in a long cycle of reincarnations; the *bodhisattvas* were saints who, having only one more birth to undergo before attaining Nirvana, chose to give up their chance to enter Paradise in order to return to earth to help others.

During those years when Crofts was sending thousands of items to Toronto, he remained a man of mystery to everyone at the museum. It is now known that he was born in 1872 and came from an English family that had moved to Ireland. Why he went to China has never been explained, but it was while working as a fur trader in that country that he became an agent for S.M. Franck and Co., the largest importer of Chinese art in England. It was officials at that company who took such extraordinary steps to keep Crofts' name a secret so that rival dealers would never discover his identity.

Buddhist saints (*bodhisattvas*), secured by Crofts for the Royal Ontario Museum, stand in the Bishop White Gallery.

Crofts' personal fortunes were always largely derived from his sale of furs to England, and he lost everything when a strike in 1924 forced him to land his furs in Europe. By the time the strike was settled, the English season for buying furs was over and Crofts was bankrupt. He was then 53 and had recently learned he was fatally ill with cancer. Within a year he was dead.

Visitors to the ROM today will find hundreds of memorials to Crofts. At Currelly's insistence, and as the museum's tribute, everything that Crofts sent to the ROM – the massive tomb sculptures, the Imperial Wardrobe, the *bodhisattvas*, the bronze and ivory pieces, the T'ang horses, and particularly the hundreds of small tomb figures that still constitute the largest and most important collection of its kind outside China – are all marked in perpetuity with cards stating they are part of 'The George Crofts Collection.'

9

'Caverhill': treasure of Rosedale

*One of the oldest of all
the mansions of Rosedale was home to a dedicated
and popular public servant.*

It is the oldest of all the mansions of the original Rosedale estate. For more than 100 years it has stood at the centre of one of that district's largest and handsomest estates.

In 1992, when this was written, the house was deserted and its future uncertain. If it were ever demolished, Toronto would lose one of its most elegant 19th century landmarks. To those who know its history, few Rosedale houses are more treasured than this one at the top of a hill, just east of Yonge Street at 124 Park Road.

For most of the year, it is largely hidden from sight behind hedges and trees, and relatively few Torontonians even know of its existence. It has been the home of a number of prominent people over the past century, but to many in Rosedale it is known as the Geary House after the 20th century figure who became the most famous of all its owners, George Reginald Geary.

In 1910, at the age of 36, he became one of the youngest and most popular mayors in Toronto's past. In 1927, when he bought this house, he named it Caverhill after his new bride, Beatrice Caverhill. It was his home until he died, and then became the home of his son until the 1980s when the family sold it. It has always been considered one of the earliest houses of Rosedale, but it was only recently that its full story was uncovered. There is now no question that it is the oldest of all the first mansions of Rosedale.

In 1824, William B. Jarvis, one of the sons of Toronto's famous Jarvis family, bought a 100-acre estate in the area that included a house overlooking the valley beside Yonge Street. When he married, his wife was so delighted by the sight of thousands of wild roses growing in the valley that she named the house Rosedale. In 1854, when Jarvis subdivided his estate to create a large new residential area in Toronto's northern suburbs, the entire district took its name from his home.

One of the first great houses to be built on the original Jarvis estate was that which now stands at 124 Park Road. Its story has recently been recorded for the first time by a longtime Rosedale resident, Elizabeth Vickers. In association with the staff of the Toronto Historical Board she has uncovered a number of previously unknown facts about both the structure and its original owners.

The house was built in 1855 with only one storey, but even then it was a handsome country villa. All its original reception rooms have survived and they are spacious and high-ceilinged. The second storey was added in 1863 and the present veranda sometime around 1904. Its first owner was a lawyer, James Boyd Davis. From 1875 to 1922 it was the home of John Stark. In 1922 it was bought by Ian Sinclair, and five years later he sold it to one of the best known figures in the city at that time, Colonel 'Reg' Geary.

Geary was the son of a small-town, southern Ontario druggist. He was born in Strathroy on August 12, 1873 and came to Toronto to study law; in 1896 he was called to the bar. He soon established himself as one of the leading corporation lawyers in the city but before he was 30 he knew that, for him, the most rewarding career would be in public service. In 1903 he became one of the youngest members of the Board of Education. In 1904 he was an alderman and in 1910, at the age of 36, he decided to run for mayor. His principal opponent based his election campaign on the need for a subway in Toronto. Geary ran on a less pretentious platform. He called for lower taxes, won by a handsome majority, and became Toronto's 'bachelor mayor.' By then he was a decidedly popular young figure among all the voters.

As almost everyone who interviewed him recorded, he bore a striking resemblance to Woodrow Wilson, the future president of the United States. In the press, Geary was constantly referred to as one of the few 'gentlemen' in the world of municipal politics. He was also one of the most ardent supporters of the city's sports teams, and many voters met him for the first time sitting on a rail fence watching a race or a match. The ease with which he moved at every level of the social world proved to be unexpectedly important during his first year in office. In 1910, he was Toronto's official representative at the funeral of Edward VII in London and returned the following year to England to represent the city at the coronation of King George V and Queen Mary.

The Geary house, oldest of the mansions of the original Rosedale

At City Hall, he became known as one of the hardest working mayors Toronto had ever had. He was always at his office by 7 a.m. but critics said there was nothing remarkable about that; he didn't have a wife or any children at home to detain him. But the public and almost the entire press world became his supporters. The Toronto *Star* called him the ideal kind of young man for a 'youthful' city that was then bursting beyond its borders. Geary was easily elected to a second and third term in 1911 and 1912 but then surprised his friends by announcing he was retiring as mayor. The city was becoming increasingly embroiled in court cases involving various public service corporations, and he was convinced that by training and temperament he could best serve the city as its corporation counsel.

In the summer of 1914, while he was fishing with friends at Temiskaming, word reached the camp that war had broken out in Europe. Everyone raced back to the city and the 41-year-old Geary was one of the first to enlist. He had no military experience and volunteered to serve in any capacity. He was sent to an officers' training camp and was soon in Europe as a lieutenant with the 35th Battalion. In later years, like many other veterans, he rarely talked about his life during the war, but he had served with distinction.

He was initially attached to the headquarters staff in London but was soon sent to the continent, where he helped locate more than 300 missing Canadians who had been interned in Switzerland. He served in the trenches of the Western Front, where he was badly gassed. By the time the war ended he had been promoted to the rank of major and had been awarded the Military Cross and the French Legion of Honour. After the war, he was a lifelong supporter of the Great War Veterans Association and in 1924 was appointed to command the Royal Grenadiers with the rank of lieutenant-colonel.

He returned to his role as the city's corporation counsel and in 1927, at the age of 54, fell in love with a Montreal woman, Beatrice Caverhill, a Montreal socialite who had served with the Red Cross in Europe throughout the war and was now one of its strongest supporters. Within the year they were married and in that same year Geary became the heir to a sizeable and unexpected fortune when a rich uncle died and left him $170,000. He immediately bought the handsome house at 124 Park Road as a home for his bride and paid the then enormous sum of $36,000 for the building and an estate that included part of a large ravine.

Within a year a daughter was born and in later years there would be a son. In 1925, Geary returned to public life as the Conservative member for Toronto South in the House of Commons. He served for 10 years until 1935, when he and his party were defeated in the election that brought Mackenzie King and the Liberals back to power.

In that same year there was a great personal tragedy. Geary's wife died very suddenly at her home on Park Road. Geary was more deeply affected by her death than most people knew at the time. He was then in his sixties, and it was soon obvious that he would never return to public life. He continued to live at the house he had named Caverhill after his wife until his own death on April 30, 1954.

Among the tributes paid at the time, it was said, 'There was nothing spectacular in his long life now ended at the age of 80, but he will be remembered as a public official and practising lawyer with faith in his country, his city and their institutions and who believed that a life spent in their service was sufficiently rewarding for a man of intelligence and ability.'

10

The teen-age triumphs of the legendary Kathleen Parlow

As a 15 year-old violinist, she was summoned to play before the Queen of England. At 16, she went to Russia. She was the darling of Europe but returned to Canada and left its young artists a lasting gift.

Just north of Kensington Market there is a small narrow house on Major Street where Kathleen Parlow lived her last years.

There had been a time when her name was known throughout Europe and North America as one of the foremost violinists of the day. In Toronto, those who once packed concert halls for her sold-out performances still tell the legends that will always surround the story of her life.

At the age of 15, during her first visit to England, she was commanded to appear before the Queen at Buckingham Palace. At 16, she became the first foreigner ever allowed to study at the famed conservatory at St Petersburg in Russia. In her late teens, she met the composers Glazunov and Sibelius and was presented at the Russian court. A wealthy admirer gave her one of the world's most valuable violins; and in the 1910s and 1920s, when she toured Europe, there was not a major work in the violin repertoire that she did not play, and play superbly.

In 1941, at the end of one of her recitals in Toronto, Sir Ernest MacMillan, conductor of the Toronto Symphony Orchestra, came onto the stage to announce to a surprised and delighted audience that Kathleen Parlow had accepted an offer to become a permanent member of the staff of the Toronto Conservatory of Music. Before he could finish his speech, the crowd was on its feet cheering. Kathleen Parlow had come home.

It had been many years since she had lived in Canada. Decades had passed since the day when, at the age of four, she had left Canada to live in the United States. She had been born in Calgary, on September 20, 1890. She adored her father but he drank heavily, and in 1894 Kathleen's mother left him and took her daughter to live in San Francisco, where relatives had settled.

The legends that would surround Kathleen's career began less than a year later. When she was five and saw a small violin in a store window, she began pleading with her mother to buy it for

The 15-year-old Kathleen Parlow
in London, about the time she
played before the Queen

her. Mrs Parlow finally agreed, but only if Kathleen promised to learn how to play it properly. Not only did Kathleen fulfil that promise, within a year she was giving recitals in public.

Her mother had been a violinist and Kathleen seemed to have been born with a talent for music. Within a few years she had been accepted as a pupil by the man who, at that time, was probably the leading teacher of music in San Francisco. He was an Englishman named Henry Holmes and had once been a famous violinist in Europe and a professor at the Royal College of Music in London.

When Kathleen was 15, Holmes insisted that she must go to England for a year of study and recitals. He would supply her with all the letters of introduction she would need and promised her that she would play before the Queen.

Neither Kathleen nor her mother had saved enough to pay for such a trip, but the congregation at their church raised the money and in 1905 Kathleen arrived in London with her mother and $300 between them. As Holmes had predicted, all the recitals that he arranged were great successes, and she played before Queen Alexandra, who had once been a pupil of Holmes.

On the eve of her scheduled return to America, Kathleen received word that Holmes had died. He was the only great music teacher that she had ever known and there was no longer any reason for her to return. One night, at a concert in London, she sat spellbound listening to a 14-year-old Russian violinist named Mischa Elman. After the concert, she hurried backstage to ask who was his teacher.

He said it was Leopold Auer, a renowned Russian violinist who, at that moment, was in London. Friends Kathleen had made in London quickly arranged for an audition. Auer was so impressed he told her if she could come to St Petersburg he would personally arrange for her to be enrolled in his class at the conservatory. Kathleen now had to raise enough money for a trip to Russia.

The Canadian high commissioner in London was Lord Strathcona, a wealthy Montrealer who was known for his philanthropy towards young Canadian artists. He readily agreed to lend her £200 and, in 1906, at the age of 16, Kathleen arrived in St Petersburg.

After a year of study with Auer, she made her professional debut in Berlin, and then began a tour of many of the principal concert halls of Europe. The young teen-aged Canadian became a particular favourite with Scandinavian audiences, and after one concert in Oslo, a wealthy Oslo family, named Bjornson, presented her with a violin that had been given by Catherine the Great to a once-celebrated violinist named Viotti. It was known as the Viotti Guarnerius, one of the world's most prized violins. It became Kathleen's most treasured possession.

In 1912, she and her mother settled in England. In 1926, the two of them returned to San Francisco. The next year, Kathleen had what has been described as a nervous breakdown. No one has ever discovered the cause, but whatever happened, her diary remained blank for a year.

In 1928, she returned to music and in 1936, at the age of 46, she moved to New York. There she attracted a large number of pupils but her public appearances were becoming increasingly rare. Eventually MacMillan persuaded her to return to Canada to teach at the Toronto (later Royal) Conservatory of Music.

During her first year back in Canada, she regained all her earlier enthusiasm and began plans for a project that had been on her mind for some time. In 1943, she announced the formation of the Parlow String Quartet. The group began appearing regularly on the CBC network and was soon touring the continent. For the next 15 years it remained Canada's most internationally known and admired ensemble of string players.

In 1954, at the end of a long illness, Kathleen's mother died at their home in Toronto. Kathleen had never married and her mother had been her constant companion throughout the past 50 years of travelling. Kathleen was so shaken that she told none of her friends about her mother's death until after the funeral. She then found it impossible to live in the house at 351 Huron Street they had shared together and moved into a smaller house at 53 Sussex Avenue. Finally she moved into an even smaller house at 129 Major Street.

She still continued to attract pupils. A new generation of young violinists who had heard of the legendary Kathleen Parlow were startled to discover she was still alive and began arriving at her home and studio. And she was still an incomparable performer. One admirer who tried to describe the magic of her playing wrote that 'she had a big, pure tone, a suave legato ... as if she were playing with a 9-foot bow.'

In the summer of 1963, while visiting a friend in Oakville, Kathleen Parlow fell while getting off a bus. There were unexpected complications and her friends in Toronto were shocked to learn she had died very suddenly of a heart attack at the hospital in Oakville.

She was buried in St James' Cemetery in Toronto. When her will was read it was discovered she had left the bulk of her estate to establish scholarships for young Canadian musicians who, like herself, needed a helping hand.

11

Sarah Bernhardt's 'scandalous' performance in Toronto

In 1881, she was the reigning star of the world's stage and loved by millions, but her performance was considered too daring for puritanical Toronto and she played to a half-empty house.

She was called 'France's greatest actress of all time.' King Edward VII and Napoleon III were among her most ardent admirers. Victor Hugo, it was said, once knelt before her. But in 1880, when she made her first tour of North America, Sarah Bernhardt caused a scandal that created a furor in the press and alarmed theatre managers.

Nowhere was the effect of that scandal more apparent than on March 19, 1881, when Bernhardt made her first appearance in Toronto. The house was half empty. She had ignored the advice of friends and, in defiance of the critics, opened her engagement in the city with the one play she had been warned not to include on her tour.

She was then 37, a woman of extraordinary beauty and, even at this early stage in her career, the most celebrated actress in Europe. But she had never performed in one of the most famous plays of that century, Dumas' *La Dame aux Camelias*, which had shocked even Parisian audiences with its story of a notorious courtesan. Bernhardt had considered the role for years. In 1880, on the eve of her departure for New York, she announced she would debut in it during her North American tour.

Frantic theatre managers who were worried about lost ticket sales persuaded her at least to change the name of the play. Thus it was a performance of *Camille* that was advertised for her first appearance in Toronto, at the newly built Grand Opera House at 9 Adelaide Street West. But in Toronto the Good of a century ago, the change of name fooled no one.

In the opening lines of his review of the performance, the theatre critic for the Toronto *Mail* wrote: 'Toronto has seen Sarah Bernhardt and Toronto is happy – at least a portion of Toronto is happy – for the possibilities are another portion is unhappy that people could be found in this fair city so horribly wicked as to go and see a woman who has sinned.'

In Montreal, the protests were even stronger. The clergy denounced the play from their pulpits, and Roman Catholics were forbidden to attend any of the performances. The controversy over *Camille* dogged Bernhardt throughout the tour, but she considered the affair laughable. She had lived a far more scandalous life than those lived by any of the heroines in all of Dumas' plays.

She herself was the illegitimate child of a notorious Dutch courtesan named Judith Van Hard, and was born in Paris on October 22 or October 23, 1844. Her father probably was a law student, Edouard Bernard, and she was known as Henriette Rosine Bernard until she adopted her famous stage name. She went to a convent school and might have become a nun, but at the age of 15 she went to a theatre for the first time and that changed her life. According to her memoirs, she was so excited that by the time she got home she was shaking and spent the next six weeks in bed with brain fever. One of her mother's lovers, a half brother of Napoleon III, realized she had a natural talent for acting and arranged for her enrolment in a government school of drama.

Shortly afterwards, she was accepted as a beginner at Paris' most famous theatre, the Comédie Française, and in 1862, at the age of 18, made her debut on its stage. It was at this time that she had the first of the many love affairs that would scandalize the public. At 20 she had an illegitimate son, her only child. She named him Maurice. His father was Henry, Prince de Ligne, whom Sarah left soon afterwards for another lover.

The legendary Sarah Bernhardt in 1879,
two years before she scandalized Toronto

By her early twenties she had developed into a fine actress with
a magnificent speaking voice, and was already referred to as 'the
Divine Sarah.' At 25 she had her first major success, playing the
part of a minstrel in Copée's play *Le Passant*. The following year,
when she appeared in Victor Hugo's *Ruy Blas*, he coined the famous phrase for her as the actress with the Golden Voice. By 1879
she had formed her own acting company and was touring most
of the major cities of Europe. In 1880, she decided the time had

come for her first tour of the principal theatres in the United States and Canada.

She opened in New York at Booth's Theatre on November 8, 1880, in *Adrienne Lecouvreur*, another famous courtesan role. In her memoirs she wryly commented, 'The house was crowded ... but there were no young girls present ... The piece was too immoral.' But she dazzled all the New Yorkers who saw her. According to Joanna Richardson, author of *Sarah Bernhardt and her World*, women in the audience ordered their escorts to find every available musician and sent them to serenade Bernhardt in the street below her hotel window.

Instead of being appalled at the thought of seeing her perform *Camille*, New Yorkers fought to get tickets. On the night of her last appearance there in that play, there were 29 curtain calls and a crowd of 50,000 people jammed the streets in the hope of getting a glimpse of the star. But the American Midwest was less charitable about *Camille*. In her memoirs, Bernhardt wrote that critics in the larger cities denounced her as the modern Magdalene; those in the small town 'threw stones.'

Her opening in Toronto was a Saturday matinée. 'It was a stormy and rainy day,' wrote one reviewer who gallantly suggested that it was the weather that caused the house to be less than half filled. For those who came, Bernhardt gave a superb performance. In the first act, her fainting scenes were so convincing that many in the audience thought, at first, she was really ill. In the second act, when she renounced her lover to send him back to the arms of his family, her portrayal was 'so grand and noble that throughout the scene the audience frequently broke into applause.'

That night, for her second and last performance in Toronto, she appeared before a packed house in a 'delicate and unobjectionable comedy,' *Frou-Frou*. 'It was,' wrote the theatre critic for the *Mail*, 'one of the best audiences, socially speaking, Toronto has ever turned out.'

'This time,' he added, 'the Wealth, Beauty and Intellect of the city braved the rain and showed themselves superior to that narrow view which would refuse a recognition to art because its exponent may not be the exact embodiment of all that is good and righteous.'

Despite the furor, *Camille* provided Bernhardt with the most famous and successful role of her career, and the tour of North America was a triumph. The year after her return to Paris she married for the first and only time in her life. Her husband was a Greek actor, Jacques Damala, a dope fiend who would soon desert her.

For the rest of her life she built her entire world around the theatre. She would later confess to the Duchess of Teck, the mother of Queen Mary, 'I will die on the stage. It is my battlefield.' She returned to perform in Toronto on four other occasions. In 1899, she built a theatre in Paris, the magnificent Sarah Bernhardt Theatre, so that she and her company could perform regularly, but it was an extravagant undertaking and cost her most of her fortune to run it.

Many of France's greatest authors wrote plays especially for her. Sardou wrote *Tosca* for her. During one performance of this play, in 1905, when Bernhardt jumped off the parapet in the final scene, she injured one of her legs seriously. Gangrene set in and the leg had to be amputated. She refused to allow the loss to keep her from the stage, and continued to tour the continent. During World War I, in her seventies, she regularly visited army camps at the front lines, performing scenes from her repertoire before enraptured troops while seated on a sofa or chair on a hastily improvised stage.

Performances throughout her career were entirely in French. In an introduction to William A. Emboden's biography of Bernhardt, Sir John Gielgud wrote, 'I was lucky enough to see her in one of her last performances ... I understood very few of the words she spoke but there was a magical stillness in the auditorium and when the curtain rose for the final curtain calls, it revealed her standing proudly upright on her one leg, her hand on the shoulder of one of her fellow actors for support ... I was spellbound.'

On the night of March 26, 1923, during a performance of *L'Aiglon* by her company at the Sarah Bernhardt Theatre, the stage manager walked suddenly onto the stage with a tragic announcement. He had just received word that Sarah Bernhardt had died at her home in Paris. The performance stopped and the entire audience left the theatre in silence. She had died in the arms of her son, surrounded by friends from the world of the theatre.

In the long tributes that appeared in newspapers throughout the world, many people read, for the first time, of the hardships she had had to face during most of her life. In London, the *Daily Telegraph* (March 28, 1923) reprinted its last interview with her and closed with her reply to the interviewer's final question: 'You ask me my theory of life? ... Life is short and we must live for the few who know and appreciate us, who judge and absolve us ... We ought to hate very rarely, as it is too fatiguing, remain indifferent a great deal, forgive often, and never forget.'

12

La Salle: the epic tragedy of one of the world's heroes

While still in his thirties, La Salle expanded the borders of Canada across the Great Lakes and south to the Gulf of Mexico, but at the height of his fame he was murdered by his own men. The wonder, wrote one historian, was not that he was assassinated, but that he was not killed years earlier.

One of the epic tales of this continent began in the autumn of 1681 when a young Frenchman led a party of 30 French adventurers and 100 Indians along the banks of the Humber River in search of a great river that legends said flowed to the southern seas.

Six months later, the expedition reached the middle of the continent. Its French members then became the first Europeans to travel down the last 700 miles of one of the world's greatest rivers, the Mississippi. On April 9, their leader, the 39-year-old René-Robert Cavelier de la Salle, raised a cross at the mouth of the river and, in honour of his king, Louis XIV of France, named all the lands at the centre of this continent Louisiana.

Americans have always claimed him as one of the most important explorers in the history of the United States. The 19th-century historian Francis Parkman, in *La Salle and the Discovery of the Great West*, wrote, 'the United States owes him an enduring memory for he guided her to the possession of her richest heritage.' In France, however, La Salle is remembered as one of that country's most tragic figures. Less than five years after his greatest discovery, he was murdered by the very men he brought to America to establish France's newest colony.

But the basis for all La Salle's enterprises was Canada, and on the day that he planted the royal arms of France at the mouth of the Mississippi River he extended the borders of Canada (then known as New France) from the Gulf of the St Lawrence River west across the Great Lakes and south to the Gulf of Mexico. Canada that day became one of the largest lands in the western world.

In the French heritage of Toronto, La Salle has always been one of its most important figures. Percy J. Robinson, the definitive historian of that period, wrote in *Toronto during the French Regime* that, of all the explorers and traders who travelled the great portage route along the Humber Valley to the lakes of the north and west, 'none stands out so visibly as the great explorer of the Mississippi.' George Wrong, the University of Toronto professor who first introduced the study of Canadian history into a Canadian university's curriculum, called La Salle 'one of the world's greatest heroes,' but he was also one of the most misguided and deluded men ever to be called a hero. In the *American Encyclopedia*, Professor W.J. Eccles of the University of Toronto added: 'The wonder is not that La Salle was assassinated by his own men but that he was not killed years earlier.'

From his earliest years in France, La Salle seemed destined to find his final career in the New World. He was born in Rouen, on November 21, 1643, in a part of Normandy that sent many of the first generations of French settlers to colonies along the St Lawrence River. He was the son of a wealthy merchant and was baptized René-Robert Cavelier but the name he made famous was the name of his father's estate on the outskirts of Rouen and he is known in all history books as Cavelier de la Salle.

He was educated at a Jesuit college in Rouen and became a teacher, but was totally unsuited for an academic life. Céline Dupré, in the *Dictionary of Canadian Biography*, described young La Salle as 'unsocial, fiery, and autocratic.' At the age of 24 he chose a new career. Rouen was part of the diocese that included the church in New France and one of his brothers, Jean, had become a Sulpician at the seminary in Montreal. In 1667, La Salle left the convent where he had been teaching and sailed to join his brother and begin a new life as a fur trader.

He was daring and ambitious and soon held the monopoly for all the French fur trade at the eastern end of Lake Ontario. He

La Salle portages through the rain on the Humber Trail, on an early stage of an expedition that would lead to the Mississippi River. The drawing is by the Canadian historical artist C.W. Jefferys.

had arrived at a time that marked the beginning of a great struggle between many of the major powers of Europe for possession of the lands in the west. France in particular was no longer content with a few scattered settlements along the St Lawrence Valley. When two Frenchmen, Louis Jolliet and Father Jacques Marquette, reached the northern headwaters of the Mississippi River and reported that it was said to flow halfway across the continent to the southern sea, the governor of New France, Frontenac, wrote to the court at Versailles that if the legend was true, French ships built above Niagara Falls could sail from the Great Lakes to the Gulf of Mexico.

At that time, Spain controlled the gulf and threatened to sink any foreign ship that dared sail in those waters. For the French, the only way to reach the heart of the continent was overland, and La Salle now became the central figure in one of the great explorations of that century.

In 1680, and during each of the next three years, he regularly visited the site of the future city of Toronto to travel north on an ancient Indian trail beside the banks of the Humber River. It led north to a lake, now known as Lake Simcoe; but at that time the lake and all the lands around it were known only by an Indian name written in a number of confusing forms by previous explorers. In his journal for 1680, La Salle described his visit to 'Lake Toronto' and became the first to use the word in the spelling that would later be adopted for the name of a capital city.

In the late summer of 1681, he undertook the grandest exploration of his career. With 30 Frenchmen and 100 Indians and 20-foot-long canoes he headed north and west. The first stage took him along the Humber trail. A scene of La Salle walking through the rain over the valley's hills became one of C.W. Jefferys' most famous historical drawings.

In February of the following year, he reached the river that Jolliet and Marquette had reported and begun the 700-mile journey downriver through lands no European had ever seen. On April 9, 1682, he reached its delta, raised the royal arms, and declared that all the lands stretching east and west from the river now belonged to France. Soon after his return to Montreal, he sailed for France and petitioned Louis XIV to provide him with two ships and enough men to establish a colony and a fort at the mouth of the Mississippi, as a base for France's war against Spain for possession of Mexico.

The king was so impressed with La Salle's proposal that he gave him not two ships but four. On July 24, 1684, with more than 300 soldiers, colonists, missionaries, and craftsmen, La Salle sailed from La Rochelle on his last and fatal voyage. But by now he had become totally unfit to command any expedition. All his life he had resented authority of any kind and was now so unstable some people called him mad. His obsessive search for a great river that might be the long-sought passageway to China had once so amused his friends in Montreal that they nicknamed his estate on the St Lawrence River La Chine, the French word for China. In a new delusion of grandeur, La Salle now saw himself becoming the governor of the newest and largest French colony in the New World.

On the last voyage to America he constantly quarrelled with the captain and angered all the men by his insistence on strict discipline. Few French farmers had volunteered to be part of a colony in an uncharted part of the world and La Salle had to settle for convicts and seamen who had been forced aboard by press gangs. When the little fleet finally reached the Gulf of Mexico, La Salle misjudged the location of the mouth of the Mississippi and the ships landed 400 miles west of the delta in Texas near Matagorda Bay.

On the voyage, one of the ships had been captured by Spanish marauders. A second had had to return to France, and, shortly after the dispirited colonists landed, the two remaining ships crashed against the shore during a storm. Tropical diseases now began decimating the colonists. By 1687 fewer than 40 were still alive. None of the expected relief ships had arrived and the entire colony would soon perish without fresh supplies and medicines. In January 1687, La Salle set out with 17 men in an attempt to travel overland and reach the French settlements on the Great Lakes. By now he had become a virtual dictator and there had been numerous plots to murder him. On March 19, while searching for game, La Salle was shot at close range by two of his men. He died instantly and his body was left to be devoured by wild animals. Only six of the original colonists survived to record the story of La Salle's final days.

More than a century later, in 1803, in one of the world's most famous land sales, the United States vastly enlarged its borders by buying all the territory along the Mississippi from France. That transaction became known in history as the Louisiana Purchase.

13

Was the founder of Upper Canada College the true hero of the Battle of Waterloo?

He is remembered as the founder of a famous private school and as a lieutenant-governor – but was Sir John Colborne also the decisive figure in the battle that ended the Napoleonic Wars?

In the centre of the quadrangle at Upper Canada College stands a large bronze statue of John Colborne, the founder of the school. In all the books ever written about this city, so rarely has his story been told that only a few Torontonians are aware of him – or that, for more than a century, he has been the central figure in one of the most fascinating legends of military history.

In most Canadian history books, he appears as a relatively minor figure who served for eight years as lieutenant-governor of Upper Canada. But, there is a definitive work, the *Dictionary of National Biography*, which records the lives of every major figure in the history of Britain and the British Empire for more than 2,000 years. In it, most names receive barely a paragraph. The story of John Colborne fills a page.

After serving as lieutenant-governor, in 1837 he became commander-in-chief of all British forces in Canada and quelled the rebellion that broke out in Lower Canada in December of that year. In 1838, he became governor-general of Canada. When he finally returned to England, he was elevated to the peerage for his services to the Empire and became Lord Seaton of Devonshire. Queen Victoria later conferred on him the highest rank she could bestow on any man in the British army and made him a field marshal. When he died in 1863, *The Times*, in its tribute, wrote: 'The fame of Wellington more and more dwarfs the reputation of all who served under him, but his subordinates also attained to greatness and would, but for his gigantic proportions, stand out before our eyes in bold relief ... and Colborne was an officer worthy of his chief.'

Three years after Colborne's death, William Leeke of Queen's College, Cambridge, who had served under him at Waterloo, published a two-volume work, *Lord Seaton's Regiment at the Battle of Waterloo*. On its title page and in subsequent chapters, he claimed that Colborne was not only a heroic figure throughout that engagement; he and his regiment had won the final battle at Waterloo. Leeke's book created a legend that has refused to die.

It was inevitable that Colborne's most enduring fame would be won on a battlefield. He was, according to the *DNB*, 'a man of singular talent for war.' He was born at Lyndhurst, in Hampshire, on February 16, 1778, the only son of Samuel Colborne. He was sent to be educated at one of England's best public (i.e., private) schools, Christ's Hospital and, in 1794, began his lifelong military career as a teenaged ensign. It was to be an exceptional career by any standards. In an age when almost all commissions were bought, Colborne earned all his promotions entirely by courage and daring.

By the outbreak of the Napoleonic Wars he had reached the rank of captain and, during the Peninsular War, one of the dying requests of Sir John Moore was that his young officer, the 31-year-old Colborne, be given a lieutenant-colonelcy. In 1811, Colborne was appointed lieutenant-colonel of the 52nd regiment, which Sir William Napier, the celebrated historian of the Peninsular War, called 'a regiment never surpassed in arms since arms were first borne by man.' On the eve of the Battle of Waterloo, it was under Colborne's command.

For three days, the battle raged across the fields of central Belgium. In the early evening of June 18, 1815, the decisive hour arrived. Napoleon had to defeat Wellington's army before any new Prussian corps arrived to tip the balance against the French. A little after 7 p.m., Wellington ordered Colborne to place his regiment at the extreme right of the British position, where it could act as the right wing of Sir Frederick Adam's brigade. During those closing moments of the battle, the fighting was at its fiercest. The French had reached a position less than 300 yards from the British, who had lined themselves along a hill overlooking the plain.

In *Waterloo*, Lord Chalfont recorded what happened next: 'Showing splendid initiative and anticipating his commander-in-chief's orders, Colborne advanced his regiment, four deep, and wheeled them into line opposite the flank of Napoleon's advancing Guards ... The movement was carried out with unhurried, drill-book precision but with devastating results. Napoleon's Guards

A memorial to Sir John Colborne stands in the Massey Quadrangle of Upper Canada College, the school he founded as lieutenant-governor.

opened fire and 150 of Colborne's men fell. But the sudden appearance of Colborne and the 52nd emerging through the smoke on the battalion's flank had taken the Guards by surprise. Colborne seized his opportunity and, as the Guards staggered under the repeated blows, he checked his men's fire and calling "Charge! Charge!" Colborne led the 52nd forward and down the hill ... The Guards, whom no previous perils had daunted, now turned and fled.'

The other British regiments, seeing the rout of the French line, now came up to join with Colborne's men and Adam's entire brigade swept down and across the field. Wellington, close at hand, could be heard shouting, 'Go on, Colborne! Go on!' Then, sensing that the repulse of the Guards was having a fearful effect on the entire French army, Wellington gave the signal for a general advance. Raising his hat, he waved it three times towards the French. 'Those who could see him, let out a mighty cheer ... and in a moment of immortal glory, every man in the allied line capable of moving was advancing down the slope in pursuit of the broken army.' The day was won. The Battle of Waterloo was over.

To the despair of all historians, a detailed account of those final moments was never written in the days immediately following the battle. In the words of the *Dictionary of National Biography*: 'Whether this charge of Colborne's really defeated the Old Guard and won the Battle of Waterloo is a point which will always be disputed ... but there can be no doubt Wellington never gave fair credit to Colborne's exploit.' Colborne's officers were furious that Wellington never mentioned in his despatches the role played by the 52nd but Colborne silenced them saying, 'For shame, gentlemen. One would think you forgot that the 52nd had ever been in battle before.' From that moment on, it became a point of honour in the regiment never to mention the Battle of Waterloo again.

In the year of the battle, Colborne received a knighthood and in 1821 was appointed lieutenant-governor of Guernsey in the Channel Islands, where he helped re-establish a once-famous boys' school, Elizabeth College. In 1828, at the age of 51, he was appointed lieutenant-governor of Upper Canada and his arrival at York (later Toronto) was described as 'like entering a hostile camp.'

William Lyon Mackenzie greeted him with a list of 31 grievances, demanding that the colony be given responsible government. The minister of St James' Church, Reverend John Strachan, called on the new governor to insist that a university be established in the town. To the practical-minded Colborne, there appeared to be more urgent matters.

The sparsely settled province needed roads and bridges and markets and he inaugurated his own 'good works.' He dismissed Strachan's plans for a university as 'madness' since there was not a single acceptable pre-university school in the province. Instead, in 1829, Colborne founded Upper Canada College. To ensure it would survive, he endowed it with land – enough to guarantee that the fees would be low and there would be adequate funds for a staff of well-qualified masters. He insisted on becoming involved in every detail in the planning of the school, and laid the foundations for a college that became one of the most renowned boys' schools in Canada.

In 1887, the province withdrew all the college's original endowment of land and gave it to the University of Toronto. Then it was the quality of its masters and the enthusiastic support of its former graduates that enabled Upper Canada College to survive the transition to a private school.

In the years following his return to Britain, Colborne was appointed commander-in-chief of the British forces in Ireland and in 1860 was made field marshal. On April 17, 1863, at the age of 85, he died at his home in Torquay, in Devonshire.

Today, in the centre of the college's new buildings at the top of Avenue Road hill, there is a large bronze statue of their school's founder. On its base, carved into the stone, are the names of the two greatest campaigns of Colborne's military career, Peninsula and Waterloo, and, in a longer inscription, these words: '... Renowned and chivalrous in war ... in peace, a generous and enlightened friend of learning.'

14

Oscar Wilde in Toronto

*He was 25 and his work was virtually unknown, but
Torontonians packed the Grand Opera House
and the pavilion at Allan Gardens to see
and hear the notorious Mr Wilde.*

When Oscar Wilde was 25 and a virtually unknown writer, he arrived in Toronto and spoke to sold-out houses at both the Grand Opera House and the great pavilion that once stood in Allan Gardens.

All his greatest successes, including *The Importance of Being Earnest* and *The Picture of Dorian Gray*, would not be written for almost another decade. But, in the summer of 1882, when Wilde arrived in North America to begin a lecture tour, he had already become one of the most celebrated and notorious figures of his time. So many people wanted to see and hear him that in many of the larger cities, including Toronto, two halls had to be booked. For someone who had published nothing except one small book of poems that almost no one had read, the success of Wilde's tour of America was astonishing.

He had left Oxford University only a few years before and, almost as soon as he had settled in London, had become one of the most talked-about young men in England. What he said and the way he dressed either shocked or angered most people, and almost every week stories about him appeared not only in the English press but also in newspapers across the United States and

Canada. When the program for his lecture tour of North America was announced, people lined up in the thousands to buy tickets. It was the outrageous and flamboyant Oscar Wilde that everyone wanted to see, and Wilde decided not to disappoint them.

Although he was now as famous as any stage star, few people knew anything about the true story of his life and almost no one knew he had deliberately embarked on a campaign to make himself notorious. His real name was Oscar Fingal O'Flahertie Wills Wilde, and he was born in Dublin on October 15, 1854, the youngest son of a prominent Irish surgeon. His father enrolled him in Trinity College, Dublin, where he proved to be a brilliant classical scholar, winning a gold medal for his essay on the Greek poets. He then entered Oxford. It was during his years there, as an undergraduate at Magdalen College, that he first began to shock his more conservative friends, along with most of the authorities at the college.

He announced he had decided he would become the apostle for his own aesthetic philosophy: Art for Art's Sake. His room at the college became notorious for its exotic splendour. Without a smile, he would confide that he hoped he might, one day, be able to live up to his blue china. He wanted to be talked about. Fame meant money and money meant freedom. And he began using his wit to open otherwise closed doors. 'To get into the best society,' he would say, 'one has either to feed people, amuse people, or shock people.' Everything else would soon fall into place.

By the time he left Oxford in 1878, he was calling himself 'professor of Aesthetics' and dressing the part. He wore his hair unfashionably long and, in those very formal and staid years of the Victorian era, he would arrive at London dinner parties dressed in velveteen breeches, a soft loose shirt, and a large, flowing pale green tie. He adopted the sunflower and the lily as symbols of his art and by 1880 was so notorious that he was being used as a character in *Punch* cartoons. In 1881, he published *Poems by Oscar Wilde*; it sold almost entirely on the notoriety of its author.

That same year Gilbert and Sullivan produced the operetta *Patience*, and in it created a character, Reginald Bunthorne, whom everyone instantly recognized as an outright parody of Wilde.

Oscar Wilde

Every night there were roars of knowing laughter whenever Bunthorne stepped to the footlight and sang: 'Though the Philistines may jostle, you will rank as an apostle in the high aesthetic band,/ If you walk down Picadilly, with a poppy or a lily in your medieval hand.'

All this publicity was making Wilde famous but it was not making him any money. And he was now desperately in need of a large amount of money. The estate left to him by his father had been heavily mortgaged and in 1882, when an American promoter suggested he embark on a lecture tour of the United States and Canada, Wilde accepted at once. To his great delight he discovered he had become as famous in North America as in England.

Gilbert and Sullivan's *Patience* was playing in cities all across the continent and American audiences were as aware as any in

London that one of its principal characters was based on Wilde. When Wilde arrived by ship at New York, he was surrounded by reporters. When he told them the trip had been 'tame' and added that 'the roaring ocean did not, in fact, roar,' one New York paper headlined its story: 'Wilde Disappointed With Atlantic Ocean.' That line was picked up by almost every leading newspaper in the country and provided him with more publicity than anything he had ever written or said before.

There was now virtually a stampede for tickets to see him and 125 lectures were booked in more than 100 cities and towns. At every stop along the route Wilde gave one or more of the same three lectures: The English Renaissance, The Decorative Arts, and The House Beautiful. In May 1882 he arrived to speak in Toronto.

In the best account published about the Canadian portion of the tour, *Oscar Wilde in Canada*, Kevin O'Brien, professor of English at St. Francis Xavier University, wrote, 'The serious-minded wanted to learn from him. The frivolous set looked with expectation for the fool of the hour.' During his time in Toronto, he stayed at the Queen's Hotel. The lieutenant-governor, John Beverley Robinson, held a banquet in his honour at Government House and, despite Wilde's known dislike for every form of outdoor sport, insisted on taking him to a lacrosse game.

On the evening of May 25, 'all the best people of Toronto' arrived at the Grand Opera House to see and hear him speak on The Decorative Arts. To Wilde, his lectures were a serious matter but he dressed for his appearance on the stage as flamboyantly as ever – on this occasion, entirely in black, a black velvet coat, black knee breaches, and black silk stockings. In his speech that night he reiterated most of his strongest beliefs: 'There is nothing in life that the touch of art cannot ennoble ... All the teaching in the world will do you no good unless you surround your workmen with beautiful things.' And he warned his audience, 'It is better to live without art than to live with bad art.'

Two days later, on Saturday, May 27, he spoke in the great pavilion in Allan Gardens which, for years until it was demolished in 1902, was one of the city's principal centres for concerts and almost every kind of social event. That afternoon, Wilde appeared on its stage dressed almost entirely in gray and spoke on The House Beautiful.

To his audience at this second sold-out house he said: 'I did not imagine until I went into some of your simpler cities that there was so much bad work done ... bad wallpaper horribly designed and that old offender, the horsehair sofa.' American homes impressed him even less. He referred to them as 'ill designed, decorated shabbily, and in bad taste' and confessed he had been particularly incensed by the large number of plates he had seen decorated with sunsets and moonlight scenes: 'We do not want a soup plate whose bottom seems to vanish in the distance.' Americans, on the whole, had disappointed him. 'Beauty has no mean-

The pavilion in Allan Gardens was the site of concerts and other cultural events before its demolition in 1902.

ing to them and the past no message ... When good Americans die, they go to Paris. Bad Americans remain in America.'

The tour was a great financial success. He attracted enormous crowds almost everywhere he spoke. But he also faced abuse. He outraged many people, and a number of newspapers, notably Toronto's *Telegram*, were openly hostile.

Soon after his return to England, he married Constance Lloyd. In 1888, with the appearance of his first major work, a collection of short stories entitled *The Happy Prince* written for his sons, he began the string of successful plays and stories that would soon make him an internationally famous author. In 1891 he wrote *The Picture of Dorian Gray*, in 1892, *Lady Windermere's Fan*. In 1895 *The Ideal Husband* opened in London's West End. In that same year, Wilde's masterpiece, *The Importance of Being Earnest*, opened in another London theatre and within a month of its opening Wilde brought an unsuccessful action for criminal libel against the Marquis of Queensbury.

As a result of that disastrous trial, Wilde was arrested and charged with homosexual acts which were offences under England's Criminal Law Amendment Act. He was found guilty and sentenced to two years in prison with hard labour.

The scandal that surrounded his trial ruined him. When he was released from prison, it was only through the help of friends that he was able to leave England and live in a small but rather shabby hotel on the left bank in Paris. During those years in Paris, he changed his name to Sebastian Melmoth and lived in obscurity. On November 30, 1900, at the age of 46, Oscar Wilde died of meningitis in his room at the Hotel d'Alsace.

15

The violinist from Vienna who founded the Toronto Symphony Orchestra

In 1923 a popular new arrival, Luigi von Kunits, organized some of his students and many of Toronto's finest professional musicians into a new orchestra. By the end of that decade it had become famous across the country.

In 1912, only a few people knew why a musician in Vienna had refused to become the conductor of the famous Philadelphia Orchestra and, instead, had accepted an offer to come to Toronto as a music teacher.

In Philadelphia, the vacant position was offered to a 30-year-old conductor named Leopold Stokowski, who accepted it at once. In Toronto, hardly anyone had ever heard of the violinist from Vienna, but every major musician in this city knew the stories that surrounded him, and his arrival marked one of the great turning points in the city's musical history. For it was this man, Luigi von Kunits, who in the 1920s became the founder of the Toronto Symphony.

He was Viennese by birth, born on July 20, 1870, within sight, it was said, of the city's fabled St Stephen's church. His family's friends included many of the musicians and composers of Vienna and it soon became obvious to everyone that the young Luigi had an extraordinary musical talent.

When Luigi was 11 years old one of his father's closest friends, the composer Johannes Brahms, selected him to play the second violin in the premiere of his latest quartet. That almost unprecedented honour for one so young was to have a profound effect on the young von Kunits. In the past, he had often skipped his violin lessons; now to the delight and sometimes despair of his family, he began getting up at 5 a.m. to practise.

At the University of Vienna, in addition to studying languages, philosophy, and law, he took classes in composition with the composer Anton Bruckner, and at the age of 21 he wrote a violin concerto considered so remarkable that he was invited to perform it with the Vienna Philharmonic Orchestra. His mother was a devout Roman Catholic and hoped her son would become a priest, but at the university friends spoke about the success that many European musicians were finding in the United States. At the age of 23, Luigi suddenly informed his family that he was quitting his religious studies and leaving Vienna to join an Austrian orchestra that had been booked to play at the World's Fair in Chicago.

When the fair closed, he decided to remain in Chicago, and for the next two years supported himself as a violin teacher. As his reputation grew, he was frequently invited to perform with the Chicago Symphony. Stories of this remarkable young composer and violinist from Vienna soon became known in a number of musical circles and in 1896 he was invited to become the concert master and assistant conductor of the Pittsburgh Symphony Orchestra. He accepted at once and the next 14 years were among the happiest of his life.

In Pittsburgh, he fell in love and married. He was still the same ardent Greek scholar that he had been at university, and he gave all his children Greek names such as Nausicaa and Astyanax. One daughter, who settled in Mississauga, was christened Aglaia. These names may have been beloved in Greece but, as Aglaia would later confess, 'As we grew up, they seemed increasingly hard to bear.'

In 1910, von Kunits requested a leave of absence. He took his family to Europe and spent the next two years performing his own violin concerto and the concertos of Brahms, Mendelssohn, and Paganini in cities across Europe. It was while he was in Vienna, visiting his family, that two unexpected letters arrived from North America.

One, from Philadelphia, offered him the kind of position he now longed to hold. He was invited to become the conductor of the city's famous symphony orchestra, but he was unable to accept. In later years, Aglaia would write that her father's life may have brought him some fame, but it brought him little fortune and a great deal of heartache. Shortly before the offer from Philadelphia arrived he had suffered a heart attack, and was warned by his doctor that he was not to undertake any strenuous form of work for at least another year. This, coupled with his wife's wishes that the family settle permanently somewhere, led him to accept the second offer, which came from Toronto, a city he barely knew.

He had visited it a few times when the Pittsburgh orchestra had been invited to perform with the Mendelssohn Choir, and a five-year contract guaranteed him an opportunity to start a new career that appealed to him. A Canadian Academy of Music had been founded in Toronto in 1911 to keep some of the more gifted students in the city and to attract outstanding teachers from Europe. Von Kunits was offered the position as the principal teacher of the violin in this new academy.

From his first years in Toronto he became one of the city's most beloved and admired figures. At Christmastime, he was deluged with gifts from his students, everything from carpet slippers to a small 'mountain' of Christmas cakes. Many of his first students, such as Harry Adaskin, Geoffrey Waddington, and Albert Pratz, would become major figures in the musical world of Canada, and in 1922 it was some of his own students who prompted him to found a symphony orchestra in Toronto.

To von Kunits, the timing was perfect. He was now strong again and the offer proved irresistible. But there was one major problem. Many of the finest musicians in the city were supporting their families by playing in orchestras in theatres and vaudeville houses. Von Kunits would not allow them to jeopardize their careers on the chance that the new symphony orchestra might succeed, so he proposed a highly original solution. All the performances would be Twilight Concerts. They would begin at 5 p.m. and end in time for the musicians to be at their theatres for the evening performances.

To play in this new orchestra he chose many of the city's finest professional musicians, but also included many of his best students and a number of enthusiastic, gifted amateurs such as Dr J. Pilcher, a bass clarinetist who was a professor at Wycliffe College. On April 23, 1923, their first public performance was an unqualified success; the reviews next day were raves. The quality of the playing was so high that Stokowski, when he later appeared as a guest conductor, said he would hire any one of the string section for his orchestra in Philadelphia without an audition.

In 1929, years before the Canadian Broadcasting Corporation was founded, the Canadian National Railways began a series of national radio broadcasts. It soon discovered that the acoustics in the Arcadian Court restaurant, on the top floor of Simpson's department store (now the Bay) on Queen Street in Toronto, made

Luigi von Kunits and the Toronto Symphony Orchestra broadcast concerts in the 1920s from the Arcadian Court restaurant.

it 'the finest broadcasting room in Canada.' On Sunday afternoon, October 20, all the dining room tables were removed and the restaurant was transformed into an enormous radio studio for 'the most ambitious broadcast ever attempted in Canada.' That historic performance became the first in a series of regular broadcasts that would make the orchestra famous across the country. In its early days, it had been known as the New Symphony Orchestra; in 1927, it was re-named the Toronto Symphony Orchestra.

The von Kunits family was now living at 29 Rose Avenue, near Sherbourne and Carlton Streets, in what was then a very fashionable part of town. It was there that he would often work long into the night transcribing scores to suit the special talents of performers in his orchestra. He was always the first to volunteer to accompany any of his favourite pupils at their first recital. He would also readily agree to appear as the guest artist at concerts staged throughout the province, even when the society or organization could not afford to pay even a token fee.

In 1931, he began to suffer from an occasional fever, but refused to allow any performances of the orchestra to be cancelled because of him. Suddenly, on October 8, almost without warning, he was dead. At the request of the University of Toronto, his body lay in state in Convocation Hall on the campus.

The following year, the members of his orchestra paid their own special tribute. During his last years, he had often confessed to them that Beethoven had always been his favourite composer. In Beethoven he had found 'the most permanent values in music.' On the night of the opening concert of its tenth season, the Toronto Symphony Orchestra performed the Funeral March from Beethoven's Eroica Symphony in honour of its founder.

On the podium that evening stood the man von Kunits had personally chosen as his successor, one who would extend the fame of the orchestra throughout North America, a 38-year-old Torontonian named Ernest MacMillan.

16

The epic tale of the Scottish Highlanders and Toronto's first Roman Catholic church

The first great wave of Roman Catholics to settle in this province came from the villages of the Scottish Highlands. Their religious leader played an important part in the history of Toronto and of Ontario.

The first great wave of Roman Catholics who settled in this province were not French-speaking or Irish immigrants. They were Scottish Highlanders. They arrived by the boatload in the early 1800s. And the first Roman Catholic church to be built in Toronto is part of their story, for its founder was the Scottish missionary priest who led them to Upper Canada in 1801.

The greatest number of the men belonged to the clan of the Macdonells, and the one who became the most celebrated of them all was the Reverend Alexander Macdonell. In the early history of Upper Canada, it is said, he played such a leading role that the story of his life is largely the early history of the Roman Catholic church in this province.

That story is recorded in the major history books in Scotland. In Canada, the importance of his later years as the first Roman Catholic bishop in Upper Canada has always been acknowledged. It is his early years as a missionary priest and the story of St Paul's, the first Roman Catholic church in Toronto, that are less well remembered.

His clan, the Macdonells of Glengarry, had been devout Catholics ever since the arrival of the first Christian priests in Scotland.

Even in the years following the Reformation, when most of their churches were destroyed, they kept to their faith. When Alexander Macdonell was born on July 17, 1762, in Glen Urquhart, Inverness-shire, there was not a single Catholic college in all of Scotland. When he chose to live his life as a Catholic priest, he had to move to France. There he enrolled in the Scottish College in Paris and completed his studies at the Scots College at Valladolid in Spain, where he was ordained at the age of 25. He returned at once to Scotland and for the next five years served as a missionary priest in the highest and least inhabited parts of the Highlands.

Most of the families he met had been farmers for centuries. But in the 1780s their Scottish landlords had begun evicting them, to turn the valleys and hills into more profitable sheep-walks. When Macdonell realized that few of the families had any place to go, he went to Glasgow and persuaded factory owners to hire them. Since these Highland families spoke nothing but Gaelic, Macdonell promised to come with them and serve as their interpreter, and hundreds of families joined him in Glasgow.

In 1794, when Napoleon ordered a blockade of all English ships, trade between England and the European continent virtually ceased. Scottish factories began closing and the Highlanders soon found themselves without a job. Macdonell realized that the only way he could now help was to make soldiers of them. England, he knew, would need all the men it could get for its armies. With the approval of government officials in London, he organized the Glengarry Fencibles, the first Roman Catholic regiment to serve in the British army since the time of the Reformation. The head of the clan, Ranaldson Macdonell, offered to serve as its commander. Alexander Macdonell would be its chaplain.

In 1801, during a period of peace, the regiment received word that it was to be disbanded and, again, the Highlanders faced a bleak future. This time, Macdonell went to London and asked that, in recognition of their service to the king, the soldiers be granted land in one of the new British colonies. Government officials were looking for settlers, and it was finally agreed that land would be given to every Highland family who would emigrate to Britain's newest colony, Upper Canada.

As soon as news of this mass immigration scheme reached Scotland, factory owners in Glasgow became alarmed at the thought of losing thousands of skilled workers. They demanded that port authorities place an embargo on all ships: none would be allowed to sail for North America with more than one passenger for every two tons of cargo. Macdonell persuaded a number of sympathetic

St Paul's was the first Roman Catholic church in Toronto. The original building, depicted by Owen Staples, stood on the site of the present St Paul's on Power Street.

captains to help him smuggle his Highland families out of the
harbours. And in 1801, vessels filled almost entirely with Scottish
Highland families began sailing for Canada.

On their arrival, each head of a family was granted 200 acres
of farmland in the eastern part of the province, in an area that
became known as Glengarry County. In the years that followed
and down to the present, it has always been renowned as one of
the largest and most ardently Scottish settlements on this continent.

When Macdonell realized there were only two Catholic priests
in the province, he began the first of many journeys to visit all
the widely scattered Catholic settlements. These journeys were
often made alone, and he would frequently travel more than 700
miles to the lands beyond Lake Superior. On his first visit to the
capital of the province, York, later named Toronto, he laid the
plans for the first Catholic church to be built there.

The threat of an imminent war with the United States delayed
all building plans, however. When war did come, in 1812, Macdonell called on his Highlanders to form a 2nd Glengarry Fencibles
regiment, and his men once again served with distinction.

Once the war was over, Macdonell's principal work became the
establishing of new churches throughout Upper Canada. During
his lifetime, 48 new churches would be built. One of these, in
1822, was the first Roman Catholic church in Toronto, St Paul's.
On land granted by the government, its site was at the eastern
end of town, near the corner of today's Queen and Parliament
Streets.

As the Reverend Edward Kelly recorded in a 100th anniversary
volume, *The Story of St. Paul's Parish 1822-1922*, Macdonell immediately came to Toronto to help raise the money to build it.
The town's Catholic community was almost entirely poor Irish
immigrants but many Protestants readily donated to the building
fund, and enough was raised to build an impressive church of red
bricks brought from Kingston. At a time when Toronto was almost
entirely a town of plain wooden buildings, the new St Paul's was
often described by travellers as its most beautiful building. It stood
for close to 70 years until a new St Paul's was built in 1889, a

The Right Reverend Alexander Macdonnell
was the religious leader of Highland
Scots who settled in Upper Canada.
(Mezzotint by Martin Archer Shee)

magnificent structure in the Renaissance style, that stands today on the site of the first St Paul's at 83 Power Street.

For more than 30 years after the provinces of Upper and Lower Canada were created in 1791, there was only one Roman Catholic bishop for the entire area, the Bishop of Quebec. In 1826, this enormous diocese was divided. A new diocese of Kingston was created and the man who was chosen to become the first Roman Catholic bishop in Upper Canada was Alexander Macdonell. Four years later, another honour followed when he was chosen by the new lieutenant-governor, Sir John Colborne, to become a member of his legislative council. Macdonell moved to York and built a house at the southeast corner of Jarvis and Adelaide Streets. He included a small chapel on his land that, in times of trouble, became known as York's 'soup kitchen.'

The one last great goal of Macdonell's life was to see a seminary established in Upper Canada. The province, he said, needed more native-born priests. In 1839 he laid the cornerstone for the seminary he hoped to build in Kingston. In the autumn of that year, he made plans to sail to Britain to raise the money to complete it. There was a huge crowd at the docks to wish him Godspeed and, as his ship pulled out into the lake, a jubilant Macdonell shouted back, 'Wait till I return ...' But it would be the last time friends in Upper Canada would see him alive.

He arrived in England during a bitterly cold winter but insisted on completing all his proposed journeys across England, Ireland, and Scotland. In the far north of Scotland he became gravely ill and on January 14, 1840, at the age of 77, he died, quite suddenly, in the town of Dumfries. By then he had became a legendary figure to the people of Scotland. When his body was brought to Edinburgh for burial at St Margaret's Convent Chapel, it was said, 'Not since the days of Scotland's royalty had so magnificent a funeral been seen in Edinburgh.'

For years afterwards, families in the Highland communities in Upper Canada continued to hope that his body might one day be brought back to this country. When a new cathedral was built in Kingston, a site was set aside for his tomb. Finally, in 1861, arrangements were approved and the body of Alexander Macdonell, the first Roman Catholic bishop in Upper Canada, was brought back to this country and buried in the cathedral near the heart of Glengarry County.

17

The blind young veteran who founded the CNIB

*At a wartime hospital in London, when a young
lieutenant was told he would never see again,
he vowed that a sniper's bullet would never cost him
independence. What he did thereafter won him
the admiration of millions around the world.*

At a glittering reception in the summer of 1954, Edwin A. Baker of Toronto was welcomed to Paris by the president of France. In 1959, by royal command, the route of a proposed tour was changed to allow Queen Elizabeth to meet him during a visit to Toronto. And in 1967, on the 100th anniversary of the founding of Canada, when the government honoured the 150 most outstanding living Canadians, Edwin Baker was among those who received this country's highest award and became a Companion of the Order of Canada. He was then 74 years old and for the past 52 years had been totally blind.

It was said of him that few men who received so many honours ever deserved them as richly as he did. He was a 22-year-old lieutenant when he was blinded during World War I. At a hospital in London, when doctors told him he would never see again, Baker vowed he would never lose his freedom or his independence because he had lost his sight. On his return to Canada, he inspired thousands of Canadians and, in 1918, became the chief founder of the now world-renowned Canadian National Institute for the Blind.

In the 1950s, when people throughout Canada raised $4 million to build a national headquarters for the CNIB in Toronto, it was the unanimous decision of all the committees concerned that the building be named after the two men who had made it possible: Lewis Wood, the financial genius behind the fund-raising, and Edwin Albert Baker, whose dream it had been. When the great building was opened on April 16, 1956, it was called BakerWood.

From its beginning in a small back room on College Street and a staff of three, the CNIB has grown into an organization with more than 50 offices across Canada. The only part of its story more inspiring than its success is the story of Baker himself.

He was born on January 9, 1893, in the house his grandparents had built 100 years earlier at Collins Bay near Kingston. In 1914, he was among the first to enlist and, on the night of October 9, 1915, while his company was moving up to Ypres, he was hit by a single shot from a sniper's rifle.

At the hospital in London, when he woke after a final operation, he found he had lost the use of both his eyes. Bitter and feeling helpless, he refused to speak to anyone; he flung the tray across the room if anyone tried to feed him in bed.

Late one night a visitor pressed a watch into his hands. It was a watch with dials that could be read with fingers and, for the first time since he became blind, Baker felt a sense of independence. Now, when he woke at night, he would never again have to call out to ask what time it was. When he asked about the visitor, he was told it had been Sir Arthur Pearson, the founder of the London newspaper, the *Daily Express*, who was going blind himself. He had sold his newspaper and had used his money to build St Dunstan's Hostel for Blinded Soldiers.

Sir Arthur had a theory, revolutionary at the time, that the blind could live reasonably normal lives and become self-supporting, providing they were offered proper training. Baker asked if he could meet him and, after their first conversation, wrote to his parents to say he would not be home for a while. He was going to St Dunstan's.

He learned how to read Braille and how to type, and soon overcame all his early frustrations. But he was not prepared for the letter from his girl back home, who wrote that she could never marry a blind man.

On his return to Canada, although he found he could help on the family's farm, he longed for the independence that could come only from a paying job. His friends were so impressed by his spirit that they arranged an interview for him with Sir Adam Beck, head of the Ontario Hydro. 'I don't want anything soft,' he told Sir Adam. 'If you'll give me a month's time, I'll make good or fire myself.' He was hired to take dictation from engineers and amazed them so completely with his accuracy that, a month later, he was on permanent staff.

Word of the extraordinary young blind veteran at the Hydro reached military officials and Baker soon became one of the most popular speakers at the war bond drives at Massey Hall. In 1917, when he learned that the Canadian Free Library for the Blind was

Edwin Baker, who lost his sight in World War I and went on to found the Canadian National Institute for the Blind, is greeted by Queen Elizabeth in 1959.

being forced to close, he persuaded the Toronto Women's Musical Club to come to its aid. The women raised more than $7,000 and the library moved into a house of its own at 142 College Street.

In a room at the back, Baker started occupational training courses for the blind and, with the first signs of success, conceived the idea of creating a national non-profit organization. On March 30, 1918, a charter was drawn up and the Canadian National Institute for the Blind was born with Baker as its vice-president and managing director.

In the months following the end of the war, large numbers of blinded men began returning from Europe and Baker was placed in charge of their training. As the scope of his work continued to grow, he resigned from Hydro in 1920 and joined the permanent staff of the CNIB. He married Jessie Robinson, daughter of the editor of the Toronto *Telegram*. In 1925, buying doors and panelling from some of the mansions that were being demolished in Toronto and by scouring the auction houses, they were able to build and furnish an attractive house at 412 Russell Hill Road in the new village of Forest Hill.

As Marjorie Wilkins Campbell wrote in a biography of Baker, *No Compromise*, his successes during the next three decades were phenomenal. As early as the 1920s, the CNIB had begun opening cafeterias and snack bars in factories and offices, all operated by blind people. Baker won government support for many new projects by proving that any investment would be repaid ten times over when the blind became self-supporting. He also became increasingly involved in projects to prevent blindness and helped to found the Canadian Ophthalmological Society. He never lost his association with the military, and was made an honorary colonel in the Canadian army.

In July 1951, Baker received word from Paris that he had been unanimously chosen to become the first president of the World Council for the Welfare of the Blind and during the following years he toured the world building that organization. After Lewis Wood's death in 1954, he was made honorary president of the CNIB and never retired from his work for the blind.

In the 1960s, the Bakers gave up their home in Forest Hill and moved to a house on a bay near Kingston where Baker had been born. It was there that Colonel Edwin Baker died on April 7, 1968, at the age of 75.

The Toronto Star headlined its tribute with these words: 'Through Sightless Eyes, A Vision.'

18

The Toronto nurse who changed her name and became Elizabeth Arden

How a struggling young nursing student decided to spend her life making people feel and look beautiful, and ended up making herself rich as well.

In the early 1900s, a young student nurse named Florence Nightingale Graham quit her job in Toronto and moved to New York. She changed her name to Elizabeth Arden and, in the words of *Fortune* magazine, 'earned more money than any other businesswoman in the history of the United States.'

By the 1930s, she had founded an empire of Elizabeth Arden beauty salons and Elizabeth Arden beauty products were being sold in almost every country in the western world. To the astonishment of every male executive who ever met her, she ran her business entirely by herself. She owned all the stock, she was chairman of the board, and president of every Elizabeth Arden company. Photographs of her that regularly appeared in the press for almost half a century rarely indicated how small she was. She was only slightly more than five feet tall and often looked rather fragile but, in the words of one admirer, 'she was about as fragile as a football tackle.'

Her story became one of the major success stories of the time but few Canadian women, even those who use her products today, are aware that she was a Canadian, born on the outskirts of Toronto in the village of Woodbridge. Her mother was an English woman from Cornwall who eloped to marry a Scot, William Graham, and, as soon as they were safely married, emigrated with him to Canada. They settled in Toronto, but Graham was not happy living in a big city. He soon leased about 200 acres of land along the upper reaches of the Humber River and moved his family to the nearby village of Woodbridge. He became a market gardener and sold vegetables in the village, and was known as an affable and popular figure, although some of his neighbours considered him an eccentric. He had always been an ardent horseman and never used anything but discarded race horses to pull his vegetable wagon.

There were soon five children in the family, and when one of the daughters was born her mother named her after an English nurse she admired, Florence Nightingale. In later years, Florence was always rather vague about her age but it appears she was born on December 31, 1884. The money that her father earned barely supported the family and the Grahams survived chiefly on a generous annual allowance sent to the children by an aunt in England. When she died, the allowance abruptly stopped and Florence had to leave school and find a job.

She was then 18. She moved to Toronto and during the next year worked at a variety of jobs, including brief periods as a cashier, stenographer, and dental assistant. Finally, she thought she had found her career when she enrolled as a student at one of Toronto's nursing schools. She never completed the course because she soon realized she did not want to spend her life looking after sick people. She not only wanted to make people well, she decided; she also wanted to make them look and feel beautiful.

She was not sure where she would find such a career but was convinced she would never find it in Toronto. In 1908 she left the city to join her brother, William, in New York. Within 10 days of her arrival she knew exactly where she wanted to work and got a job as an assistant in Eleanor Adair's beauty salon.

Adair was a European who had opened the first salon in America that offered revolutionary new beauty treatments known as 'facials.' She had also begun to attract a great deal of publicity by recommending that women use skin tonics and creams to improve their complexion. Even as late as the turn of the century, no 'respectable' woman used any cosmetics except, perhaps, some talcum powder and a little rose water. It was considered almost as scandalous for a woman to 'paint' her face as it was for her to smoke. But in the years immediately preceding World War I, a new kind of freedom emerged for women. Even *Vogue* magazine dared to suggest that 'a little colour applied discreetly' could enhance a woman's appearance.

To Florence, the benefits of facial massages and skin creams were obvious, and she knew she had found her true career at last. She quit her job and became a partner in a beauty shop run by an acquaintance, Elizabeth Hubbard. It was a stormy partnership and soon broke up. Florence immediately borrowed $6,000 from her brother and took over the shop. It would need a new name and she knew that no government official in his right mind would allow her to register a beauty shop under her own name of Florence Nightingale. She wanted a name with a sense of style, and since her favourite book at the moment was Tennyson's *Enoch Arden* she decided that Arden had the right kind of ring to it.

There have always been two versions about how she decided on the second name. One story is that it came from another of her favourite works, *Elizabeth and Her German Garden*. A more outrageous version is that since the store already had the name Elizabeth Hubbard, it would save money if only one of the two words had to be repainted. Whatever the truth behind the story, Florence Nightingale Graham was now Elizabeth Arden.

From the beginning she knew exactly the combination of exercises and beauty treatments she would offer her clients and, in the words of the *New York Times*, 'she soon convinced women that they could attain that mysterious thing called beauty if they permitted themselves to be steamed, rolled, massaged, and bathed in wax in her sumptuously decorated salon.' Once her salon was successfully established she began to consider the idea of selling her own line of cosmetics in stores all across the country. In her opinion, all new face creams coming onto the market were either 'too hard' or 'too sloppy.' She wanted something 'like whipped cream' and when she introduced her Cream Amoretta it became

Elizabeth Arden left Toronto and found riches in New York.
(Portrait by Rawlings)

the basis for a line of cosmetics that by the 1930s would be a
multi-million dollar business.

She was solely responsible for the introduction of more than
300 Elizabeth Arden products and by the 1940s had opened more
than 100 Elizabeth Arden beauty salons in America and Europe.
She was one of the first to make the world of cosmetics seem
glamorous, and her advertising campaigns with headlines such as

'Every woman has a right to be beautiful' became classics.

The competition began fighting back, claiming that most of her products were made of quite ordinary ingredients and said that one of them was in fact made of nothing but castor oil and water. Arden's answer was that she always based her products on natural ingredients. There was a famous story at the time about one of her client's cooks, who had discovered a jar of Elizabeth Arden's Orange Skin Cream in the refrigerator and had mistakenly used it in making a cake. As the cook's employer happily informed Elizabeth Arden, the cake had been served to the entire family, it had been considered delicious, and there had not been the slightest sign of any ill effect.

By the 1940s, Elizabeth Arden owned the most prestigious beauty salon business in America and the clients at her main Fifth Avenue salon included many of the leading names in New York society as well as the Begum Aga Khan, Clare Booth Luce, Beatrice Lillie, and Mrs Dwight D. Eisenhower. In 1947, she was offered $17 million for her business but refused even to acknowledge the offer.

Like her father, she had always been interested in race horses and, as her one principal hobby, she began buying thoroughbreds and won more than $4 million with her stable. She married twice but both marriages ended in divorce.

During the last 30 years of her life, she lived in a 10-room duplex apartment at 834 Fifth Avenue, decorated almost entirely in pink. Very early in life, she had discovered that the most flattering colour for women was pink. She not only wore pink; she added pink to her hair colour, and it became the signature colour of her entire line of cosmetics.

In 1954, during its 50th anniversary year, the Canadian Women's Press Club honoured her as one of Canada's most remarkable women. Later that year, she was invited by the executives of the Humber Valley Conservation Authority to return to Toronto. On September 25 she helped dedicate the new Dalziel Pioneer Park in the Humber Valley near Woodbridge and planted a ceremonial maple tree on the land that had been her playground as a child. That tree now is part of a small grove on the site of today's Black Creek Pioneer Village.

On October 18, 1966, Elizabeth Arden died at the age of 81, of a heart attack, in New York. Shortly afterwards her company was sold, and is now owned by Unilever Ltd. In her will, she left many generous gifts to her family and friends, including $4 million to be divided among longtime employees, but there was no mention about the future of her business. In the words of the editors of *Notable American Women*, 'Apparently she could not conceive of a life for Elizabeth Arden after Florence Graham was gone.'

The informal Elizabeth Arden in 1954, planting a
maple tree in a historical park, now part
of Black Creek Pioneer Village

19

Bea Lillie: 'The funniest woman in the world'

She was a reigning star of Broadway and London, but until the Duke of Edinburgh unveiled a plaque to her, few Torontonians knew she had been born in this city, just north of the railway tracks.

For more than 30 years she dazzled the international theatre world. In the 1930s and 1940s she was the star of some of the most famous shows on Broadway and in London's West End. Noel Coward wrote songs for her. The *New York Times* theatre critic, Brooks Atkinson, once described her as 'quite simply the funniest woman in the world.' In 1989, when Canadian newspapers reported she had died in England, many Torontonians were startled to learn that she had been born in Toronto in a small, narrow house near the corner of Queen Street and Dovercourt Road.

For years, there had been plans to mark the house with a historical plaque, but the family that lived there in the 1980s weren't interested. They had never heard of Beatrice Lillie. They weren't alone. Even some of her most ardent fans have forgotten what a truly legendary figure she was.

On the night of December 7, 1944, she was the star of the most glittering opening night that Broadway had seen since before the war. Billy Rose had spent a fortune restoring the historic old Ziegfeld Theatre and, for its opening show, *The Seven Lively Arts*, he had booked many of the greatest theatrical celebrities from both Europe and America. Cole Porter and Igor Stravinsky were commissioned to write the music, and the cast included Bert Lahr, Broadway's favourite comedian, Benny Goodman, America's most popular jazz artist, and the world's reigning ballerina, Alicia Markova. But the undisputed star of the show was Toronto's Bea Lillie. The moment she stepped on stage, the audience gave her a five-minute standing ovation.

There are hundreds of stories still being told about her, and many of the best are the ones she told about herself, especially about her early years growing up in Toronto. 'We were located,' she said, 'half way up the social ladder. Or half way down. It depends on which way you're looking.'

Her father, John Lillie, was an Irishman 'who made a habit of running away from home.' Her mother, the former Lucie Shaw, was half Spanish, half English and an accomplished concert singer. The house where Beatrice Gladys Lillie was born, on May 29, 1894, is a narrow, red-brick eight-room building that still stands at 68 Dovercourt Road, although the front has been greatly modernized. 'It had a garden in front,' Bea remembered, 'as big as a handkerchief.'

The house stands only a few blocks north of the Canadian National Exhibition grounds and, as a small child, Bea always looked forward to her days at the CNE. 'I'd have been happy to spend every day of my life there.'

At the age of five, she became a pupil at the Gladstone Avenue School, now re-named the Alexander Muir School after its headmaster, the author and composer of *The Maple Leaf Forever*. Almost every day, she would wait for Muir at the school gates and walk beside him on her way home.

Her mother became a leader of the local choir and was determined that both her daughters would become professional musicians. Muriel, Bea's older sister, had the talent to become a concert pianist, she decided. Bea, a promising soprano, would be a concert singer. By the time Bea was in her early teens, her mother had organized the Lillie Trio, and the three women were touring concert halls across the province.

But by then Bea had discovered that, in her own words, she was 'a natural born fool.' One Easter, she was thrown out of a local choir for leaning over the choir stalls and nonchalantly fanning herself with a palm leaf until the congregation was in hysterics. When Muriel won a scholarship, Mrs Lillie put Bea in a boarding school for safekeeping, and she and Muriel sailed for Europe.

Bea hated the school and hated being separated from her mother and sister. Within a year she joined them in London. Her mother helped her get bookings as a ballad singer in variety houses, but the turning point in her career came in 1914 when she auditioned for a French producer, André Charlot, who had become famous for his 'intimate revues.' Bea never believed for a moment he would hire her and decided she would simply enjoy the audition. She had discovered she could make audiences laugh by injecting irrelevant gestures into a song. She decided to sing for Charlot the most outrageous song she knew: 'The Next Horse I Ride On, I'm Going to Be Tied On.' She followed it with an Italian street song during which she kept frantically waving a bunch of grapes. The producer was slightly bewildered but delighted, and at the end of the audition offered her a three-year contract at £15 a week.

During the wartime years that followed, Bea gradually acquired a reputation as a promising young comedienne-singer on the London stage. In 1919, almost every major newspaper in Canada carried the story that 'the popular Ontario-born singer,' the 25-year-old Beatrice Lillie, had become engaged to 21-year-old Robert Peel. He was the great-grandson of one of the famous figures in British history, Sir Robert Peel, a former prime minister of England and the man who had created London's first permanent police force. Londoners had nicknamed policemen 'Peelers' and 'Bobby's Boys' and, finally, simply 'Bobbies' in honour of him.

None of the family attended the wedding of his great-grandson to a West End actress and the marriage would not be a happy one. The young Peel had almost no money of his own, and was an inveterate gambler. Within a year Bea was back on the London stage earning enough money to support the two of them. Shortly afterwards, there was a son. He would be their only child, and was christened Robert Peel.

By the early 1920s, Bea had become one of the principal performers in André Charlot's revues. In 1924 he took his latest show

to New York. The moment Bea came on stage as a slightly de-
mented 'Britannia,' she was an instant success. By the 1930s she
had become famous for her irreverent sense of fun. 'Nobody,' said
The Times of London, 'was ever nastier in a nicer way than Bea
Lillie when she set out to murder a sentimental ditty.' She would
select some simple love-sotted ballad and before she had sung its
first line there was a distinct glint in her eyes that assured her
audience that she didn't mean a single word of what she was
singing.

Beatrice Lillie appeared as a mermaid in the
stage production 'Inside USA' in 1948.

In 1925, her father-in-law died. Her husband assumed the family's hereditary title and became Sir Robert Peel. Bea became Lady Peel. Nine years later her husband died, leaving her with debts of £10,000 and a 13-year-old son to raise. When war broke out in 1939, Robert was 18 and enlisted in the Royal Navy. Bea spent most of her time entertaining the troops.

In April 1942, she was in Manchester when a cable arrived at the theatre informing her that Robert was missing in action. That night, Bea posted this message on the cast's bulletin board: 'I know how you all feel. But let's not talk about it, darlings. Bless you. Now let's get on with the show.' Months later, it was confirmed that he had been killed during an attack on his ship by Japanese planes somewhere off the coast of India.

When the war ended, Bea returned to her full-time role on the stage and appeared in a long list of successes. She also starred in a number of Hollywood films but was never happy or completely successful as a film actress. She missed the live audience.

In 1975, while living in New York, she suffered a stroke that left her partially paralysed. She was seriously ill for months, and stories in the press reported that she had been forced to sell her furniture and paintings to pay her medical bills. But none of the stories was true. She had saved enough money to buy a comfortable home at Henley-on-Thames in England. As soon as she was well enough to travel, she returned to England, and it was there that she died on January 20, 1989, at the age of 94.

She had long been a favourite of the royal family, and for years there had been plans to have a member of the royal family unveil a historical plaque to her in Toronto. In 1989 an ideal site was found. At 1115 Queen Street West, near her home, there is a large Edwardian building that had been the local public library when Beatrice Lillie was living in the area. It has now been handsomely renovated and turned into the District Office of the Toronto Department of Public Health. On March 14, 1989, during a stay in Toronto, the Duke of Edinburgh unveiled a plaque on the building and dedicated it as the Beatrice Lillie Building, a lasting memorial to her.

20

Why Mackenzie King built a replica of Pasteur's tomb in Toronto

Mackenzie King's youngest brother, Max, was his closest and most trusted friend. King's final tribute was the tomb he chose for him in Mount Pleasant Cemetery.

In 1922, when his younger brother died, William Lyon Mackenzie King ordered a tomb built for him in exactly the same style as the tomb of Louis Pasteur in Paris, and buried him beside the graves of their father and mother in Mount Pleasant Cemetery.

His brother had been King's closest friend for many years and his death was the last in a series of personal misfortunes that would deeply affect Mackenzie King's life. In the space of a few years, his older sister, his father, and his mother had all died. Their graves, close by, are marked by a large Celtic cross.

Mackenzie King's grandfather was William Lyon Mackenzie, the Scottish immigrant who led the rebellion of 1837 that attempted to overthrow a Provincial government he believed was corrupt. His grave in the Necropolis Cemetery in Toronto is marked with the same type of monument, a cross that was used for centuries to mark the graves of the ancient kings and heroes of Scotland. But for his brother King chose an entirely different design. The reason is known to relatively few who come each year to the cemetery to see the grave of the older brother who, for more than 20 years, was prime minister of Canada.

Both Mackenzie King and his brother, Dougall Macdougall King, were born in Kitchener. Their mother, Isabel, was the youngest daughter of William Lyon Mackenzie. She had married a young and promising lawyer in Toronto and they settled in Kitchener where John King soon established a successful practice. The Kings had four children – Willie, Max, Isabel, and Janet. In his biography of Mackenzie King, *The Incredible Canadian*, Bruce Hutchison wrote: 'The Kings were small gentry when gentility still counted for something. The town knew them as good citizens and friendly neighbours. Mrs King's treasonable origins had been forgiven or forgotten.' She was always intensely proud of her father and her pride was deeply shared by her oldest son, whom she had named after her father.

In 1893, John King secured a position at Osgoode Hall. The family moved to Toronto and into a large house at the corner of D'Arcy and Beverley Streets. It now bears a Toronto Historical Board plaque in memory of Mackenzie King.

Both Willie and Max attended the University of Toronto. After graduation Willie became an outspoken reformer, like his grandfather, and was soon writing newspaper articles exposing the working conditions in Toronto where women were being paid three and four cents an hour to make uniforms. He demanded the establishment of minimum wage laws, and, in 1900, at the age of 25, was offered the post of deputy minister of labour and moved to Ottawa. Eight years later he was elected to parliament and in 1909 became minister of labour under Sir Wilfrid Laurier. In 1919 he succeeded Laurier as leader of the Liberal Party.

Max chose a career in medicine. When the South African War broke out in 1899, he joined the army and served as a corporal in the medical corps. The conditions under which he lived during the next few years in remote outposts in South Africa would permanently affect his health. In 1913, shortly after opening a medical practice in Ottawa and becoming the father of twin boys, he became critically ill with tuberculosis. He had to move his family to a warmer climate where he could recuperate in a sanitorium and for the next two years he lived in Colorado.

The following year, war broke out in Europe and, as Max's health gradually began to improve, he decided to write a book he would call *The Battle of Tuberculosis and How to Win It*. He was aware that many veterans would be returning from this war, as he had from the last, with their health affected and prone to the same illness he had contracted. And he believed there would be a great need for a book, written by someone who had won the battle, that would give hope to all who read it.

He could work for less than an hour at a time and it took two years to complete the book. Then, just when he felt well enough to resume his practice, he contracted a far graver illness, muscular atrophy. This time he knew there could be no hope of recovery. All he could look forward to was gradual paralysis and the slow approach of death.

The thought of spending the last years of his life in prolonged inactivity was unthinkable and he began work on a second book. He knew that he would steadily become weaker and prone to nervous diseases but he knew that the experience of what he would be living through could, once again, be of use to others. He called his new book *Nerves and Personal Power*. Again, it would be a book filled with hope of a victory over illness.

During those last years, Max and Mackenzie King grew even closer together. Max, in fact, became the only friend and critic that Mackenzie King would listen to. After his death, there would be no one who would replace him.

In 1921 Mackenzie King was elected prime minister. The first telegram he sent was to Max and four weeks later he left by train for Colorado for what both of them knew would be their last meeting. On March 18, 1922, Max died.

Many have said it was the tragedy of four close deaths in so short a time that drove Mackenzie King to spiritualism to keep the memory of his family alive for him. According to Reginald Hardy, in *Mackenzie King of Canada*, King had seen in his brother's life the same devotion to science and medicine that had symbolized the career of the great French scientist Louis Pasteur, whose work had done so much to help eradicate tuberculosis. King became an avid reader of Pasteur's writings, particularly his philosophical works, and believed his brother had made a not unimportant contribution to the history of medicine. For his tomb, Mackenzie King ordered a copy to be made of the tomb of Pasteur that rests in the crypt of the Pasteur Institute in Paris.

Mackenzie King resigned as prime minister in 1948, after an unprecedented number of years in that office. He died on July 22, 1950, and was buried beside the graves of his parents and his brother. His monument, unlike the others, has no lengthy inscription. It is the simplest of the three, a plain slab of the strongest Canadian granite bearing only the words 'Mackenzie King.'

Mackenzie King's grave is marked by a simple
slab in the family plot. The Celtic cross
commemorates his parents and sister; the more
ornate tomb, a copy of Louis Pasteur's,
he built for his beloved brother Max.

21

The true story behind Charles Dickens' visit to Toronto

Charles Dickens told no one – except his publisher – the real purpose behind his visit to North America in 1842. The novel he wrote after it outraged Americans.

No one in America knew the real reason why Charles Dickens arrived in the summer of 1842 to tour most of the major cities of the United States and Canada.

At the time Dickens was still a relatively young man. He was barely 30 but had already written three highly successful novels and would soon become one of the most popular and perhaps the greatest of English novelists. His first major book, *Pickwick Papers*, written in 1836, had established him as one of England's most promising writers. His next two novels, *Oliver Twist* and *Nicholas Nickleby*, won him international fame.

He had become the most eagerly sought-after new celebrity in Britain. Everyone wanted to meet him. In 1840, he was invited by the Duke of Wellington to spend the Christmas holidays at his country estate. There Dickens met the chief justice of Upper Canada John Beverley Robinson.

When Dickens visited Toronto two years later, the major social event of his time in this city was a banquet given in his honour by Robinson at Beverley House, Robinson's home close to Osgoode Hall. Curiously, it was almost the only event that has ever been documented about Dickens' visit to Toronto. Despite the enormous crowds that turned out to see him in many American cities, there was apparently no public reception for him in Toronto, and the newspapers virtually ignored his visit. But the greatest mystery surrounding his tour was the purpose behind it.

None of his friends and none of his hosts in North America, only his publisher in London, knew that the reason why Dickens had embarked on such an exhausting tour was to collect material for a travel book. It was published a few months after his return to England. When copies arrived in North America there was a storm of protest from almost everyone in the United States who read it. The following year, when Dickens used some of the notes taken on his tour as material for a new novel, *Martin Chuzzlewit*, there was an even greater outcry from American readers.

Dickens never understood the furor he created and the story of his tour, particularly the Canadian portion, has always been largely glossed over in most of his biographies. But, to those who knew him, it was not surprising that he would use the people and places he had visited as material for his books. Dickens constantly used the people he met, even members of his family, as principal characters in his work. Even his father, it is said, was the model for one of his most beloved characters, Mr Micawber in *David Copperfield*, the novel which was as close to an autobiography as anything he would ever write.

Dickens' father, John Dickens, was working as a clerk in the Navy Pay Office in Portsea, near Portsmouth, when a son was born on February 7, 1812, and christened Charles John Huffam Dickens. The elder Dickens always wanted to be seen as a gentleman but had little sense of money or responsibilities and was constantly in debt. When Charles was 12 his father was sent to a debtors' prison and Charles was forced to leave school and start earning his own living. The only job he could find was pasting labels on bottles in a filthy factory. That part of his childhood became the darkest period of his life, and the humiliations he suffered during the next few years would leave lifetime wounds.

When his father was finally released from prison, Charles vowed he would never face poverty again. He got a job as an office boy, learned shorthand, and was soon hired as a newspaper reporter. By the time he was 20 he was writing short, usually humorous pieces for a number of London magazines. In 1836, when he was 24, he was asked to write the text that would accompany a series of sporting prints. Dickens elaborated the texts into a story of English country life and it became his first successful novel, *Pickwick Papers*. *Oliver Twist* followed in 1838; *Nicholas Nickleby* in 1839. He was now happily married and, early in 1842, he and his wife decided to make a six-month tour of North America.

Charles Dickens

Throughout the early 19th century there had been a number of highly unflattering reports, written by Englishmen, about their visits to America. Largely because of his own personal background, Dickens had become an avid social reformer and was a great admirer of the new republican institutions that had been introduced in the United States. He decided he would write a travel book that would refute these earlier accounts and, to avoid being overwhelmed by patriotic speeches by overeager hosts, he told no one but his publisher what he proposed to do. He simply announced that he was taking a quiet holiday. But he completely underestimated the fame and publicity of his books in America. In the words of one of his biographers, Stephen Leacock, 'The country went wild over him.'

There were lavish banquets in his honour in both Boston and New York. But within weeks of his arrival Dickens was totally disillusioned. On March 22, 1842, he wrote from Baltimore to a friend in England, W.C. Macready: 'This is not the Republic I came to see. This is not the Republic of my imagination ... Even England, bad and faulty as the old land is, and miserable as millions of her people are, rises in the comparison.'

He was shocked by the living conditions in all the prisons he visited. He was offended by the Americans' 'boastful patriotism' and was incensed by their harsh treatment of their slaves, especially in the South. 'He didn't like the South,' Leacock wrote in *Charles Dickens: His Life and Work*, and added: 'The West was to finish him.'

In his travels down the Mississippi River Dickens was appalled by the seemingly endless number of settlements of ill-built homes rotting away along its banks. In his public speeches he began telling Americans what he thought of them and their country and the crowds got smaller. Even the press stopped reporting on his tour.

By the time he headed north and crossed into Canada, it must have become a virtually private tour. Otherwise it is difficult to explain why none of his major biographers or any Canadian writers have ever written in detail about his visit to Toronto. Almost all that we know of his days here are the impressions that he later recorded in his book.

After his disillusionment south of the border, Dickens thoroughly enjoyed his stay in the new British colony of Canada. When his *American Notes* appeared, he wrote largely in praise of everything he saw in Toronto: 'The country round this town being very flat, is bare of scenic interest but the town itself is full of life and motion.' The stores along King Street, then Toronto's main shopping centre, he said were 'excellent' and 'would do no discredit to (London) itself.' He visited Upper Canada College, and there is a legend at the school that he spoke to the students in Prayer Hall, but he never recorded such an event.

The one thing that deeply shocked him was his discovery that the Irish settlers in Toronto had brought the 'troubles' of Ireland with them to Canada. Dickens sadly noted in his book a recent incident involving an Irish Orangeman who had fired on a group of politicians, killing one of the people in the crowd.

A major Toronto sight that particularly interested him was a broad new thoroughfare (later to be named University Avenue) that had been built leading north from the city to the site of the province's first university (soon to be named the University of Toronto). It is, he wrote in his *American Notes*, 'a long avenue which is already planted and made available as a public walk.' And he praised Toronto's many well-laid 'footways,' adding: 'The town is well adapted for wholesome exercise at all seasons.' At the time of his visit, the view looking north on University Avenue was particularly impressive, with its rows of trees seeming to stretch to the horizon. For decades afterwards the avenue continued to be used as a private roadway to the university, with gates at its southern entrance at today's Queen Street.

The anger that erupted in the United States when Dickens published his *American Notes* in 1842 was nothing compared with the furor that greeted the appearance of his next novel, *Martin Chuzzlewit*. In it, Dickens sent the hero to seek his fortune in a town in the American Midwest surrounded by fever-ridden swamps and settled by some of the most vulgar people he had met on his tour. He modelled the town after Cairo, Illinois, and sarcastically renamed it Eden. It was years before his American readers, especially those in the West, forgave him.

By the time he returned for a second visit in 1867, Dickens was in his fifties, the author of *Great Expectations*, *David Copperfield*, and *A Tale of Two Cities*, and had become one of the most beloved writers in the English-speaking world. By then many, but not all, of the past differences between Dickens and his American readers had been forgotten.

On his return to England, his friends were concerned to see how

The College Avenue (now University Avenue) in 1868, a generation
after Dickens remarked on the trees newly planted along its length.
This picture comes from the first book of photographs of Toronto.

pale he had become. He had also grown noticeably thinner but
few realized how very sick he was. Despite his ill health, he now
conceived the idea of reading from his books at public performances and embarked on an exhausting series of 'recital tours' of
the principal cities in Britain and the United States, primarily to
add to the amount of money he hoped to leave his family.

His marriage had ended in a separation but his books had earned
him enough to buy Gad's Hill, a home in Kent he had admired
ever since he first saw it as a small child. In 1870, he began work
on a new novel, *The Mystery of Edwin Drood*, but never lived to
finish it. On June 9, 1870, Dickens died of a stroke at Gad's Hill
at the age of 58.

Generations of English families had grown up knowing and
loving his novels, and throughout Britain his death was seen as a
national calamity. In the words of *The Times*, 'Statesmen, men of
science and philanthropists might pass away and yet not leave the

void which will be caused by the death of Dickens.'

Dickens had always detested pomp and the kind of extravagance that had surrounded the funerals of many public figures and had directed, in his will, that his funeral be 'inexpensive, unostentatious ... and strictly private.' But as soon as his death was announced, people throughout Britain began saying that he should be buried in Westminster Abbey. The Dean of Westminster wrote to Dickens' family and his body, in a plain coffin, was brought in secrecy to London. There he was buried, with only the family and a few friends present, in the Poet's Corner in Westminster Abbey.

By nightfall, all of London knew that Dickens had been buried in the abbey. The next day, people came in the thousands to place wreaths and bouquets near his grave until the floor of the entire south transept of the abbey was covered with flowers.

22

How Leo Tolstoy and a Toronto professor brought the Doukhobors to Canada

It was called the largest mass immigration Canada had ever handled. The principal Canadian figure in the story was a professor who is remembered as 'the Aristotle of Toronto.'

At the very end of his life, Leo Tolstoy, the greatest Russian author of his day, returned to writing fiction. The sole reason behind his last great novel was to raise money to help thousands of Russian families emigrate to Canada.

It was called the largest mass immigration which Canada had ever handled. In January 1899, the first of close to 10,000 Russian families began arriving at our eastern seaports on their way to new homes in the Canadian West. They were a devoutly religious people who called themselves the Doukhobors (Wrestlers for the Holy Spirit). The man who had persuaded the Canadian government to approve of this great immigration scheme was a professor at the University of Toronto, James Mavor.

The novel Tolstoy wrote to help finance the expedition he titled *Resurrection*. He had written *War and Peace* when he was in his thirties, *Anna Karenina* in his forties. He was now 71. Mavor, at the time, was a comparatively young man, only 37, and had only recently emigrated to Toronto from his native Scotland. His involvement with the Doukhobors has always been among the most highly publicized stories of his life, but in his twenties Mavor was already an admired, even notorious, figure in Britain. If his name is unfamiliar to most Torontonians today, the name of his daughter, the late Dora Mavor Moore, is remembered by many Toronto theatregoers and his grandson, Mavor Moore, is a prominent Canadian playwright.

James Mavor never planned to emigrate to Canada, but there is a saying repeated by generations of Scottish historians: 'Scotland has always sent most of her educated sons abroad, because she is too poor to keep them at home.' He was born on December 8, 1854, at Stranraer, the son of a school teacher and the eldest of nine children. It was a time when Glasgow was one of the world's centres of both the arts and sciences and the young Mavor soon became involved in both fields.

His friendship with inventor William Thompson led to an interest in electrical engineering; his talents as a writer earned him a position as editor of the *Scottish Art Review*. His engineering work brought him into close contact with a large number of workers in the factories of Glasgow. There he first became aware of the appalling conditions faced by most of the workers and their families, who were living in ill-managed and overcrowded tenement buildings. The discovery turned him toward socialism.

He became one of the original directors of Glasgow's Working Men's Dwelling Company, and joined the then notorious Fabian Society. At the meetings of this society Mavor met the Irish playwright George Bernard Shaw. Shaw was so impressed by the zeal of the young man that when he later wrote his play *Candida*, he named Candida's husband James Mavor as a form of tribute to him.

By the time Mavor was in his mid-thirties he had become one of Britain's leading authorities in the fields of co-operative societies, labour unions, and labour colonies in Europe. He became increasingly interested in political economy, the one scholarly subject that encompassed not only industry and the arts but also religion, government, law, and even the manners and customs of society. In 1889, at the age of 35, the highly regarded young Mavor was appointed professor of political economy at St Mungo's College in Glasgow.

Three years later, an unexpected but attractive offer came from

Canada, inviting him to become professor of political economy at the University of Toronto. In the autumn of 1892, Professor James Mavor arrived in this city.

In 1975 Rachel Grover organized an exhibition, 'James Mavor and His World,' at the University of Toronto's Rare Book Library. The commemorative brochure that accompanied the exhibition described Mavor's arrival in 1892 'as though a small tornado had hit Canada.'

He wore a long beard and, although only 37, looked like a man of 70. He was careless about his clothes, disdainful of anyone with an average incompetence, and totally overwhelmed his students. He lived in a house (now demolished) that stood on the campus at 8 University Crescent, near the site of today's Convocation Hall, and soon attracted a wide and influential circle of friends. To those who came to know him well, it was said, his knowledge of the world came as a breath of fresh air. He enthusiastically committed himself to aiding any young writer of promise, and was a member of the founding committee of the Art Gallery of Ontario. Six years after his arrival in Toronto, a letter from a Russian, Prince Peter Kropotkin, whom he had met in Britain, led to Mavor's involvement in the emigration of the Doukhobors.

The origins of that sect are still obscure, but it is believed it first arose among a peasant group in southern Russia. They were dissidents from the traditional Orthodox Church, and were persecuted because they rejected all forms of worldly governments and were avowed pacifists. Many of their leaders preached the idea of communal living that would later be advocated by Tolstoy in many of his writings. In the 1890s, when the Empress of Russia finally granted permission for the Doukhobors to leave Russia, no country was willing to accept them, until Tolstoy wrote an impassioned article to plead their cause.

Prince Kropotkin sent a copy to Mavor in Toronto. Correspondence began between Tolstoy and Mavor that eventually led to Mavor formally approaching the Canadian government to secure permission for the Doukhobors to settle here. Tolstoy announced that he would write a novel and would donate the entire royalties to help pay for the emigration expenses. British Quakers, who

James Mavor, first professor of political
economy at the University of Toronto

enthusiastically shared the Doukhobors' belief in pacifism, also
offered support.

In January 1899, the first wave of these Russian immigrants
arrived in Canada. They settled on land the government had provided for them in the West, but their later and permanent settlements would be in British Columbia. They would face difficult
years, particularly during World War I when they refused to enlist
in the armed forces. They also bitterly resented the government's
plans to build schools on their property and take over the responsibility for the education of their children.

When the first of the Doukhobors arrived, Mavor travelled to
the West to ensure they were being treated well. In July 1899 he
also visited Tolstoy at his home in Yasnaya Polyana, near Moscow,
to report on the success of the venture. When Mavor arrived on

a later visit in 1910, he learned that Tolstoy had left home and was now living with his daughter Tatiana at Mzensk, where Mavor finally joined him.

Tolstoy, 'the Pre-Revolution Revolutionary,' had grown to despise property in all its forms. He was now giving away his valuable manuscripts and had become totally unconcerned about royalties or any other form of foreign payments he might receive from his books. There had been mounting quarrels with his family, particularly his wife, and Tolstoy had abruptly abandoned her. It would be the last time Mavor would see Tolstoy alive. Two months later, on November 20, at the age of 82, Tolstoy was dead.

For years, Mavor had been fascinated by the complex history and the diverse culture of the Russian people and had even learned to speak and read Russian. On his return to Canada, he began work on two enormous projects. Out of his years of struggles against social injustice and his new and deep interest in Russia emerged two classics: *An Economic History of Russia*, published in 1914, and *The Russian Revolution*, published posthumously in 1928.

In 1910 Mavor (*at right*) visited Leo Tolstoy in Russia. With him are P. Nikolaiev and (*centre*) the novelist's son, Count Leo Leovich Tolstoy.

In 1923, when he retired from the university, his friends arranged for the publication of his memoirs. Mavor titled his book, *My Windows on the Street of the World.*

Although neither his work at the university nor his international fame as a writer had ever brought him more than a modest income, he was always passionately fond of travelling, and spent many of his summers travelling alone through Europe and Asia. In 1925, on his way to visit friends in the south of France, the man who was once called 'the Aristotle of Toronto' died in Glasgow and lies buried there in the family plot.

23

The Grange: an architectural treasure

One of the most romantic landmarks of Toronto is a Georgian house, built in the early 1800s in the middle of a forest. Today it stands in the heart of downtown.

There is only one house in Metropolitan Toronto that the Canadian government has declared one of the architectural glories of this country. It stands almost in the centre of downtown Toronto, but when it was built in the early 1800s it was in the middle of a forest. So dense were the woods that stories were told of young British officers becoming lost in them, then suddenly entering a clearing and finding themselves in front of a magnificent Georgian country house.

It was built in 1817 for a man considered so unimportant in Canadian affairs that his name appears only as a passing reference on one of the historical plaques now standing in front of the house. But D'Arcy Boulton was not a minor figure in Toronto's history. He was in his early twenties when he and his parents came to live in Upper Canada, and few histories of 19th century Toronto omit this family, who dominated much of the early social and political history of the city.

The family's home was originally in Lancashire, in northern England. D'Arcy's father, D'Arcy Boulton, Sr, studied law at the ancient and renowned Middle Temple in London but soon gave up all plans for a law career to become a merchant. When his business failed he emigrated with his family to the New World. They settled first in the United States, in 1797, but in the early 1800s, with the promise of greater opportunities in the new British colony of Upper Canada, they moved north and settled in York (later renamed Toronto).

There were few qualified lawyers in the province and almost none with the kind of formal training Boulton had received in London. In 1804, when the solicitor-general died suddenly, the post was almost immediately offered to him. Ten years later he was the province's attorney general and the family was securely established.

The eldest son, D'Arcy Boulton, Jr, was 21 when the family settled in York. Two years later he allied his family with the man who would become one of the most powerful and influential in the province when he married Sarah Anne Robinson, the sister of John Beverley Robinson, the future chief justice of Upper Canada.

D'Arcy had studied to become a lawyer like his father but had little interest in the world of law courts. Many of his friends were growing rich by becoming merchants and shortly after his marriage he opened a store at the corner of King and Frederick Streets, in the heart of the town. By 1817, he had enough money to indulge himself in a grand project that had been on his mind for years. He bought 100 acres of land to the west of town and began planning a large and handsome home that would be the family's 'seat' for generation of descendants.

D'Arcy had always had a flair for architecture and decided to model his home in the style of the great Georgian homes that dotted the countryside of England. He would call it 'The Grange,' a name used for centuries in England to mark the residence of a country gentleman. D'Arcy personally supervised all the plans for its construction, often leaving his office for days at a time. When it was complete, it was one of the handsomest homes in the province. A large measure of its glory was its park-like setting and the magnificent forest of tall trees that surrounded it.

That early grandeur became the subject of a number of paintings of 19th century Toronto, notably one titled simply *The Grange*, by the Alsatian artist, Henry Perre. In the definitive history of the building, *The Privileged Few*, John Lownsbrough wrote that the house also became a symbol of social importance: 'The Grange testified to the position D'Arcy Boulton had established for himself in the community.'

Despite his distaste for days in court, D'Arcy had accepted the office of Master in Chancery, and would later accept a position of some importance as chairman of the board of magistrates for the Home District. In the late 1820s, when there was a depression in Upper Canada and he was in need of money, he sold the northern half of his estate, and it became part of the site for a new college that in 1850 became the University of Toronto.

During his later years, the Grange became increasingly the centre of all the pleasures of his life. He planted large orchards and laid out cricket and lacrosse fields and built a race course, the St Leger, to the north of the house. When all his children had grown up, he turned the nursery and one of the large bedrooms on the second floor into a music room. And he expanded the main-floor drawing room until the house became one of the greatest showplaces of the new young city.

Boulton was never a particularly robust man, and what he regularly referred to as his 'enfeebling illness' proved to be a form of serious heart disease. On April 10, 1840 he died at the Grange. Those who succeeded him as masters and mistresses of the Grange would become far more celebrated.

D'Arcy's son, William Henry Boulton, served as mayor of Toronto from 1845 to 1847, and again in 1858. After his death in 1874, his widow married one of the most celebrated English writers of that time, Goldwin Smith. For the rest of that century and well into Toronto's Edwardian years, the Grange was renowned as the home of the only internationally famous author in Toronto. Neither Goldwin Smith nor his wife had any children. In the early 1900s a close friend, Sir Edmund Walker (later the founding chairman of the Royal Ontario Museum), suggested to them that they leave their home and all its land to the city as the setting for Toronto's long-awaited first public art gallery. Both of the Smiths warmly approved of the plan. After their deaths, the first exhi-

The Grange, first building of the Art Gallery of Ontario, was still a private home when Henri Perre painted it in 1880.

bition in the Grange of the new Art Museum of Toronto (now the Art Gallery of Ontario) opened in the spring of 1913 and was held in the second-floor music room. By then the acres of land in front of the house had been turned into a new public park.

In the decades that followed, the art gallery added large modern wings to the north of the house, but by the 1960s the Grange had fallen into a serious state of disrepair. In 1967, the directors of the AGO asked the Women's Committee if it would help to organize the complete and authentic restoration of the Grange to its appearance in its most elegant period, the 1840s. The Women's Committee launched a fundraising campaign that was an overwhelming success.

Today, the Grange is open to the public, and is staffed with knowledgeable volunteers dressed in the style of costumes worn by servants, cooks, and parlour maids in the 1840s. D'Arcy Boulton's former home has become one of the most graceful and important 'living museums' in the country.

In the 1980s, the Canadian government placed two historical plaques in front of the house to commemorate Goldwin Smith and Edmund Walker. In 1984, the Grange became one of the few buildings in Canada to be awarded *three* federal plaques. In that year the government designated the Grange one of the architectural treasures of Canada.

The Grange has been restored to its 19th century elegance as one of Toronto's finest 'living museums': this is the drawing room.

24

The extraordinary story of a dog named Beautiful Joe

One of the greatest publishing successes in Canada's history is a book about a dog that has sold 7 million copies and is still loved by children around the world.

In 1892, Margaret Saunders began her newest book with one of the most famous opening lines in Canadian literature, 'My name is Beautiful Joe.'

The book told of the adventures of a mutilated dog who had been named Beautiful Joe by a group of small children who adored him; and it became one of the greatest publishing phenomena of its time. It was translated into more than 14 languages including Japanese, Chinese, and Bulgarian. By the 1930s, it had worldwide sales of over 7 million copies and is still in print to this day with the Toronto firm of McClelland and Stewart.

In 1914 its author moved to Toronto, and to generations of school children one of the highlights of their lives was a visit to a small cottage at 62 Glengowan Avenue to meet the most beloved writer most of them would ever know. To Canadians, she was more famous than the author of *Black Beauty*. She wrote more than two dozen books but none of them, even *Beautiful Joe*, ever made her a wealthy woman. She never published the story of her life and thousands of her readers today are probably unaware that she was a Canadian or that she was once one of Toronto's most popular celebrities.

She was born in the Maritimes and was a descendant of one of the ministers who arrived with the Pilgrim Fathers on the *Mayflower*. In 1761, a branch of the family moved north from New Hampshire and settled in Nova Scotia, where Margaret Marshall Saunders was born on May 13, 1861. Her father was a Baptist minister in the village of Milton, in Queen's County, and her earliest memories were of growing up in a house filled with books and pets.

Her father sent her to boarding schools in Scotland and to a Protestant School in France to improve her French, and she seemed to have inherited his love for all animals. In later years, she would often tell the story of how she had studied at the school in France with a mouse tucked up her sleeve. When she returned to Canada she became a teacher, but her life in Europe had made her restless and she spent several years travelling across the United States and living in California.

By the time she returned home, her father had become the minister of the First Baptist Church in Halifax and later would become a prominent historian of the Maritimes. Margaret had still not decided what she wanted to do with her life until a friend of her father, Dr Theodore H. Rand, chancellor of McMaster University, suggested one day, 'Why don't you write of the winter's beauty of Nova Scotia's woods?'

As she would later confess, she found herself 'enchanted' by the idea of becoming a writer, but her sister suggested that, instead of writing about scenery, she write something 'with blood and murder in it – lots of blood, people like that.' And so her first story became a tale of an unhappy marriage and a terrifying robbery in Spain, two things she knew absolutely nothing about. She called it *My Spanish Sailor*, sent it to an American magazine, and was astonished to receive a cheque for the then huge sum of $40.

Dazzled at how easy it was to be a successful writer, she told her father she had found her profession. But all her next stories were rejected by every editor who saw them. Several years passed before a small book, *Daisy*, was accepted. It was not until 1892, when she visited Ontario, that she found the subject for the book that would make her famous.

Sir Charles Tupper, another of her father's friends, had found a job for her brother, Jack, in Ottawa as a civil servant. There, he had fallen in love with Louise Moore, a boarder in the rooming house where he lived, and married her. In 1892, when Margaret visited them, she was invited to Louise's home in Meaford, Ontario, on the shore of Georgian Bay. During that visit she heard the story of a mongrel dog that had been cruelly mutilated by its original owner. The man had cut off its ears and tail and the dog would have died if Louise's father, Walter Moore, the local miller, had not rescued it and made it the family pet. As everyone in Meaford remembered, the grateful animal became a one-man-dog for the rest of its life.

Margaret was touched by the story. Soon after her return to

Margaret Marshall Saunders,
author of *Beautiful Joe*

Halifax, she read about a contest being conducted by the American Humane Education Society. It was offering a prize of $200 for a story 'illustrative of the kind or cruel treatment of domestic animals or birds.' What the society really wanted was a book that would do for other dumb animals what a popular new book, *Black Beauty*, had done for horses.

She decided to enter the contest with a book about the Ontario dog. She would write it in the form of an autobiography written by the dog itself and she would call him Beautiful Joe. She filled it with all the incidents in the life of a small dog that she knew would delight every child, but she also filled its pages with sound, practical advice about how to care for a pet. In the words of a later reviewer, 'It breathed a passion against all cruelty to dumb animals.'

It won first prize, but when someone offered only a few hundred dollars for all publishing rights, Margaret's father was indignant. 'It cost me $100 for your typewriter ribbons alone,' he said. Margaret sent her book to a long list of American publishers and was finally accepted by the American Baptists Publication Society.

Her book became an instantaneous success. In addition to all its foreign editions, it was the first Canadian novel to be published in the universal language of Esperanto. But it never made Margaret Marshall rich. 'Royalties were never very good,' and she had only moderate success with later books, written mainly about other pet animals.

In 1914, when she was in her fifties, she came to Toronto and moved into rooms on the top floor of a boarding house at 66 St George Street. There her first friend was a squirrel that regularly scratched on her roof at night. When her father died, Margaret's younger sister, Grace, came to live with her and they moved into the small, attractive cottage at 62 Glengowan Avenue that still stands there today.

The house was always filled with pets, and she had a habit of naming each one after the place where they had been found. There was a pigeon named 38 Front Street and a dog called Johnny Doorstep. Thousands of small children came to visit her. She became known over the years as the Children's Comrade, and the

Friend of the Helpless, for she was one of the world's born 'protectors.' She also became Canada's national symbol of what one person could do in the cause of a more humane treatment of defenceless animals.

For years, she was also one of Canada's most popular speakers. At writers' clubs she would regularly denounce those Canadian professors who were discouraging students from becoming writers because they could never reach 'the standards of Oxford and Cambridge.' This 'colonial mentality,' she said, was destroying our most promising writers. She was realistic enough to know that most authors would have to move to the United States to make a living or give their stories American locales before a publisher would accept them. She herself had had to turn Beautiful Joe into a dog from Maine rather than a dog from Ontario before her book was accepted. However, she constantly urged writers to stay in Canada. 'Americans have fine writers of their own. They do not need ours,' she said.

She also recognized another problem. Women authors were not popular. She herself had had to adopt the masculine-sounding name of Marshall Saunders to make her books more acceptable to publishers. (Marshall was her middle name.)

In 1931 there was a great public celebration at the Royal York Hotel to mark her 70th birthday. Three years later, when she was told that she had been honoured in the King's birthday list as a Commander of the Order of the British Empire, she was so touched that she could not speak to reporters and simply broke down and cried. During her final years, she became increasingly ill and unable to leave her home. On February 15, 1947, she died there at the age of 85.

In 1963, in Meaford, close to the site where the original Beautiful Joe lies buried, a new park was created and named Beautiful Joe Park. On its lawns the Ontario government placed one of its historical plaques to ensure that the story of Margaret Marshall Saunders would always be remembered.

25

The international (and surprising) tale of Mrs Morrison's opera house

Only the Metropolitan Opera House in New York, it was said, had a more legendary past in the musical life of North America.

More than a century ago, there was a Grand Opera House in downtown Toronto, and it was one of the most famous on this continent.

For more than 30 years, it was one of the very few theatres in North America where nearly all the great singers and performers of the time regularly appeared. Hector Charlesworth, who knew the theatre's history well, once wrote: 'Of all the stage doors in America, the one that is richest in associations is probably that of the Grand Opera House in Toronto – with the sole exception of the Metropolitan Opera House in New York.'

This was where Europe's Sarah Bernhardt, Ellen Terry, and Henry Irving appeared when they first toured North America. In 1899, this was where the Metropolitan Opera Company performed on their first visit to Toronto. But all the stories about the Grand Opera House have been overshadowed by a single legend that has nothing to do with anything that appeared on its stage.

One afternoon in December 1919 the owner of the Grand Opera House deposited $1.5 million in his Toronto bank account, and that was the last time he was seen. His body was never found. The mysterious disappearance – and possible murder – of Ambrose

Small is now almost the only story told about Toronto's once-fabled opera house. But there are memories of the building that date back to its very beginning.

From the night the theatre opened on September 21, 1874, in its splendid new building at 9 Adelaide Street West, it seemed destined for years of success. The money to build it had been raised by a joint stock company founded by a number of wealthy Torontonians, and the first manager of the theatre was one of the most admired actresses in Canada.

It was a time when many of the great theatrical companies of Europe and America were run by actor-managers. Sarah Bernhardt and Henry Irving both founded their own theatre companies. The actress who was the unanimous choice as manager of Toronto's elegant new 1,644-seat opera house was Charlotte Morrison. She was the daughter of the owner of the Royal Lyceum Theatre in Toronto and had been a popular performer in the city for a number of years. She was so well-known, in fact, that the new theatre was originally known as 'Mrs Morrison's Grand Opera House.'

For the first opening night she chose a play with a perfect part for her, as Lady Teazle; its performance would also serve as a tribute to the theatre's principal patron. She had persuaded the governor-general, Lord Dufferin, to be her theatre's honorary patron; and the play was one of the great classics, *School for Scandal*, written by Lord Dufferin's ancestor, Richard Sheridan.

The Grand Opera House enjoyed a large number of early successes, including performances of Handel's *Messiah* by the Philharmonic Society of Toronto. But Mrs Morrison was a better actress than a theatre manager, and the house was soon in serious financial difficulties. It was saved from bankruptcy by Alexander Manning, one of the wealthiest men in Toronto, who had served as mayor in 1873, and who bought it in 1876. Three years later, it lay in ruins, totally destroyed by fire, and the curious events surrounding its destruction would haunt Toronto's theatre world for years.

On Friday, November 28, 1879, the night of the fire, the Grand Opera House was offering the play that all actors consider the world's most 'cursed' drama, Shakespeare's *Macbeth*. So many unexplainable and frequently deadly incidents have occurred during performances of it that many actors refuse to speak its name, and refer to it only as 'the Scottish play.' An entire book has been written solely to record some of the most famous disasters surrounding its production: *The Curse of Macbeth* by Richard Huggett.

In Toronto, on that November night, nothing unusual appeared to have occurred during the performance. But shortly after midnight, a fire that had been lit by the three witches, which everyone believed had been extinguished, began to smoulder again. By 3 a.m., the entire building was ablaze. By dawn the Grand Opera House was a smouldering mass of bricks and stone.

Its new owner, Alexander Manning, immediately announced he would rebuild the theatre in all its original splendour. In the incredibly short time of 51 days, it reopened. In the years that followed, many of the greatest singers and theatre companies from New York, London, and the European continent performed in Toronto's Grand Opera House.

In February 1883, Mme Emma Albani sang *Lucia de Lammermoor*. That same year, the Polish actress Helena Modjeska, one of the great international actresses of her time, starred in *As You Like It*. In October 1884, Sir Henry Irving, the first English actor to be knighted, appeared as *Hamlet*. A record of those performances, together with rare copies of original theatre programs, was compiled by the opera house's engineer, Thomas Scott, and is now part of the special collection of the Arts Department at the Metro Toronto Library.

The Grand Opera House continued to prosper throughout the closing decades of the 19th century, but with the opening of the even more elegant Royal Alexandra Theatre in the early 1900s the years of its greatest successes were coming to an end. The last of its famous legends began in 1903 when the theatre was bought by the notorious Ambrose Small.

Hector Charlesworth, one of the major theatre critics in Toronto's past and editor-in-chief of *Saturday Night* in the 1920s, was always fascinated by the 'Ambrose Small Affair,' because the magazine's early home had been in rooms in the Grand Opera House. In his books, *Candid Chronicles* (1925) and *More Candid Chronicles*

The Grand Opera House on Adelaide Street was the setting for a
performance of Handel's *Messiah* in 1875.
(Engraving from a sketch by F.M. Bell-Smith)

(1928), Charlesworth related some of the legends that surrounded
the opera house and his own version of the story of the life and
passing of Ambrose Small.

Small's entire career was centred around the opera house. His
father owned a hotel at the corner of the opera house lane at 13
Adelaide Street West, and Ambrose's first job was as a bartender
for his father. In his teens, he was hired as an usher at the opera
house, but he was hot-tempered and quarrelsome and after one
particularly violent incident he stormed out of the theatre, saying
he would never return until he owned the building. In 1903, when
he had made a considerable fortune through what have been described as 'treacherous dealings,' he returned as the theatre's new
owner. But he had also made a host of enemies. There was a
saying around Toronto, 'Someone will get Ambry one day.'

In 1919, he sold a large chain of theatres he had acquired, and
on the afternoon of December 2 deposited the then enormous sum

of $1.5 million in his Toronto bank account. Then he disappeared. A $50,000 reward was offered, but nothing more was ever known about him. Some said he had been killed in the Grand Opera House, but the last time he was seen he was walking briskly away from the theatre. Charlesworth never had any questions in his own mind about how the story ended: 'Beyond doubt, Small was murdered.'

Small's wife became the theatre's new owner. In *Look at the Record: An Album of Toronto's Lyric Theatres 1825–1984*, Joan Parkhill Baillie recorded the major successes and eventual collapse of the Grand Opera House. By World War I it had been turned into a vaudeville house. By the early 1920s it was a movie house. One of its last small moments of triumph came in 1924 when *Dorothy Vernon of Haddon Hall*, the latest film of Toronto's most famous actress, Mary Pickford, received its world premiere under its roof. By the end of that year, the doors were closed for the last time, and the building was boarded up. Three years later, it was demolished.

26

The Reverend John Strachan's grand deception

In 1819, Toronto's most distinguished religious figure masterminded one of the most curious cases of forgery in Canadian literature. His book attracted tens of thousands of willing immigrants to Canada.

In many ways it is the most surprising deception in Canadian literature.

In 1820, publishing houses throughout Europe and North America were printing travel guides for a new generation of adventurous world travellers. In the spring of that year a small publishing house in northern Scotland, D. Chalmers & Co., issued one of the first important guide books about Canada.

It was titled *A Visit to the Province of Upper Canada in 1819*, and its author was said to be an obscure Scottish merchant named James Strachan. The book became a great success throughout Britain; a century later it was still considered so valuable that it was reprinted by S.R. Publishers of England. It was not until 1946 that the true identity of its author came to light. It happened when the Archivist of Ontario, George W. Spragge, was preparing the publication of a collection of the Anglican bishop of Toronto's private papers (*The John Strachan Letter Book, 1812–1834*).

From letters written in the 1820s, Spragge discovered that the guide book had not been written by some 'obscure Scottish merchant.' Its author was in fact the subject of his research, one of the best known, most admired, and most powerful figures during

137

the first half century of Toronto's history, the bishop of Toronto himself, John Strachan.

In the definitive, multi-volume work, the *Dictionary of Canadian Biography*, where many of the great figures in Canada's past can be covered in a page, the summary of John Strachan's life fills more than 14 pages. He is remembered as the founder of the largest university in Canada, the University of Toronto, and countless stories have been told about his heroism during the War of 1812. The curious and, at times, quite hilarious story of his deception in one of the first important books about Upper Canada is possibly the least known story about him but is also one of the more revealing.

There is a legend that when he was born on April 12, 1778, at Aberdeen, it was high noon and high tide and the very hour when most of the villagers were at church. To his mother, this was a clear sign that her son was destined to be a minister. He was the youngest of six children and the son of a local quarry worker. When his father was killed during an accidental explosion at the quarry, Strachan was 16 and immediately became a teacher to help support the family. He later received a grant to study at King's College, Aberdeen. After graduation, since there were few opportunities to earn a living as a school teacher in Scotland, he accepted an offer to teach in the new British colony of Upper Canada, and founded a school in Cornwall that quickly became known as the finest in the province.

In 1807, he married the prettiest and wealthiest young widow in Cornwall, Anne Wood McGill. Strachan had been a close friend of her late husband, Andrew McGill, and it was Strachan who had suggested to Andrew's brother, James, that he leave the bulk of his estate to found a college. When it was finally established in Montreal it was named McGill University.

To secure his future in the New World, Strachan was ordained as an Anglican minister and in 1812 accepted an invitation to come to Toronto (then called York) as the new minister of St James' church. During the American invasion of the town in 1813, Strachan's courage and defiance of the American generals made him a hero, and the war changed Strachan's thoughts about his future career. He had originally planned to return one day to Scotland but his admiration of the settlers, and particularly of the militia whom he believed were the true heroes of that war, made him an ardent Upper Canadian. He resolved to spend the rest of his life in this province.

In the years following the war, the province desperately needed more settlers. By 1820, Strachan had lived in Upper Canada for 20 years and knew the province well. He decided to write a book

John Strachan, first Anglican bishop of Toronto and founder of two of its universities

that would tell of the many opportunities that awaited any immigrant prepared to work hard. Since he was the rector of St James, he could not be seen as the author of a book as commercial as a guide book, and decided to substitute the name of his older brother who was still living in Scotland.

He never informed his brother of his plan and the idea of the deception thoroughly appealed to Strachan's sense of fun. It would be one of his better practical jokes and would, of course, remain a very private joke among the family. As to the format of the book, he decided to base it on his brother's visit the previous year. He began his book with one of the best lines in the joke: 'Not having seen my brother for 25 years, who is respectably settled in Upper Canada, and having some leisure, I determined to pay him a visit.'

The following chapters are filled with a record of the dangers and adventures of crossing the Atlantic. When the ship finally docks at Quebec, Strachan's joke becomes even more elaborate: 'Although my brother resides at York, in Upper Canada, a distance of nearly 600 miles, he was well known and I received attention on his account.' After arriving at York and a reunion with 'my brother,' Strachan devoted the remainder of the book to a fascinating account of life in this province.

There is an entire chapter on 'How The Land Is Cleared.' Another on the province's game laws included this cheering news for all immigrant sportsmen: 'Game laws are unknown in this country. Deer are numerous and you may shoot every one you meet.' One important chapter records how settlers could receive 100 to 200 acres of land 'for nothing except the trifling fee.' Even retail prices in Toronto are generously itemized: 'Beef 7 shillings 6 pence ... China tea 8 shillings a pound ... French brandy 12 shillings a gallon.'

In Strachan's opinion, too many immigrants to Upper Canada had been political malcontents from Britain. He was determined to use his book to attract more farmers, factory workers, and middle class British families who were, in overwhelming numbers, choosing to settle in the United States rather than in Canada.

When the book appeared in shops in Britain, James Strachan was 'in a fume' when he discovered his name had been used as author. He angrily wrote to his brother denouncing the flagrant and outrageous deception. Strachan was still delighted with his practical joke and wrote back, 'I applaud your resolution to have nothing more to do with it but you might ask some of your London correspondents whether they would undertake a corrected and enlarged edition.' His brother was not amused.

The book proved to be an even grander success than Strachan had anticipated. As he later confided to the still furious James, 'The best proof that the book is useful appears from this, that every one of the immigrants who have come out this summer possessed of it say it represents all things as fairly as they are and hides none of the difficulties which they have to encounter.'

Strachan was 42 when the book was published and still largely unknown outside the town. During the next 40 years he became one of the most powerful and influential figures in the life of the province. Religion and education continued to dominate his interests, and in 1827 it was Strachan who sailed to England and secured a royal charter to establish the province's first university. He called it King's College after his old college in Aberdeen, and wanted it to be totally under the direction of the Church of England, in the style of the colleges of Oxford and Cambridge.

His plan antagonized every other religious denomination and in 1850 the government took over control of the college and made it a non-denominational university, renaming it the University of Toronto. Angered by this substitution of a 'godless' university, Strachan sailed again to England and returned with another royal charter. With it, in 1852, he founded another Church of England university, Trinity College, in Toronto.

By then, Strachan had become the first Anglican bishop of Toronto. When a new cathedral was to be built in the 1850s, he insisted that the city was both pious enough and rich enough to deserve and warrant one on the scale of the great medieval cathedrals of Europe. When its huge spire was finally completed, many years after Strachan's death, it became the tallest cathedral in Canada.

By the time Strachan died in Toronto on November 1, 1867, at the age of 89, all old battles were forgotten. On the day of his funeral the entire city closed down, and his body was buried with great pomp beneath the high altar of St James' Cathedral.

Today, every English student knows the name of Cardinal Wolsey, who built Hampton Court Palace and who, in the 16th century, founded what many have called the greatest of all the Oxford colleges, Christ Church. In France, even the youngest students know the name of Robert de Sorbon who, in the 13th century, founded the Sorbonne in Paris. In Canada, one can only wonder how many Canadians recognize the name of John Strachan, who was possibly unique in history as the principal figure in the founding of three universities: McGill, Toronto, and Trinity.

During the ceremonies in 1977 that marked the 125th anniversary of the founding of Trinity, Archbishop Robert Seaborn recalled the importance of the events in its early history and the life of its founder. He closed with the words of an old Russian proverb: 'If you dwell on the past, you lose the sight of one eye. If you forget the past, you lose the sight of both.'

St James' Cathedral in 1868: the spire, added later, would be the tallest in Canada. Strachan insisted that Toronto deserved a cathedral on the scale of those in Europe.

27

Bernard Lonergan: perhaps the finest philosopher of the 20th century

In 1947, in a seminary on Wellington Street, a Jesuit priest wrote a book he proposed to title Insight. *He feared that if he wrote it in Latin, Rome would never allow its publication. So he wrote it in English.*

In the 1940s, during his free hours, Father Bernard Lonergan wrote a book that is now hailed as one of the most important books to be published in this century. Its publication in 1957 passed almost unnoticed by the public. But by the early 1960s, editors of magazines such as *Time* and *Newsweek* began sensing the excitement that his book was creating on college campuses and sent reporters to cover his appearances at major conferences.

Newsweek described him as a philosopher who had set out to do for the 20th century what no philosopher of the Golden Age of Christianity had been able to do for the 13th. *Time* wrote: 'Bernard Lonergan is now considered by many intellectuals to be the finest philosophic thinker of the 20th century.' By the early 1970s, his writings were being translated into French, German, Italian, Polish, Chinese, and Japanese. Today, there are nine Lonergan Research Centres in major cities around the world. University students throughout Europe and the United States use his writings as the basis for doctoral theses.

When Lonergan died at a Jesuit seminary in Pickering, Ontario, in 1984, he was largely unknown to the majority of Canadians, but the news of his death and tributes to him appeared not only in the *New York Times* and *The Times* of London, but in the Belfast *Irish News*, the Hong Kong *Sunday Examiner*, and scores of other leading newspapers around the world.

He had never lived as a recluse, but all of his life he had avoided personal publicity. He had many close friends and they knew him as an inveterate film goer, a man who loved music, Beethoven in particular, and a hand of bridge, and who relaxed at night with a copy of the *New Yorker* magazine. It is not surprising that the press rarely quoted any of the more extraordinary remarks that he made during his lectures at the seminary. All his lectures were always given in Latin and, half-jokingly, he would often tell his students that he read English at night 'to keep in contact with the language.' 'He was,' wrote the *National Catholic Register*, 'a quiet shy man whose shadow has already fallen far into the next century.'

He was 79 when he died, and had spent almost his entire life as a teacher and lecturer. He never had any strong desire to see his works published. 'He was content,' added the *National Catholic Register* (December 7, 1984), 'to be a teacher of teachers rather than a prophet in the public eye.'

His ancestors were Irish. In the early 1800s, a branch of the family emigrated to Canada and settled in Buckingham County, Quebec, where Bernard Joseph Francis Lonergan was born on December 17, 1904. His father was a civil engineer, and the young Bernard was sent to the local school for his education and, later, to the Roman Catholic Loyola College in Montreal.

As reported in the *Compass*, a Jesuit journal (Spring 1985), 'It was in the course of a two-hour ride across Montreal in a streetcar that the 17-year-old Bernard Lonergan made the decision to become a Jesuit.' With his family's approval, he left Quebec and spent the next two years at the Jesuit Novitiate at Guelph, studying the humanities, including Latin and Greek, then left Canada to study philosophy at Heythrop College in Oxfordshire.

In 1930, he obtained his bachelor of arts degree from the University of London, and two years later in Rome was ordained a priest. He was then 28 and would spend more than the next 20 years of his life as a teacher in Catholic schools and colleges in Europe and Canada. In 1947, he arrived in Toronto to teach philosophy at the great Jesuit seminary that once stood on Wellington Street just west of Spadina Avenue. Most of this vast complex of buildings, including a magnificent chapel, had been built by the Sisters of Loretto in the late 19th century. In 1930, when the Sisters moved to a new convent, the Society of Jesus acquired the buildings and turned them into a college where young men could be trained to be priests. In the 1960s, when the seminary acquired new buildings elsewhere, all of these buildings were demolished.

When Father Lonergan arrived as a new teacher at the seminary in 1947, he had already begun to search for a way to overcome what he called, 'the terrible fragmentation of knowledge.' In the words of one theologian, 'He had found it impossible to teach theology correctly without first establishing a viable underlying

The Jesuit seminary, formerly the convent of the Sisters of Loretto, that stood on Wellington Street just west of Spadina Avenue. It was demolished in the 1960s.

philosophy which led him to consider the fundamental question: "What does it mean to know?"'

The method he eventually found would prove so radical it would affect not only the teaching of theology and philosophy but the teaching of mathematics, economics, and even history. In the year he arrived at the seminary he started to put his thoughts into a book. He titled it *Insight: A Study of Human Understanding*, and in its opening pages he clearly defined what he meant by insight: 'In the ideal detective story,' he wrote, 'the reader is given all the clues, yet fails to spot the criminal – for the simple reason that reaching the solution is not the mere apprehension of any clue, not the mere memory of all, but a quite distinct activity of organizing intelligence that places the full set of clues in a unique, explanatory perspective ... Insight is not any act of attention or memory, but the supervening act of understanding.'

Although his book encouraged readers not to fear the answer to even the most awesome question, it was not an anti-religious philosophy. It was solidly grounded on the writings of the great 13th century Italian philosopher, Thomas Aquinas, whose work on reason and faith had formed the basis of Christian thought ever since the 'Golden Age of Christianity' in the Middle Ages. Lonergan feared that if he wrote his book in Latin it would appear to be an authoritative work and Rome would never allow its publication. So he wrote it in English.

When it appeared in 1957, it immediately caught the attention of the intellectual world. Articles by and about him quickly followed. Langdon Gilkey, a Protestant theologian at the University of Chicago, summarized the revolutionary change in thinking that followed its publication: 'I used to read Jacques Maritain or Etienne Gilson to find out what Roman Catholic intellectuals are thinking. Now, I read Father Lonergan to find out what I am thinking.'

Many honours followed. Twelve leading universities conferred honorary doctorates. In 1967, in Canada's centennial year, he was awarded the highest honour that this country can bestow on one of its own citizens, the Order of Canada. In 1974, a Lonergan Workshop at Boston College attracted scholars from all across North America, and Lonergan workshops have been held in that city every year since then.

By the late 1970s, Father Lonergan was in his sixties and had become gravely ill. One of his lungs had to be removed to prevent the spread of cancer, and the last years of his life were spent largely in seclusion, studying and writing. On November 26, 1984, he died in his room at the Jesuit seminary at Pickering.

Five years after his death, the University of Toronto Press and the Lonergan Institute in Toronto embarked on a major project of international importance, the Collected Works of Bernard Lonergan, a work that when completed will fill 22 volumes. In his review of the first volume, *Collection,* Edward MacKinnon, writing in *Thomist,* described it as 'the most readable introduction to the sometimes frustrating, often irritating but ever enlightening thing that is the thought of Bernard Lonergan.'

28

Canada's Margaret Anglin, 'one of America's greatest actresses'

No one was more Canadian: she was born in the Parliament Buildings at Ottawa. In the early years of this century she was a star Sarah Bernhardt called 'one of the few dramatic geniuses of the day.'

In 1958, an 81-year-old actress died in obscurity in a nursing home on the outskirts of Toronto. But the day after her death tributes began appearing in all the major New York newspapers. 'For decades,' wrote the critic of the *New York Times*, 'Margaret Anglin had been one of America's greatest actresses.'

At the age of 22, with the president of the United States in the audience, she had created her first great success. In the often repeated words of the *New York Times*, 'The morning after, she woke up to find herself famous.' During the years that followed, she appeared in more than 80 plays on Broadway and on tour. One memorable evening, Howard Lindsay recalled, she was introduced to the reigning queen of the American stage, Minnie Maddern Fiske, and it was Mrs Fiske who kissed *her* hand. To Sarah Bernhardt, she was 'one of the few dramatic geniuses of the day.'

Other Canadian actresses, such as Mary Pickford, Marie Dressler, and Norma Shearer have become better known, but Margaret Anglin outclassed and out-acted them all; and, as more than one writer has observed, no other Canadian actress ever had a better right to represent this country. Margaret Anglin had been born in the Parliament Buildings in Ottawa.

Her father, Timothy Anglin, was an Irishman who immigrated to Canada in the late 1840s and began his career as a newspaper editor in New Brunswick. In 1867, he became a member of Canada's first Parliament and in 1874 was elected speaker of the House. Two years later, his daughter Mary Margaret was born in the Speaker's Chambers, a private residence reserved for the speaker and his family inside the Parliament Buildings.

In 1883, her father left politics and moved the family to Toronto to return to the newspaper business as editor of the Toronto *Tribune*. Margaret grew up in the great house he bought on University Avenue. The Anglins were staunch Roman Catholics and Margaret, or Mary as she was always known to her friends, was enrolled in the Loretto Abbey School.

Even as a young girl, she had a remarkable speaking voice and was invited to appear in a small part in a French drama at school, but she had little interest then in becoming an actress. She had her heart set on a far less controversial career: she wanted to become a recitalist as a reader of Shakespeare. Her father was against the idea of his daughter appearing on any kind of stage, but her mother became her principal supporter and secret benefactor. She sold some of the family's prized point-lace flounces and gave Margaret enough money to study for a year at the renowned Empire Dramatic School in New York. So, at the age of 16, Margaret quit school, left home, and moved to the United States.

In New York, she became a regular theatregoer. The night she first saw Ellen Terry in a Broadway play she began to think of changing her mind about a career. A Broadway impresario, Charles Frohman, who had an interest in the Empire Dramatic School, heard her read and was so impressed that he gave her a small part in his next production, *Shenandoh*. The excitement she felt during her first night on Broadway marked the turning point in her life. Shortly afterwards she gave up all thoughts of becoming a professional reader; she wanted to be an actress.

She had to settle for years of touring the country in a series of unsatisfactory plays. Then, in the autumn of 1898, when she was 22, she was given the chance to play opposite Richard Mansfield as Roxanne in a new production of the great French classic, *Cyrano de Bergerac*. Though she was still a comparatively unseasoned actress, she was a fighter, like her father. When Mansfield questioned whether she was beautiful enough to play the part of an enchanting heroine, Margaret snapped back, 'If you can make yourself ugly enough for Cyrano, I can make myself pretty enough to be Roxanne.'

On opening night, before a distinguished audience that included President Benjamin Harrison, she gave one of the great performances of her life. The critics were ecstatic. One called Margaret Anglin's performance 'perhaps the most extraordinary personal achievement of the year.'

Within five years, with her gray-green eyes, red-gold hair, and haunting voice, she became one of the most popular and commanding personalities on the American stage. She joined Henry Miller and his company, and legends are still told of her years with that fiery-tempered actor. Perhaps the most famous story is of a night in Pittsburgh when Miller noticed people leaving the theatre. He angrily walked to the front of the stage and shouted 'Get back to your seats.' A few minutes later, when he saw other couples leaving, he yelled, 'Knaves and varlets, back to your seats!' An exasperated Anglin finally had to cross the stage and tell him, 'Stop acting like a jackass. The theatre's on fire.'

She appeared in numerous stage hits with James O'Neill, father of the playwright Eugene O'Neill, who once told her 'You must play Shakespeare; you have the Irish Sea in your voice.' Although she had 50 generations of Irish blood in her veins she always confessed she never understood what O'Neill had meant; but in 1908, when she was offered the chance to tour Australia in some of her favourite Shakespearean roles, she accepted at once and won new acclaim playing Katharina in *The Taming of the Shrew* and Viola in *Twelfth Night*.

On her return, she was offered the chance of appearing in a huge, open-air Greek-style theatre which had recently been given to the University of Berkeley. She announced she would appear as Sophocles' *Electra*. On opening night more than 10,000 people cheered her to the skies. She repeated her performance in cities across America and arrived in New York for sold-out performances at Carnegie Hall and the Metropolitan Opera House.

She was now staging her own productions and had insisted that this production be in the style of bigness and simplicity that the Greeks themselves had loved. The New York *Herald Tribune* praised her for finally making American audiences like and understand Greek drama; the paper's slightly awe-struck theatre critic wrote, 'She acted with a sort of cold square-jawed intelligence reminiscent of Greek architecture.'

In 1909, Anglin announced she was tired of ending every performance holding a damp handkerchief. She said she wanted to

In the opening years of the 20th century Margaret Anglin was a commanding personality of the American stage.

do comedies and began appearing in plays by Oscar Wilde, who had once bounced her on his knees at her father's home. Dozens of starring roles in both contemporary plays and the classics followed. But by the 1920s she was being locked out of almost every theatre on Broadway and the reason had nothing to do with her acting.

In 1911, she had married a young author and playwright, Howard Hull, and was now insisting that he be given a major role in all her productions. Hull was no actor, and when the theatre managers began objecting Anglin walked out of her contracts. By the early 1930s no theatre in New York would book her. She virtually disappeared from the American stage except for a brief return in the 1940s when she agreed to play the part of the dowager Fanny in Lillian Hellman's play, *Watch on the Rhine.* When that production appeared at the Royal Alexandra Theatre in 1943, there was a rush of new interest in her as reporters rediscovered 'Canada's own Margaret Anglin.' But when the play closed, she went into complete retirement.

In 1952, she returned to Toronto to spend her last years in the city she had known as a child. When she died on January 7, 1958, she was buried beside her father in the Anglin family site in Mount Hope Cemetery in north Toronto. There, at the foot of an enormous stone cross, is a name only her most steadfast fans would recognize: Mary Margaret Hull.

But the theatre world of Canada has never forgotten her. In 1971, when a great complex known as the National Arts Centre was built in Ottawa, Herbert Whittaker, drama critic of the *Globe and Mail*, wrote, 'Ottawa should be naming one of the theatres after Margaret Anglin to remind Canadians – and the rest of the world – that Canada's theatrical tradition includes at least one star of the brightest rank.'

29

How a beloved 'dictator' built the Hospital for Sick Children

No hospital in North America ever raised so much money to build a hospital for children. The story of that success is largely the story of Dr Alan Brown.

There are three extraordinary figures in the story of Toronto's first Hospital for Sick Children: the woman who founded it, the millionaire who built it, and Dr Alan Brown, who not only made it rich, he made it famous. Brown was also, beyond question, the most controversial figure in the hospital's history. For more than 30 years he ruled over it like a virtual dictator, terrifying not only the staff but also the parents of the children.

Of the hundreds of stories that have been written about him, none is more famous than his arrival at the hospital in 1914. He was then in his late twenties. There was probably not another doctor in Canada who could match his qualifications, yet – possibly just *because* he was so well qualified – no hospital would hire him.

When Brown learned of the appalling number of children who were dying in the wards, he forced his way into the office of the head of the hospital and told him, 'Put me on staff and I'll reduce the infant mortality rate in your wards by 50 per cent within a year.' He was granted his trial period and within the year he lowered the death rate exactly as he said he would. Four years later he was made physician-in-chief.

For the next 30 years no doctor was more feared by the staff. He tongue-lashed any nurse who allowed a child to develop a diaper rash; any student arriving a minute late for any of his lectures was locked out of the room. Parents became so flustered by his attitude that they usually forgot to ask questions; if they did ask why they were to follow a certain procedure, the only answer they got was 'Because I say so.' But the children adored him. To them, he was like a perennially smiling uncle. He personally cared for so many children that thousands of Torontonians grew up proudly calling themselves one of 'Alan Brown's babies.'

He attracted the best medical staff he could find and by the 1930s had made the hospital famous throughout the medical world. Torontonians grew increasingly proud of the institution and in 1950 they oversubscribed a drive to raise $12 million for a new building. It was a remarkable achievement, for no city in North America had ever raised such an amount. Boston had to cancel its plans to build a similar hospital when it could raise only half as much. On the night in February 1950, when Torontonians packed the Arts and Letters Club to celebrate their success, there was never any question in anyone's mind that the man who had made the drive a success was Dr Alan Brown.

Alan was one of four children. From the time he was 12, the only career he ever wanted was to be a doctor. His father was a businessman; his mother, Georgina Gowans, was one of the first two female students to be admitted to Toronto's School of Medicine, but gave up her career to raise a family. He graduated from the University of Toronto with honours and spent the next three years at the Babies' Hospital in New York, studying under a renowned paediatrician, Emmet Holt. Then he left for Europe to complete his postgraduate studies in Vienna, Berlin, and Paris.

He had made the decision to confine his practice to the new field of paediatrics, and on his return to Toronto he was one of the best qualified specialists in baby care on this continent. It has been said that his expertise was probably the principal reason why he found it so difficult to find a position in Toronto. Many local doctors openly resented the brash young Canadian with his 'European background.'

Alan Brown, the dynamic and dictatorial
baby doctor who built the Hospital
for Sick Children

To Brown, paediatrics was, above everything else, a preventive science. To build the kind of hospital staff he knew he would need, he brought people like Angela Courtney from New York to establish a research laboratory and hired the brilliant young Frederick Tisdall to work in the field of nutrition. He established Canada's first psychological clinic for children, and in 1923 wrote *The Normal Child* to guide women in the proper care and feeding of children.

He also became one of the most militant crusaders in the cause of safer milk. In the 1930s, when he became convinced the Ontario government was stalling in its plans to make the pasteurization of milk compulsory, he invited – some say he commanded – the premier of Ontario, Mitchell Hepburn, to come to the hospital and see for himself the hundreds of children who were suffering and dying from bovine tuberculosis. A few weeks later the government passed the new legislation.

In October 1930, two of the doctors on his staff, Tisdall and Theodore Drake, produced a new cereal to ensure that small children received the necessary amount of vitamins and minerals in their daily food. It was marketed commercially as Pablum and was an international success. Neither Brown, Tisdall, nor Drake would ever consider accepting any share of the profits: they directed that all royalties be given to the hospital.

Over the next 25 years the millions of dollars that poured into the hospital from Pablum financed other research projects. Brown, in the meantime, was becoming increasingly notorious through speeches that were regularly becoming front page news. He told women who refused to breast feed their children that they were 'subletting their duty to a cow.' He told parents to stop spreading diseases by kissing their children on the hands and mouth; if you must kiss a child, he said, kiss it on the head or forehead where you will do the least damage. To his male audiences he said, 'Don't marry a pretty girl without a brain in her head and then bring me your idiot children.' And he warned parents they were turning their children into potential criminals by picking them up every time they cried. A baby of two weeks soon learned, he said, 'how to put it over its parents' and would eventually end up in juvenile court.

In his own life he set standards few of his staff could match. He spent his mornings at the hospital, but never accepted any money for his work there in all the years he served on its staff. He had decided his income would come solely from his private practice, and his afternoons were spent at his office in the Medical Arts Building at Bloor and St George Streets. He made so many house calls in the evenings that he finally installed a bed in his car so that he could sleep near the home of any child who was dangerously ill, and won the admiration of thousands of parents.

The hospital, which was always at the centre of his life, had been founded in 1874 by Elizabeth McMaster. In 1892 a large new hospital building had been built at the corner of College and Elizabeth Streets, primarily through the generosity of John Ross Robertson, who had made his fortune by founding the Toronto *Telegram*. By the 1950s, however, that building had become totally inadequate, and a public drive was launched to raise $12 million for the much larger building that stands today at 555 University Avenue. When it was completed in 1951, Brown retired. He had been the drive and the inspiration for the new hospital and few have ever questioned that it stands today as his finest memorial.

An element of confusion has always surrounded the year of his birth. One legend says that in the 1940s he changed it from 1885 to 1887 so that he could postpone his compulsory retirement by two years until the hospital was safely in its new building. It was, after all, as he always said, 'his hospital.'

30

The man who founded the Canadian Opera Company

In the 1940s, Arnold Walter vowed to establish an opera company in Toronto that would be unique in North America. He would use only Canadian singers. Before long he had attracted some exceptional talents.

Late one night in 1933, while Arnold Walter was working alone at his newspaper office in Berlin, the telephone rang and a voice warned, 'Don't go home tonight. The Reichstag is in flames.' By midnight almost all his fellow editors had been arrested by Hitler's Gestapo. By morning Walter, the newspaper's 31-year-old music critic, and his wife had escaped from the city and were on their way to Spain.

Three years later, when civil war broke out in Spain, friends helped them escape to England. In London, Walter met most of the country's leading composers. When he received a letter offering him an opportunity to live in Canada, Ralph Vaughan Williams was among those who tried to persuade him to remain in England where, in Williams' words, 'he was needed.' But Walter had had enough of Europe. He was tired of running, tired of having to leave everything behind and escape to some new country. He was also convinced that a major war was imminent in Europe. In 1937 he accepted the offer from Canada and arrived in Toronto as the new music teacher at Upper Canada College.

Toronto became his home for the rest of his life. During more than 30 years, he became one of the most important figures in the history of music in this country and the principal founder of a cultural landmark of this city, the Canadian Opera Company.

Arnold Walter was born on August 30, 1902, in Moravia, a part of the old Hapsburg empire that became a province of Czechoslovakia. It is an area visited by few tourists but known to every historian of music; Leos Janacek is only one of many famous composers born there. Walter grew up in a family where everyone was either a composer, violinist, pianist, or singer. In later years in Toronto he would tell his students that he usually had to go out into the garden at home and climb a tree to find enough peace to compose music.

Both his father and grandfather were schoolmasters. Neither of them believed that the world of music offered any form of financial security for a young man, so when he was in his late teens Arnold registered in the law school in Prague. By that time, however, he was convinced that the only career he wanted was to be a composer. He broke the laws of Austria by enrolling in two universities at the same time, and secretly became a student at the school of musicology in Berlin.

In the late 1920s Berlin was the mecca of all musicians in Europe. By the time Walter completed his music studies, hundreds of other young composers were also looking for work there. It was then, as he would later write, 'I was suddenly "discovered" as a writer.' He had started writing articles for the local newspapers to support himself, and his features on music had attracted so much attention that he was offered the position of music editor of *Die Weltbühne* and later became the music critic of *Vorwarts*, the city's leading socialist paper.

He married and started plans to settle permanently in Berlin until the night that Hitler and his party came to power. After fleeing Germany, he and his wife lived on the Spanish island of Majorca, where he soon found a job as a music teacher. He found himself fascinated by Spanish folk music, and was beginning to make a serious study of all folk music when civil war broke out in Spain in 1936. As a suspected socialist he again had to leave. With the help of friends, he and his wife boarded a British destroyer bound for England.

In London, because of his new love of folk music, he started attending the workshops at Cecil Sharp House where he met Ralph Vaughan Williams, Imogene Holst, and many other British composers. 'I have never met such nice people,' he later wrote. 'They helped us, protected us, sustained us – we were after all, poor as church mice.' In 1937 an unexpected letter arrived from the headmaster of Upper Canada College, William Grant, offering him the position of music teacher. Walter accepted almost at once.

The invitation offered the first chance in years for some kind of peace and financial security. He and his wife soon became part of the musical life of the city. Godfrey Ridout would often speak of the many evenings when Walter and his wife would invite him and other young composers and musicians to their flat 'tucked up under the roof' at the college.

The first two years were happy ones but Walter soon found the daily routine of a school teacher too restricting. In 1943 he quit to gamble on a career as a freelance musician and composer. By then he had become so determined to build his life in Canada that he had become a Canadian citizen. In 1945 he was hired by the Toronto (now Royal) Conservatory of Music and immediately began to establish a graduate and professional school similar to the one that existed at the Juilliard School of Music in New York. And it was now, in the words of the *Encyclopedia of Music in Canada*, that he began his 'master plan for music in Canada.'

He had found a wealth of musical talent in this country and was convinced that one of his primary roles was to find audiences for Canada's singers and musicians. In 1946 he took the first steps towards one of the grandest achievements of his career when he created the Royal Conservatory Opera School. It would eventually grow to become the Canadian Opera Company.

Toronto, he said, deserved to hear more opera. He remembered the nights in Berlin when there had been performances at three different opera houses on the same night. To ensure the lasting success of his new opera school he began hiring the best teachers he could find. He brought in Nicholas Goldschmidt as the school's first music director. In 1948 Herman Geiger-Torel became the company's stage director. Within two years there were performances of Smetana's *Bartered Bride* at Eaton Auditorium. As Ruby Mercer, editor of *Opera Canada*, recalled in a profile of Walter in the May 1969 issue, to make that production both handsome and authentic, costumes were borrowed from Toronto's Czech community.

From the very beginning, Walter insisted that his opera company would be unlike most other opera companies on the continent. Foreign artists would not be hired to sing the principal roles while local talent was used only in the chorus: principal roles would be sung by Canadians. Soon singers from across the country were enrolling in the new opera school. Among them was a promising young tenor from the west, Jon Vickers, as well as an extraordinarily talented young woman from Toronto, Teresa Stratas.

In November 1950, the company became the Opera Festival Association of Toronto. In 1960, it was officially reorganized as the Canadian Opera Company, and the following year began its regular performances in its new home, the O'Keefe Centre.

In 1952, Walter was appointed director of the Faculty of Music at the University of Toronto and held this important position for the rest of his career. During all the years in Toronto he continued to write articles and compose music. But he preferred to compose music in the then unfashionable pre-World War I style of Mahler and Schoenberg, and today his compositions remain largely unknown even to Toronto audiences.

In 1961, when the university announced its plans to build a major music building, to be called the Edward Johnson Building, Walter was one of the principal figures who determined its final design. It would not only have the finest concert hall and auditorium possible; Walter ensured it would have the finest music library in Canada and one of the finest on the continent. It would also include another of his creations, the first electronic music studio in Canada.

On April 25, 1968, on the eve of his retirement, hundreds of colleagues and friends filled the Great Hall of Hart House for a memorable night of music and tributes. Godfrey Ridout wrote a special fanfare for the occasion entitled 'A Flourish of Fond Farewell,' and during the banquet the Orford String Quartet arrived to play some of his favourite music. Many people that night spoke of the enormous contribution Walter had made to the musical life of Canada in such a relatively short time. In his own remarks that evening, he himself confessed, 'I look back in wonder that so many things became possible.'

Five years later, on October 6, 1973, at the age of 71, Arnold Walter died in this city. He had always attended the first major public recital of all his students. The year after he died, as a form of lasting tribute, the concert hall in the Edward Johnson Building was renamed Walter Hall.

Walter Hall in the Faculty of Music building, University of Toronto, honours a teacher and composer who founded an opera company in this city.

31

The Toronto riots of 1832 and William Lyon Mackenzie's 'greatest moment'

He is remembered as Toronto's first mayor and leader of the Rebellion of 1837. But it was the riots in Toronto five years earlier and events of that year that made Mackenzie a hero throughout Canada.

It was a curious site for his monument. In 1940, directly in front of the main entrance to the lieutenant-governor's suite, on the west lawn of Queen's Park, an enormous statue was raised to William Lyon Mackenzie, who was hated by more governors of this province than probably any man in history.

In 1824, when Mackenzie was a newspaper editor, Lieutenant-Governor Peregrine Maitland discovered that Mackenzie had buried a copy of his newspaper in the cornerstone of the Brock Monument at Queenston Heights. Maitland immediately ordered that the almost completed monument be torn down so that the newspaper could be removed. Eight years later, Mackenzie called for the impeachment of another governor, Sir John Colborne. In 1837, he led a band of rebels down Yonge Street in an attempt to overthrow the government and end the power of all future governors.

A century passed, and in 1937 a memorial to Mackenzie was proposed for Queen's Park. The artist chosen to design it was the Toronto sculptor Walter Allward, who had been selected by the government of Canada to design the Vimy Ridge Memorial in France. For the sculpture in Toronto, Allward created a memorial to the 'legendary' Mackenzie; in the words of F.H. Armstrong and R.J. Stagg in the *Dictionary of Canadian Biography*, 'As a legend, Mackenzie had a role and importance that Mackenzie the man could never achieve.'

Despite hundreds of works that have been written about him, Mackenzie still remains one of the least understood men in Canadian history. And the greatest moment in his career did not occur during the famous 1837 rebellion, but in the year of the almost forgotten 'York Riots of 1832.'

Mackenzie was born in Springfield, Dundee, in Forfarshire (Angus) Scotland on March 12, 1795, at a critical point in the history of western Europe. It was the age of revolution in France, and during the next half century there would be rebellions in most of the major countries of Europe as people rose against the old order and tried to create democratic societies.

When Mackenzie was 15, he became the youngest man in the newsroom of a local newspaper. In his late teens, with his father dead, he and his mother ran a library and general store near Dundee. In 1820, aged 25, he immigrated to the New World and for two years worked in a number of general stores in Upper Canada until his mother joined him. She brought with her Isabel Baxter, the woman she had chosen to be Mackenzie's wife.

In 1824, Mackenzie quit his job as a merchant in Queenston to start a new career and founded a newspaper, *The Colonial Advocate*. That year he also moved his family to Toronto, then known as York, and Toronto became his 'spiritual home' for the rest of his life. By then, he had become the most outspoken advocate of the Reform movement that was attempting to end the powers of the governors that Britain sent to administer the colony. Through his newspaper, he became the champion of all reformers. In 1827, when he was elected a member of parliament for the county of York, he was able to use both his newspaper and his seat in the assembly to attack the governor and his supporters.

During the next few years, he was repeatedly expelled from the House for his slanderous and libellous attacks. Nonetheless he was rapidly becoming one of the most popular figures in the province and was re-elected every time by his growing number of supporters. On January 2, 1832, following another expulsion from the House, he was re-elected in such a landslide victory that thousands of his friends and followers formed an enormous procession that included 134 sleighs. They triumphantly escorted Mackenzie down Yonge Street to take his seat. 'It was,' in the words of Armstrong and Stagg, 'Mackenzie's greatest moment.'

Five days later, he was expelled again when he called for the impeachment of the lieutenant-governor. The Tories and the Reformers were now on the verge of a head-on collision across the province. A major clash occurred on Friday, March 23, the day of the infamous 'York Riots.'

Mackenzie had called for a public meeting and had asked his supporters to sign a petition to be sent to the King demanding an end to the dictatorial power of the lieutenant-governor. On the morning of that meeting, carriages and wagons crowded with Reformers began arriving from all the surrounding towns and villages. Four days before the meeting, the Tories had been plastering the town with posters calling on their own supporters to attend the meeting to voice their loyalty to the governor and the King. The site of the meeting was to be in front of the Court House on King Street, just east of Yonge. Almost as soon as the meeting began, so did the fighting.

Armstrong gave an account of that day in *Ontario History* (Volume 55, 1963). When Mackenzie's friends started to address the crowd from one of the wagons they were attacked and the wagon demolished. Then someone called out that Mackenzie was flying a French tricolour flag from the roof of his newspaper office. A mob of Tories headed for Church Street and started throwing rocks that shattered every window in the building.

The 'tricolor flag' that had provoked this particular riot was, in fact, a simple banner that Mackenzie had used during his victory march down Yonge Street on January 2, a red and white piece of cloth bearing the words, 'Liberty Of The Press.' But the situation had grown almost completely out of control and rioting continued throughout the day and well into the evening. It was said, 'no one in York slept that night.'

The Tories declared the day 'an unequivocal defeat of the

Yankee Republican party,' but the riots would have a profound effect on Mackenzie's future power and influence. In the following months Mackenzie was no longer considered simply the champion of the people; he had become a martyr in the cause of freedom. In 1834, when the Town of York became the City of Toronto, Mackenzie was chosen to be its first mayor.

Three years later, when he became convinced that a peaceful solution to the province's political problems could never be found, he led a rebellion. When it failed, he fled to the United States. There he lived in exile until 1849, when Robert Baldwin and his Reform Party introduced responsible government that would represent the will of the people and end the autocratic rule of a governor.

Mackenzie received a pardon from the new government and was allowed to return to Toronto, where he lived until his death on August 28, 1861. In the years that followed, he gradually came to be seen by many people as one of the early heroes in Canada's history. In the words of Armstrong and Stagg, 'Fortune let him initiate a rebellion which, to later generations, seemed crucial in forging Canadian institutions and in establishing a national spirit of democracy, justice, and freedom from oppression.'

The house at 82 Bond Street where he spent the last years of his life has now been preserved. Under the direction of the Toronto Historical Board it has been refurnished in the style of the 1850s when Mackenzie lived there, and is now one of the city's most important 'living museums.'

In 1937, on the 100th anniversary of the ill-fated rebellion, a William Lyon Mackenzie Centennial Committee was formed and plans were made to build a memorial to him. In her book on the history of the province's art collection, *The Ontario Collection*, Fern Bayer records that a site was chosen in Queen's Park and donated to the project by the Ontario government; a public subscription raised all the money needed for an imposing work.

It was to be a memorial to the Mackenzie of legends. In its final design, sculptor Walter Allward placed a bronze bust of Mackenzie high above the ground on a granite pedestal. In the background, he placed the figure of a youth striding across a field; in the field

William Lyon Mackenzie, Toronto's most historic rebel, now is honoured in Queen's Park with a bronze and granite memorial.

lies a half-buried ploughshare, symbolizing the neglect of land during the years of unrest. On the young man's left arm, there are traces of the thongs that once held him in bondage. In his right hand, he carries the book of Wisdom that has always set Man free.

32

The forgotten story of a Frans Hals masterpiece

In 1924, a Toronto collector bought it for more than five million of today's dollars. In 1955 he left it to the Art Gallery in Toronto – along with works of other masters and a foundation to buy more.

For centuries, one of the most important private art collections in Europe has been in England, at Althorp, in the family home of Diana, Princess of Wales. In the 1920s one of its most prized paintings was bought by a Torontonian, Frank P. Wood. In today's dollars he paid the Spencer family more than $5 million for it.

The painting is a masterpiece by the 16th century Dutch painter Frans Hals, and for years it hung in Wood's unlocked home on Bayview Avenue. His house was considered of such great architectural beauty that Columbia University asked for its plans and they are now in its archives in New York. The Hals was not the only masterpiece in Wood's collection. By the 1950s, in the words of R.H. Hubbard, then chief curator of the National Gallery of Canada, Frank Wood had acquired the most distinguished private collection in Canada. When he died in 1955, he left the Hals portrait and most of his greatest paintings as well as his home to the Art Gallery of Ontario.

It was, said the gallery's director at that time, 'the single most important gift of works of art the gallery has ever received.' The magnitude and importance of the legacy raised the gallery from a provincial museum to the international level. In the opinion of

Frank Wood left his magnificent home on Bayview Avenue to the
Art Gallery of Ontario. It was to be sold and the proceeds
used to buy paintings.

a number of today's leading art critics, if a tourist guide were
published that listed all the greatest art treasures of the world,
Toronto's portrait by Hals of his friend, the silk trader Isaak Abra-
hamsz. Massa, would be ranked, like the ratings in a Michelin
guide, as 'worth a 300-mile detour.'

When he made a gift of his home to the gallery, Wood asked
that it be sold and the money used to establish a foundation to
buy paintings in the future. Today, beside many of the most famous paintings in the gallery, including works by Rembrandt, Van
Dyck, and Gainsborough, you will see a small card stating 'Gift
of Frank P. Wood' or 'Purchase: Frank P. Wood Foundation.' His
is an unfamiliar name to most visitors today, for Wood always
avoided personal publicity, but there are a number of reasons why
his story deserves to be better remembered. In the words of the

Toronto *Star*, he was not only one of Canada's greatest benefactors, he was 'one of the world's great art benefactors.'

His family had lived for centuries in Inniskillen, Ireland, but in the late 1840s, in the aftermath of a series of famines and epidemics, three brothers emigrated to North America. One settled in Peterborough in Upper Canada and became a school principal; one of his grandchildren would become a great art benefactor.

In his late teens, Frank Wood left home and found a job as a clerk in Montreal. In light of later events, one of the family's favourite stories about him is that he used most of his first month's salary to buy a small painting. Collecting art became a passion, and on frequent trips back to the family home in Peterborough he would often bring a painting as a gift for his mother.

As a businessman Wood had a talent that would soon make him one of the youngest millionaires in Canada. He came to Toronto and became a founding member of a stockholding company, Baillie, Wood and Croft, and was later president and chairman of Burlington Steel in Hamilton. In the last years of his life he served as vice-president of National Trust, one of the major financial houses in Toronto, and was a director of numerous companies in this city. But when he died in 1955, newspaper headlines recorded not the passing of a major business leader but the death of one of the country's great philanthropists.

Only a few people at the time knew the extent of his personal art collection. The search to acquire some of the world's most important paintings had become a major part of his life. On business trips to New York and Europe he regularly took his wife and their three daughters with him. One of the daughters told a reporter that many of her first and most vivid memories of her father were of their visits together to art museums and to the showrooms of art dealers such as Duveen and Wildenstein.

He always hoped that his family would discover the same pleasure he had found in paintings, and would never buy anything that his wife and children did not like. When he once brought home a Van Gogh the children called it 'terrible' and his wife told him 'I could never live with that'; back it went. So did a particularly austere portrait by Van Dyck. The actual number of paintings he bought was never large but everything was extraordinary. He bought one of Gainsborough's largest and finest works, *The Harvest Wagon*; a painting of this size and importance by the great 18th century English artist may never come on the market again.

As he became more and more interested in art, he became one of the earliest and strongest supporters of the Art Gallery of Toronto (now of Ontario). He served for many years as one of its directors and during his lifetime donated many of his paintings, including Van Dyck's *Daedalus and Icarus* and a statue of Eve by Rodin.

In 1924 he bought the painting from the Spencer family that every major museum in the world would consider one of its greatest treasures. It is a portrait by Frans Hals. In the opinion of David Wistow of the Art Gallery of Ontario, it is one of the most important single portraits by this 16th century Dutch master painter. Even its composition is extraordinary for its time. In an age when all patrons expected to be posed in a formal manner, Hals seated his friend before a small window, and painted him as if he had just turned in his chair, momentarily distracted by an unseen visitor. It was also an age when artists painstakingly finished their portraits so that not a brush mark would show. Hals was one of the world's first great portrait painters to produce likenesses with bold, rough, unpolished strokes of pure paint and became a leader in a new style of painting that would not be seen again for 200 years in the Impressionists.

A portrait by Hals is considered a treasure in any gallery's collection. The Art Gallery of Ontario has two. Both were gifts from Frank Wood. He paid the Spencers $195,000 for Hals's portrait of Massa, an astonishing price for a work of art in the 1920s. At that time, a row of houses in Rosedale could be bought for less than $190,000. In the 1920s he also bought one of the last great works by Rembrandt, a portrait of *A Lady with a Lap Dog*. It too was left to the AGO and today is one of its most famous and popular works.

As architects for his home at 2365 Bayview Avenue he selected the New York firm of Delano and Aldridge, but it is now known that Wood himself was chiefly responsible for its design. When it was finished, it was hailed as 'one of the finest examples of pure Georgian architecture on this continent.'

After his death on March 20, 1955, the gallery sold the house as directed in his will. It was bought by Garfield Weston, head of Weston Bakeries, who made it his home for many years. In the 1970s it was purchased by the directors of the Crescent School and it became the home of that private school for boys.

Stories of Canadian benefactors such as Frank Wood deserve to be better known for reasons far beyond the generosity and magnitude of their gifts. Only a small portion of the millions of its visitors are aware that, unlike the National Gallery of Canada, the Art Gallery of Ontario receives no government aid to buy paintings. From its very beginning, early in this century, it has had to rely entirely on the generosity of private donors to develop its collection.

In tribute to one of its first and grandest benefactors, one of the largest exhibition halls in today's AGO is named the Frank P. Wood Gallery.

The AGO's Frans Hals,
gift of Frank Wood

33

Egerton Ryerson and a famous letter to the editor

It was an extraordinary letter, 12,000 words in length. It filled almost the entire edition of a newspaper, and it transformed an obscure young minister into a national figure.

It was one of the most famous letters ever published in a Canadian newspaper. When it appeared in the spring of 1826, people could be seen holding copies of the newspaper and arguing furiously. Many wept openly in the street.

The letter had been written anonymously, and all that week rumours flew about who would have dared to write such a thing. When speculation settled on the names of two politicians, the real author wrote a second letter and this time signed his name, Egerton Ryerson.

When his father learned what Ryerson had done, his only comment was 'My God, we are ruined.' Ryerson was then 23 years old and had only recently become a Methodist minister. The letter was his angry reply to remarks made by John Strachan, the minister of St. James' church, and it made Ryerson's name famous throughout every city and town in Canada.

Today, at the top of Bond Street in downtown Toronto, in front of the Ryerson Polytechnical Institute which was named after him, stands a bronze statute of Ryerson. On its base, there is an inscription of only seven words which most people have always assumed described the one great achievement of Ryerson's life:

'Founder of the school system of Ontario.' But, in the words of C.B. Sissons, Ryerson's biographer and the definitive historian of the Methodist Victoria College, the inscription is not only inadequate, it is misleading. Ryerson, said Sissons, was more than an educationist: 'He contributed more to the entire social history of Canada than any other person of his time and understood Upper Canada more widely than did perhaps any other of its citizens ... And the primary and dominant motive of his life was religious.'

The turning point in Ryerson's career was the publication in Toronto of that now celebrated letter in William Lyon Mackenzie's newspaper, the *Colonial Advocate*, on May 11, 1826. At the time, Ryerson was largely unknown. He had grown up in Upper Canada on his father's farm in Norfolk County and his first ambition had been to become a lawyer. But at the age of 18 he had had a profoundly moving religious experience. He had been seriously ill and there was concern that he might die. For weeks he had been too weak to write even in his diary; on the night the fever broke, among the first words he wrote were, 'God saw fit to show me the uncertainty of earthly things.' As soon as he recovered, he announced he was going to become a Methodist minister. The Methodists were a comparatively new group of Christians who had broken away from the increasingly worldly Church of England. They had established a new form of Christian worship based on the words of the Bible, the meaning of Holy Communion, and a life devoted to service to others.

In 1825, Ryerson was appointed to serve in the circuit that included Toronto. Each month, he and the other minister on the circuit arranged to meet with the town's small group of Methodists. At one of these meetings in the spring of 1826, the main subject of all conversations was a recent sermon given by John Strachan.

The head of the Anglican church in Canada, Bishop Jacob Mountain, had recently died. Strachan, in his sermon of tribute, had used the occasion to speak not only of the importance of the Anglican church in Canada but to ridicule the beliefs of the former members of his church, the dissident Methodists. It was a cruel attack and it hurt and angered the entire Methodist community. In Toronto, it was agreed that Strachan's charges must be an-

Egerton Ryerson: a steel engraving
by Thomas A. Dean

swered. Ryerson and the other local Methodist minister were each asked to prepare a letter of reply. The better of the two would be published.

Ryerson wrote his at the end of each day's travels. A month later, when he returned to Toronto, he learned that the other minister had written nothing. When Ryerson read his letter, he startled everyone with the force of his words. There was unanimous agreement that his letter must be published at once. Ryerson's sole concern was that no one would seriously consider the remarks of a relatively young and inexperienced Methodist preacher. It was agreed accordingly that his letter would be published anonymously. In place of a signature, only the words 'A Methodist Minister' would appear.

The town's most notorious rebel, William Lyon Mackenzie, was delighted to publish the letter in his newspaper, knowing it would antagonize Strachan and every member of the Family Compact which dominated the city's life. When it appeared, the letter ran to more than 12,000 words; there was almost nothing else in Mackenzie's newspaper that day. Ryerson started by calling Strachan's statements 'ungenerous, unfounded, and false' and referred to Strachan himself as 'a fountain of slander.' As to Strachan's charges that Methodist ministers were lazy, Ryerson asked if he meant those 'indolent, covetous men who travel 200 to 300 miles and preach 25 to 40 times a month and continue their labour year after year at the enormous salary of $25 per annum.'

The Methodists had yet to establish their own college and Strachan had called the Methodist ministers 'uneducated, itinerant men who had forsaken their proper calling to preach what they did not understand.' Ryerson asked if Strachan had ever heard of the uneducated, itinerant fishermen whom Christ had chosen to be his disciples.

Strachan claimed that all government land allotted to 'the Protestant church' in Canada belonged to the Anglican church since it was 'the established church' in Canada. Ryerson reminded Strachan that, for three centuries, the early Christian churches were not only without the aid of government, they were 'most violently opposed by it' yet never had the Christian church been 'so prosperous or so pure.'

Point by point, Ryerson proceeded to destroy all Strachan's arguments. Finally, in an obvious and personal reference to the socializing Strachan, he denounced 'those venerable successors of the apostles who spend two or three nights a week at the card table and ballroom and then preach by their pious example the doctrines of Christian purity.' 'The apostles never had the zeal to do it though they sometimes preached Jesus in the streets, at the tribunal and in prison,' thundered Ryerson, and closed with these words: 'I take my leave of the Doctor's sermon at present. He may trust in legislative influence, he may pray to the Imperial Parliament, but we will trust in the Lord our God and to him will we make our prayer.'

Methodists wept to read their cause so well defended. Overnight, Ryerson became the new champion of the Methodist faith in Canada. It was Ryerson who sailed to England in 1835 and obtained a charter for the first college in the British colonies that would not be under the domination of the Church of England. The Methodists later named it Victoria University after the new young Queen, and Ryerson became its first president.

The university was founded in Cobourg, Ontario, but after it became one of the federated colleges of the University of Toronto, it moved in 1892 to this city. Near the northeast corner of Queen's Park, it built the great Romanesque building that has remained a principal architectural glory of the university to this day.

In 1844, because Ryerson had constantly championed the cause of free education, he was appointed superintendent of education, a role he held for 32 years. When he retired in 1876 he had made it possible for children of every faith to be taught by qualified teachers in free public schools throughout the province.

He died in Toronto on February 18, 1882. An enormous crowd walked behind his coffin in the procession to his grave in Mount Pleasant Cemetery. It was said that never in Toronto's history had such an honour been paid to a man in death.

During his early years, when he had fought against the most powerful men in Canada, one lieutenant-governor, Sir George Arthur, had called him 'a dangerous man.' But the country's first prime minister, Sir John A. Macdonald, would later write of Ryerson: 'His country guards and cherishes his memory.' The celebrated letter had not ruined the family name as his father had feared. In Sissons' words, it caused Ryerson 'to leap at one bound into greatness.'

34

The choir that wouldn't die

The Mendelssohn Choir was born in a church and soon grew to become 'the finest body of singers on this continent.' Herbert Fricker, introduced the choir to Handel's Messiah *and made it an annual Toronto tradition.*

1917 was the year when almost everyone in Toronto said the Mendelssohn Choir should be disbanded.

The choir was at the first great height of its fame. The leading music critic in the country, Hector Charlesworth of *Saturday Night*, had called it 'the finest body of singers on this continent.' All Canada knew of the choir's success when it had appeared in Carnegie Hall in New York in a triumphant performance of Beethoven's Ninth, the 'Choral' Symphony.

The choir had been in existence for almost a quarter century and had become Canada's first internationally renowned choir. But in 1917 its leader and founder, the 56-year-old Augustus Stephen Vogt, felt he had reached an age when he must retire. To the choir and to most people in the city it seemed impossible that anyone could be found important enough to succeed the man who had led the choir to fame.

In the spring of that year, Vogt startled everyone by announcing that he had found his successor, a man scarcely anyone had ever heard of, an Englishman, Herbert Austin Fricker. A few months later, Fricker arrived in Toronto and spent most of the winter months in rehearsals with the choir. His first public appearance as its conductor, on February 18, 1918, became a legend in the musical life of this city, for he had invited a friend he had known in England to join him, and the friend, Leopold Stokowski, had arrived with the entire Philadelphia Orchestra.

The concert that night was to mark the beginning of an extraordinary era of success for the Mendelssohn Choir. Fricker's name is unfamiliar to most people today but it has been known to generations of music lovers, not only to audiences but to those who have visited the music library in the Arts Department of the Metropolitan Toronto Reference Library.

Shortly before his death, Fricker bequeathed his enormous collection of music books, manuscripts, and scores to the library. At the time of its 75th anniversary in 1958, the library paid tribute to four of its greatest benefactors. John Hallam's library had formed its nucleus; John Ross Robertson gave it thousands of Canadian historical books and pictures; Edgar Osborne gave it a famous collection of children's books; and Herbert Fricker's gift, especially the British material, constituted one of the first important cores of the music library.

The story of Fricker deserves to be better known but it has always been overshadowed by the story of the legendary Vogt, the choir's founder. Vogt was an ardent young musician from Elmira, Ontario, who, after years of study in North America and Europe, returned to Canada to become the organist and choirmaster at the Jarvis Street Baptist Church. It was there, in 1894, that he embarked on a longtime dream to create one of the world's great choirs. He enlarged his church choir to 75 singers and named it after Felix Mendelssohn. Soon its membership grew to more than 160. By the early 1900s, the choir had won an international reputation.

Fricker was only a few years younger than Vogt when he took over the choir, and was already a man of considerable fame in Europe. The son of a schoolmaster, he was born in Canterbury, Kent, on February 12, 1868. His father gave him his first lessons in vocal music, and from the time Fricker was a very small boy music was the centre of his life. He happily entered the Canterbury Cathedral Choir School, even though it was notorious for its strict

The Mendelssohn Choir, founded in 1894, still flourishes. At this performance in Roy Thomson Hall in 1982, it performed Handel's *Solomon* with the Mainly Mozart Orchestra and soloists including Kathleen Battle and Mark Pedrotti.

discipline. While still a young student there he became an exceptionally fine musician. In his teens he began travelling weekly to London to study with the celebrated organist of Westminster Abbey, Sir Frederick Bridge.

Sir Frederick rarely gave private lessons to any young musician, but he was impressed by Fricker and personally helped him to prepare for the demanding examinations set by the Royal College of Organists. Fricker graduated easily, and was offered a position as music master at Kent College in Canterbury. Shortly afterwards, he was appointed organist and choirmaster at Holy Trinity Church in Folkestone. In 1898, on a day he always referred to as 'the turning point of my life,' he noticed an advertisement for a position as city organist at Leeds, decided to apply, and to his utter astonishment, at 30 years of age was offered the post. Testimonial letters from people such as Sir Frederick had undoubtedly influenced the city fathers.

His primary responsibility at Leeds was to give regular public organ recitals, but Fricker rapidly increased the sphere of his work and was soon one of England's most prominent musical figures. In the early 1900s he founded the Leeds Symphony Orchestra, was appointed choirmaster for the Leeds Festivals, and became known to musical conductors throughout the British Empire.

There was never any question in Vogt's mind that here was the perfect man to succeed him as conductor of the Mendelssohn Choir. From the night of Fricker's first, widely publicized concert in Toronto when he shared the podium with Stokowski, he established himself as a major figure in the musical life of Canada. It was said that if Vogt had given the choir its 'diamond-like purity of tone,' Fricker added 'a softer tone, with a darker hue.' He also added a major new work to the choir's repertoire.

In 1932, he led the choir in its first performance of Handel's *Messiah*, now an annual tradition in Toronto. But to generations of choir members, he was known as 'the dictator.' In exasperated moments, he would call the sopranos 'angelic screech owls' and accuse the tenors of having 'less intelligence than brass monkeys,' but the choir remained in awe of him and, it was said, even loved him for his insistence on absolute perfection.

By the 1940s, his health began to fail, and he had no choice but to resign. His plan to simply 'go home and rest' was tragically brief. Less than nine months later, on November 11, 1943, he died in his sleep at his Toronto home at 9 Powell Avenue.

He is remembered as a reserved man, but he had been prouder and happier with his life and work in Toronto than many people suspected. Shortly before his death he drew up his final will, and left to the Toronto Public Library his entire collection of music books and manuscripts, including a rare copy of Dr Samuel Arnold's edition of *The Messiah* (c. 1790) and original works by such prominent 19th century British composers as John Field and C.V. Stanford. To friends Fricker had confessed that he had always wanted to make his collection a gift to the citizens of Toronto. It was to be 'an appreciation of their kindness' to him since the day he had arrived here.

35

How a world-famous statue of Peter Pan came to Toronto

For more than a half century, a statue of Peter Pan has stood at the corner of St Clair and Avenue Road. The little known treasure is signed with the name of Peter's creator, J.M. Barrie.

On a morning in May 1912, as if by magic, a statue of Peter Pan suddenly appeared in the middle of Kensington Gardens in London. Questions were immediately raised in the House of Commons. The affair of the unexpected statue threatened to become an 'incident' until members of the House were informed that permission had come from Buckingham Palace.

Today the statue is listed in all major tourist guides as one of the sights of London, and has become a favourite attraction for generations of children. In the 1920s, an exact duplicate of the 14-foot-high statue, fashioned by its original creator, appeared, almost equally without notice, in a park in Toronto at the corner of Avenue Road and St Clair Avenue. The story of these two statues and who donated them is a story few visitors to the parks are ever told. It began with one of the most legendary opening nights in the history of the theatre.

The play was a new work by one of England's most popular authors. It was announced as *Peter Pan, or the Boy Who Would Not Grow Up* and everyone, except the author, believed it would be a disaster. Reporters had been barred from rehearsals and, on the night of December 27, 1904, when a distinguished audience in full evening dress arrived at the Duke of York's Theatre in London, none of them knew what to expect.

The curtain went up on a scene in a nursery with a large dog preparing a small boy for his bath. There was a gasp of astonished delight and for the next two hours, in the words of one reviewer, 'the entire audience succumbed to the author's spell.' At the end of Act One, after Peter Pan led a troop of laughing children through the nursery window to fly over the rooftops of London, there was thunderous applause. Later, in Act Four, a fairy-like sprite named Tinker Bell lay dying and Peter Pan ran to the front of the footlights to tell the audience they could save her if they would only clap their hands to say they believed in fairies; the response was so overwhelming, the actress playing Peter Pan burst into tears.

The play was a resounding hit and was an even greater success when it opened in New York. Since then it has returned to the stage almost every year during the Christmas season to delight new generations of children (and their parents). The author who had always believed in his play was James Barrie. He was the son of a Scottish handloom weaver and was born in the village of Kirriemuir in Scotland on May 9, 1860. *The Times* of London once wrote of him, 'If any man was a born author, it was Barrie.'

He became a newspaper reporter and wrote short stories in his free time. When London publishers started buying them, he moved permanently to that city. In 1888, a collection of his tales about life in a Scottish town, *Auld Licht Idyllis*, established him as a promising writer. In 1891, with a novel, *The Little Minister*, he became an important writer, and when he later turned it into a highly successful play he became a wealthy writer. He was then 40 and the plays that followed, *Quality Street* in 1901 and *The Admirable Crichton* in 1902, established him as one of England's leading playwrights.

It was during those years that he became a friend of the family of a London lawyer, Llewelyn Davies. Barrie had married but was soon divorced, without children. In the summer of 1897, when he was taking one of his walks in his favourite park, Kensington Gardens, he met two of the Davies children with their nurse, and through them he met the rest of the family. The five small Davies children prompted him to write his one play that will probably be performed for as long as there are theatres.

Barrie had nothing in common with the elder Davies: the two men were from totally different backgrounds. Nonetheless, to the surprise and frequently the annoyance of Davies, Barrie 'adopted' the family as his own. He even moved to the north side of the park to be closer to them and almost every week took the family to the theatre or to dinner. The Davies children became the children he never had.

On his walks with them in Kensington Gardens he started telling fantastic stories that enchanted all of them. In one tale, he told them that all children had once been birds and that was why nursery windows had bars – children kept forgetting they no longer had wings and would try to fly through the window. One of the characters he used in many of his stories was a small boy named Peter Pan. He was able to fly 'because his mother had forgotten to weigh him at birth' and he had escaped through an unbarred window and now lived in Kensington Gardens.

In 1902, Barrie published a children's book, *The Little White Bird*; six of its chapters were later revised and published as a separate book called *Peter Pan in Kensington Gardens*. It became so popular that whenever Barrie walked in the park he was besieged by children demanding to know where they could find Peter Pan.

In 1903, he decided to turn his story of Peter Pan into a play. Producers told him he was mad. His plans for the play would require massive sets and a cast of 50, including pirates and redskins, and four of the principal characters would have literally to fly. He had also written a play that seemed to be a children's story but much of its dialogue was as sophisticated as any West End drama.

On opening night, the success of the play astonished even the cast. One reviewer wrote, 'The audience flung off the years ... whistling their childhood back.' *The Times* said, 'Peter Pan is from beginning to end a thing of pure delight.' In 1911, Barrie turned the play into a children's book that, under its original title, *Peter and Wendy*, and its later title, *Peter Pan and Wendy*, has never gone out of print to this day.

When Barrie later authorized the publication of the play, he dedicated it to the five Davies children: 'I suppose I always knew that I made Peter by rubbing the five of you together, as savages produce a flame with sticks ... That is all Peter Pan is, the spark I got from you.' Towards the end of his life, Barrie confided in his journal, 'Long after writing Peter Pan, its true meaning came to me. Despite all attempts to grow up, I can't.'

In 1906, Barrie began plans to place a statue of Peter Pan in Kensington Gardens. He commissioned one of the leading British sculptors of that time, Sir George Frampton, to design a statue with Peter Pan dressed in the costume he had worn when he first appeared on a stage. Around the high bronze base of the statue there would be the fairies and animals that once lived with Peter in Kensington Gardens. It took years before Barrie was satisfied with the design but finally, and in great secrecy, he had it trundled into the park late one night. On the morning of May 1, 1912, it 'magically' appeared in the park to the astonishment of all.

Seven years later, the City of Toronto acquired two small squares at the corner of St Clair Avenue and Avenue Road and announced it planned to landscape them as public parks. A wealthy Toronto real estate man, H.H. Williams, offered to donate to one park a replica of the fountain at the Peace Palace at The Hague. The local members of the College Heights Association (named after the nearby Upper Canada College) asked that the other park be a children's garden and offered to raise all the money needed to acquire a copy of one of the world's most popular sculptures with children, the Peter Pan statue in Kensington Gardens, London.

On Saturday, September 14, 1929, at the end of an afternoon of colourful ceremonies which included children dressed as pirates, the statue was unveiled. The next day's edition of the Toronto *Star* carried a front-page story headlined, 'Peter Pan Comes to Stay in Toronto.'

The statue is not only signed by the artist, Sir George Frampton. If you look very closely, half-way up the base among the fairyland figures and animals you will see the signature of J.M. Barrie clearly written into the bronze.

Eight years later, on June 19, 1937, the man *The Times* called 'the best loved of our dramatists' died in London. Shortly before his death, Barrie made a singularly generous gift. He had become a popular and regular visitor in the wards of the Hospital for Sick Children in Great Ormond Street, London. In his will he bequeathed to this hospital all the worldwide rights to *Peter Pan*.

Peter Pan and other figures from J.M. Barrie's classic live in bronze at Avenue Road and St Clair Avenue.

36

The man who helped Sigmund Freud escape from the Gestapo

Ernest Jones, who once lived on Brunswick Avenue in Toronto, was one of Freud's closest friends and his official biographer.

Few people remember the Toronto years of Ernest Jones. Only years later, after he helped Sigmund Freud escape from the Nazis in 1938, did he become an international figure.

Almost on his own, Jones had persuaded U.S. President Franklin D. Roosevelt to use his influence to force the Gestapo to release Freud and his family. Jones was present to meet the Freuds when they arrived to live in exile in London. During Freud's last years there, Jones was one of his closest colleagues and one of the family's most trusted friends.

A few years after Freud's death, the family decided that an authorized account had to be written to correct all the lies that had been written about him. They asked Jones to write it. The task took him almost 10 years to complete. In 1953, when his massive three-volume *Life and Work of Sigmund Freud* was published, it received great praise. *The Atlantic* called it 'The definitive life of Freud.' The *New York Times* called it 'one of the outstanding biographies of the age.' *Time* magazine called it 'A masterpiece ... from its pages suddenly emerges a tough, jealous, ferocious figure.'

When the book appeared, Jones was almost 80. A few years later he, too, died in London. In its obituary, *The Times* described him as 'the most eminent figure in the world of psychoanalysis since the death of Freud.' The medical world had long known of his importance, but it was not until the publication of the biography that the general public knew anything about him. During his last years, in fact, Jones often joked that if he should ever achieve immortality it would not be as a pioneer in the science to which he had devoted his life but as the biographer of Sigmund Freud. Today, even among Canadians who prize their copy of his biography, almost nothing is remembered of his years in Canada or the tragic affair that forced him to leave England and begin a new life in Toronto.

He lived so many years in London that writers still refer to him as an English doctor, but he was born in Wales on January 1, 1879, in the village of Rhosfelyn, near Swansea. His father was a self-made man who had started his career as a clerk in a coal firm and had risen to become a director of one of the largest coal mines in the country.

In his autobiography, Jones later wrote, 'I was born to be a doctor' and could never imagine himself in any other profession. He began his medical studies at University College of South Wales in Cardiff and completed them in London at the University College Hospital. After graduation, he was offered a position on the staff of the hospital. It was during his years as a house physician there that he first became interested in the field of neurology that would dominate the rest of his life. In his own words, 'The diseases of the nervous system are themselves fascinatingly precise but are mostly of unknown origin ... and are singularly unamenable to treatment.'

He began visiting an asylum outside London every Sunday, during his free time away from the hospital, to speak with its patients. He was still in his early twenties and was barely earning enough to support himself. To earn extra money, he undertook research projects for a number of London's leading neurologists. In 1904, when he was 25, he and a group of his colleagues opened a practice in a house at 13 Harley Street. Three years later, the incident occurred that would temporarily end his career in England.

A young girl, one of his patients at the London hospital, boasted to her friends that the youthful Dr Jones had been talking to her about 'sexual' matters. It was a rule at almost every hospital in Britain at the time that no sexual topic could be discussed with any child. The head of the hospital was furious when he heard of the girl's comments. Although Jones explained that he was simply trying to help her understand her illness, he was abruptly asked to resign. The affair was widely reported and, as Jones later wrote, 'All hope vanished of my getting on to the staff of any neurological hospital in London.'

A few months later, he heard that Dr C.K. Clarke, professor of psychology at the University of Toronto and dean of its medical faculty, was looking for someone to serve as the director of a new mental health institute (later to be named after him and called the Clarke Institute). Jones applied and, with letters of reference from Canadian friends in England, was offered the position.

Before sailing, he attended a conference in Salzburg, Austria, and for the first time met Sigmund Freud, an Austrian doctor who had been publishing a series of highly controversial papers on neurology since 1895. Jones' first impressions were of an 'unaffected and unassuming man.'

After his return to England, he sailed in September 1908 on board the *Empress of Canada* 'for a fresh start' in a new country. On his arrival in Toronto, he was welcomed 'with true colonial hospitality' but found a form of intolerance in this city he had not expected. He discovered English people were not particularly popular, and many factories posted signs stating, 'No English need apply.' He began referring to himself, correctly, as Welsh. 'This went down better, especially among the Scottish doctors.'

He moved into an attractive home in the Annex at 407 Brunswick Avenue, 'which at that time was on the outskirts of the city.' Then followed some of the most prolific literary years of his life. He published *Nightmares* and his first treatise on *Hamlet and Oedipus*, one of his most revolutionary works. When Freud made his first and only visit to America in 1909, Jones was one of the doctors who met him in New York. Freud thoroughly disliked his visit to America. 'It is gigantic,' he said, 'but a gigantic mistake.'

By 1912, Jones had grown homesick. When one of his closest friends in London became mentally ill and planned to leave for Vienna to be treated by Freud, Jones wrote saying he would accompany her. During those months in Vienna, he recorded in his journal, 'Freud has taken a liking to me and seems to want to open his heart to someone not of his own milieu.' Jones found himself spending most of his evenings at Freud's home, and the two men would often talk together until 3 a.m.

Freud's theories about the importance of dreams and the role of sex were provoking a storm of controversy across Europe, and a group of his friends and colleagues decided to form 'a sort of international guard around him' to safeguard his reputation. Freud was delighted. He called it 'a secret council of the best of our men.' The group became known as 'The Committee' and Jones was welcomed into it as the only non-German-speaker.

In 1913, Jones decided to return to London and establish the kind of organization he believed was needed in Britain. When war broke out in 1914 he went on special wartime duty. The year after the war ended, he was instrumental in founding the British Psychoanalytical Society. The following year he was elected its president and remained president for the next 24 years. By the 1930s he was recognized as one of the leading psychoanalysts in Britain. His private practice grew so large he could no longer treat all the patients who came to see him.

In March 1938, German troops invaded Austria. Freud and his family, together with thousands of other Jewish families, were arrested by the Gestapo. As soon as Jones learned of this, he immediately began plans to gain Freud's release. Few countries in the world at that time were accepting European refugees, especially Jewish ones. But Jones managed to enlist the support of President Roosevelt and, with the curious condition that Freud sign a statement stating that he had been well treated by the Gestapo, he and his family were finally permitted to leave Austria.

England had agreed to accept the family as exiles and on June 6, 1938, Freud arrived in London. Jones was at Victoria Station to meet him and take him to his first home in London, a house on Elsworthy Road. Freud was then 82 and had been in constant pain from throat cancer for 16 years. He refused to take any form of pain-killing drugs, saying he preferred to think in torment to not being able to think clearly. Barely a year later, on September 23, 1939, he died.

Jones was asked by the family to deliver the funeral oration at the cemetery at Golders Green. Shortly afterwards he was approached by a number of members of the family and asked to write the first full and true account of Freud's life. Freud had never wanted his biography published and had, on several occasions, destroyed all personal papers. It took Jones close to 10 years to complete a work that would hide nothing of Freud's failings but

Sigmund Freud arrives at his new London home in 1938 with Dr Ernest Jones, who had secured his freedom from the Gestapo.

would also record for the first time the greatness of his achievements. It was a massive work that included full details of Freud's largely misunderstood love affair with Martha Bernays and his early experiments with hypnosis and cocaine. It also recorded all the years of personal slander until the final decades of fame.

When the book was published in 1953, Ernest Jones was 74 and gravely ill. He suffered the first of two coronary attacks, and it was then discovered he had cancer. During the final months of his life he began work on his autobiography, *Free Association: Memoirs of a Psycho-analyst*, but never lived to complete it. It was published posthumously.

During his last days, when he knew he was dying, he asked to be taken to the hospital where he had started his medical career. There, at the University College Hospital in London, he died on February 11, 1958. His body was cremated and the ashes taken to Golders Green, where they were interred close to the grave of Sigmund Freud.

37

Canada's first black doctor: a hero of the American Civil War

The son of parents who had escaped to freedom in Canada, Anderson Abbott became the first native-born black Canadian to graduate from a Canadian university as a doctor.

In the winter of 1863, guests at a reception at the White House in Washington grew suddenly silent and stared at the young black doctor who was approaching the receiving line. It was most unusual at that point in the history of the United States for a black man to be invited to a presidential levée. It was likely the first time most of the guests had seen a black man wearing the uniform of a captain in the American army. When the young officer reached the presidential party, he was warmly greeted by President Abraham Lincoln. The president's wife would remember that meeting in years to come.

Dr Anderson Abbott, the black doctor who made such an impression that night, was one of the heroic figures of the American Civil War. But he is an even more important figure in the history of Canada, for he was this country's first native-born black doctor. He is a particular hero to Toronto's black community for he was born in Toronto and died in this city, and his body lies buried here in the Necropolis Cemetery beside the grave of his father, who was one of the thousands of blacks who fled to freedom in Canada.

The story of the Abbott family is one of many that appear in

The Freedom-Seekers: Blacks in Early Canada, by Daniel G. Hill, the former chairman of the Ontario Human Rights Commission. The book records more than 350 years of a virtually unknown part of Canada's history and refutes misconceptions that have existed for generations.

It is often thought that there were never slaves in this province, but the truth is that an anti-slavery act sponsored by the first lieutenant-governor, John Graves Simcoe, never did free a single black slave. For years after the passing of that act there was open, even hostile, anti-black prejudice. Yet one major event occurred at that time in which all Torontonians can take pride. Although every other large community introduced segregated schools, Toronto alone refused to permit them, and the anti-slavery sentiment became so strong in this city that the Canadian Anti-Slavery Society was born here.

The full history of slavery in Canada is almost as old as the history of the country itself. The very first French governors had prohibited slavery in New France but in 1709, when the need for labourers became crucial to the survival of the settlements, King Louis XIV of France gave approval for the importation of as many slaves as the settlers wanted.

After 1759, when British forces conquered New France, the customs of slavery introduced into Canada were virtually the same as those in the British colonies to the south. When the 13 southern colonies rebelled against Britain, the Loyalists who fled north to Canada brought their slaves with them. This was the beginning of many of the early black settlements in towns throughout the Niagara Peninsula.

In 1793 Simcoe tried to introduce an anti-slavery act, but found himself opposed by almost all his principal officials who owned slaves. Much against his will, he was forced to accept a compromise: no slaves then living in Canada would be freed, but every black child born in Canada would become free at the age of 25, and all blacks entering Canada in the future would become free the moment they crossed the border.

Simcoe's act gave impetus to the famous 'Underground Railroad,' as word spread throughout the United States that Upper

Canada had become the first land to offer freedom. The Underground Railroad was not in fact a railway. It was a secret society of men and women, black and white, whose common bond was a hatred of slavery. To help the black families escape to Canada, they adopted railway terms to confuse both the public and especially slave owners as to the true nature of their mission. 'Stations' were places where blacks were transferred from one group to another – usually barns or cellars or attics where escaping slaves could be hidden. 'Conductors' were those who helped guide former slaves to freedom in the north.

The tens of thousands of blacks who escaped to Canada became ardent Canadians. They were among the first to join the fighting units to defend the country when American troops invaded Canada in the War of 1812. Later, in 1837, they formed black companies to fight on the government's side against William Lyon Mackenzie and his rebels.

It is impossible to know exactly how many thousands of blacks found freedom in Canada. Conservative estimates quote numbers of more than 30,000. Whatever the true figure, the 'railroad' was a success, but many of the former slaves who arrived with little more than their freedom faced racial prejudice. In a number of towns in southern Ontario, white townspeople attempted to evict all poor black families. But the blacks, who had already risked their lives for freedom, refused to accept the eviction notices and began fighting back peacefully through the medium of the press. They founded their own newspapers and used them to remind whites that other immigrants, especially those from Ireland, were also arriving with little more than the clothes on their backs, yet were not facing similar discrimination.

Of all the stories that could be told of the many blacks who became a part of the history of Canada, few are filled with more glory than that of Anderson Ruffin Abbott. His father, Wilson Ruffin Abbott, and his mother were both among those who had escaped to freedom in Canada. In 1835 they settled in Toronto, where Anderson was born two years later.

From the time he was a small child, Anderson had only one ambition, to become a doctor. He enrolled as one of only three

Anderson Abbott, Canada's
first black physician, was a
medical officer with the Union
army in the US Civil War.

black students at the Toronto Academy of Medicine and graduated
from the University of Toronto as the country's first Canadian-
born black doctor.

He was 26 when word reached Canada that the United States

army was attempting to raise 150,000 black troops to fight in the Civil War, and desperately needed black doctors to staff army hospitals. Abbott wrote at once to the secretary of war volunteering his services, and on September 2, 1863, became one of only eight black physicians to serve in the army of the Northern states. His record for bravery and service during the war, in the words of one historian, was 'astonding' and he was invited to Washington to meet the president and Mrs Lincoln.

On his return to Canada, he practised in southern Ontario and eventually, in the 1890s, settled in Toronto, buying a large house in the west end of the city at 119 Dowling Avenue. Its great gabled roof has completely disappeared, but its outline suggests it was one of the grand homes of the original Parkdale.

Abbott received many honours during his life, but perhaps the most telling testimonial came early. In 1865, shortly after the assassination of her husband, Mrs Lincoln sent him the shawl that her husband had worn on the way to his first inauguration as president of the United States. Lincoln had worn it that day, at the insistence of friends, as part of a disguise to escape assassination by those who were denouncing his policies, particularly his belief that everyone has a God-given right to be free.

38

Did Captain Roy Brown really kill the Red Baron?

It is still a worldwide controversy. Newspapers hailed him as a hero, but Roy Brown never once said he had shot down the legendary German flying ace, von Richthofen.

It has been called the most controversial 60 seconds in the history of aerial warfare.

On an April morning in 1918, Germany's greatest aviator, Baron von Richthofen, the famous 'Red Baron' who had destroyed 80 Allied aircraft, was shot down and killed in a battle in the skies over northern France. Within days, newspapers throughout the world reported that he had been shot down by a 24-year-old Canadian pilot, Captain A. Roy Brown. The victory became one of the legendary stories of the war. But rumours about what had really happened during those 60 seconds would trouble and haunt Brown for the rest of his life.

When the war ended and he settled in Toronto, he was besieged by reporters but refused to be interviewed. In 1927, when a sensational story, 'My Fight With Richthofen' by A. Roy Brown, appeared in the American magazine *Liberty*, Brown denied having written it and said he never saw it until a copy of the magazine arrived at his home. When he died on the outskirts of Toronto in 1944, tributes in countless newspapers continued to hail him as the man who had defeated the Red Baron. But the story of Richthofen's death had already created an international furor, and mystery continues to surround the event.

Never once during Brown's life did he ever publicly declare he had killed the Red Baron. Yet he was a more gallant hero than most of his biographers have revealed.

Arthur Roy Brown was born in Carleton Place, Ontario, on December 23, 1893, and attended schools in Carleton Place and later in Edmonton. When war broke out in 1914, he was 21 and determined to serve as a pilot. At his own expense he enrolled in the Wright Flying School in Dayton, Ohio, and was soon a member of the Royal Flying Corps. During the four years of the war, he was officially credited with shooting down a dozen enemy aircraft and was awarded the Distinguished Service Cross for extraordinary courage and gallantry.

On the morning of April 21, 1918, the day of his encounter with Richthofen, all the aerodromes along both sides of the battlefront were blanketed by a deep fog. At the German base where Richthofen was in command of Fighter Group 1, the ace was so convinced that all regular dawn patrols would be cancelled that when he got out of bed he simply tugged on his flying suit and went for coffee. That is the true story behind the 'romantic' legend that, when his body was removed from the crash site several hours later, he was found unshaven and wearing silk pyjamas under his flying clothes.

That spring Baron Manfred von Richthofen was 25. He had been born into a prosperous German family. The name Richthofen means 'Courts of Justice,' a title given to the family by Frederick the Great. There was a strong military tradition in the family and when World War I broke out the young baron first served as a captain in a cavalry regiment. When the war bogged down into a trench warfare, he asked to be transferred to the Imperial Air Force. By 1918 he was his country's greatest air ace, and because of his fancifully decorated scarlet plane was known throughout Germany as the Red Baron.

At a British air base near the front on that April morning, Captain Roy Brown was flight commander of 209 Squadron. One of its newest members was Wilfred R. May, from Carberry, Manitoba. He had been one of Brown's classmates at a school in Edmonton, but when he arrived at the base he scarcely recognized the captain.

Brown had grown thin and his face was lined with fatigue from the endless succession of patrols. He had lost all his early love of flying. It was now simply 'flying to kill,' and on that morning he was so ill he should never have been allowed to fly.

To everyone's surprise, the fog suddenly cleared, and Brown and six of his men were ordered into the air. At about 9.40 a.m., they sighted more than 20 German planes that had also hurriedly taken to the air. The British planes dove to attack, and in the words of one of the British pilots, 'All hell broke loose.' At the height of the battle, May found that both his guns had jammed. He broke away to head back to base. One of the German planes immediately flew in pursuit. When Brown saw May being attacked, he raced to his defence. Neither Brown nor May knew at the time that the pursuer was Richthofen.

May was an almost totally inexperienced combat pilot and made none of the recognized tactical moves to escape his attacker. His erratic flying must have confused Richthofen, who was determined to add another plane to his list of kills. The German broke one of his own cardinal rules by failing to notice he was now flying dangerously low over enemy lines.

Brown closed in, firing rapidly. Seconds later, May looked back and saw the German plane crash into the ground. As soon as the ground troops discovered that the pilot was Richthofen, the news became a front page story throughout the world. Brown was awarded a bar to his Distinguished Service Cross, but, as he repeatedly admitted, he never witnessed the crash of the German plane. As he banked away, one of the wings of his plane had hidden what had happened next.

From the day of the crash, rumours started to circulate that Richthofen had been shot down by fire from troops on the ground. Mysteriously, the fatal bullet in Richthofen's body – which might have proved conclusively how he had died – was lost after the autopsy. Rumours also began to spread that Britain had needed a new wartime hero and that Brown had been ordered by the British Air Ministry to say nothing about the affair.

The rumours continued to grow for almost half a century until the full story broke with the publication of two books: *Who Killed the Red Baron?* by P.J. Carisella and J.W. Ryan in 1969 and *The Day the Red Baron Died* by Dale M. Titler in 1973. In a definitive work, *Canadian Airmen and the First World War: The Official History of the RCAF*, published in 1980, S.F. Wise could conclude only that Richthofen had been 'apparently killed' by Brown. There was by that time mounting evidence that the bullet that killed Richthofen may, in fact, have come from one of the soldiers of the Fifth Australian Division who had fired point-blank when Richthofen passed less than 40 feet above him.

When the war ended, Brown returned to Toronto and ran an air transport company. On March 9, 1944, he died of a heart attack at his farm near Stouffville. Titler reported that, 'his family, who knew and loved him as a father and husband, never heard him discuss his victory score with anyone.'

In Germany, Luftwaffe commanders refused to admit even the possibility that their greatest pilot could have been vanquished in the air. For decades millions of Germans remembered and mourned the day when it was said the legendary Baron von Richthofen had been shot down in a rain of fire from the ground.

39

The actor who became governor-general

In the 1920s, young Vincent Massey was one of the leading figures in Toronto's theatre world. Thirty years later he became the first native-born governor-general of Canada.

In the words of those who knew him well, Vincent Massey was one of the most misunderstood men in Canada's history.

Even in Toronto, where he was born, hardly anyone remembers that his first major contribution to Canada was not in the field of public service but as a leading member of a Toronto theatre group; yet in the 1920s Vincent Massey was one of this city's best-known actors. His brother, Raymond Massey, became the star of Broadway plays and Hollywood movies, but it was always said that Vincent was the better actor and could have had a far more brilliant career on the stage.

Today, he is remembered almost solely as the first Canadian to become governor-general of Canada. Before that he was a distinguished diplomat, so well informed, so intimately acquainted with so many international figures, so courteous in manner, that a British peer was prompted to make his celebrated remark, 'Vincent is a dear fellow but he makes all of the rest of us such frightful savages.'

Those who have heard that remark repeated have rarely known anything of the younger Massey who plastered his face with greasepaint, wore shabby clothes, and appeared on a Toronto stage as a Cockney burglar. He was then in his early thirties and president of a large international corporation, but he had become obsessed by the world of theatre. Presidents of other companies became increasingly suspicious about this young head of Massey-Harris, who was cavorting on the stage and spending most of his evenings at the Arts and Letters Club. But Massey was more than a dilettante actor. By 1919 he had become one of the most significant figures in the cultural life of Toronto. The background to one of his greatest later accomplishments, as chairman of the Massey Commission which revolutionized the arts world of Canada, can best be understood in light of the stage-struck young man of the 1920s.

He was born into one of the wealthiest families of old Toronto. His grandfather was Hart Massey, the founder of a farm imple-

Vincent Massey, future governor-general of Canada, played a Cockney burglar (*at left*) caught redhanded in a Hart House production in the 1920s.

ment company, later known as Massey-Ferguson, that became the most successful company of its kind in the British Empire. At the turn of the century, during the final years of his life, Hart Massey became one of the great benefactors of Toronto. It was his money that built Massey Hall and the Fred Victor Mission; and when he died Hart Massey left the bulk of his estate to public institutions and charitable causes. To fulfil his wishes the family established the Massey Foundation, with one of Hart's son's, Chester Massey, as its president.

Chester's two sons, Raymond and Vincent, became the most famous of all the Masseys. Both were rebels. Raymond shocked his Methodist family by leaving the country to earn his living on the stage. Vincent's rebellion was of a different kind – against the strict, puritanical rules of the Methodist church.

Despite family pressure, Vincent refused to enrol in the Methodist Victoria College. Instead, he chose the non-denominational University College. He majored in modern languages and history and, after graduating in 1919, studied at Oxford and then returned to Toronto as a lecturer in history at the university. Several years later he joined the family's business as a senior executive.

In 1919, a new university centre, called Hart House, was presented to the University of Toronto. It was a large handsome building, which included a magnificent dining hall, library, and swimming pool. The alumni of the university would later raise enough money to add a great tower at its western end as a memorial to former students who had died in service during World War I. Vincent Massey became so involved in the design of Hart House that many people assumed it was a gift from him. It was, in fact, a gift from the Massey Foundation; but there is a far more important connection between it and him than its architectural history.

By the time the building was completed in 1919, the world of the theatre had become a major part of Vincent's life. Whenever he was in London or New York on business, he would spend almost every free evening and afternoon at the theatre; his diary over the next decades would read like a record of great performances in the English-speaking world.

Hart House, seen here before the memorial tower was added, was
planned by the young Vincent Massey as a centre for the
University of Toronto.

Late in the planning of Hart House, a large, well-equipped theatre was added for student performances and other theatrical productions. As soon as it was in operation he became a regular visitor.
He would often bring dinner guests to see a performance.

He also became one of the principal actors on that stage. He
had a slight, boyish figure, with his mother's dark, attractive col-
ouring, but he rarely played the part of the hero. Instead, he
preferred character parts and usually appeared as some elderly,
unconventional figure. In one celebrated success, he appeared as
a cockney burglar in the Canadian play *The Point of View*. In
another he played Pope Pius VII in a play by the French dramatist
Paul Claudel.

By the early 1920s, he also was playing various management
roles within the theatre; he started to produce plays; and he

directed one of its greatest successes, *Outward Bound*. He was involved in choosing the theatre director. He sometimes commissioned stage sets and costume designs. On one memorable opening night in 1924, the three one-act plays had set designs by Lawren Harris, Arthur Lismer, and J.E.H. MacDonald, all members of the Group of Seven artists; Healey Willan composed and performed the music.

In his biography, *The Young Vincent Massey*, Claude Bissell wrote: 'The Hart House Theatre was the first of Vincent Massey's contributions to the cultural life of Canada – the first, in time and, some would say, in importance.' Massey's second contribution was in the field of music. In 1921, he became the principal founder and benefactor of four talented musicians who became known as the Hart House String Quartet. For 20 years they were Canada's most internationally renowned group of musicians.

Massey could easily have spent the rest of his life as a patron of the arts. Instead, he became increasingly restless. Hart Massey had instilled in the family a belief in 'creative philanthropy' and Massey had decided that his role would be in the field of public service. Since his work in the theatre was unlikely to lead to a public career, he turned to the only other principal interest in his life and became active in education. He was soon appointed president of the new National Council on Education and became its principal speaker.

In Ottawa on the night of January 26, 1924, one of the men in his audience was Prime Minister Mackenzie King. King noted in his diary that evening that he had found a man with 'a fine discernment of the underlying principles in our national life' and began to cultivate this wealthy young Toronto intellectual who came from a city that had almost abandoned the Liberal party and its causes. King made Massey a trustee of the National Gallery and in 1925 appointed him a cabinet minister. To avoid any conflict of interest, Massey resigned as president of Massey-Harris, and this marked the end of his family's direct association with the company. When he failed to win election to the House of Commons he resigned from the cabinet and accepted King's offer to become Canada's first minister to the United States. Thus began a public career that would lead to the positions of high commissioner to London, chancellor of the University of Toronto, and, in 1952, first Canadian-born governor-general of Canada.

To many, however, his greatest contribution came in 1949 as chairman of a royal commission that came to be known as the Massey Commission. It had been called to review the place of the arts, letters, and sciences in Canada. The final report was written almost entirely by Massey.

Throughout all the years, the arts had remained very close to the centre of Vincent Massey's life. That report called for the creation of a new institution that would help Canada's artists survive, and flourish. And out of that recommendation, by a former Toronto actor, was born the Canada Council.

40

The first forester of the New World

When Bernhard Fernow arrived in North America, millions of acres of forest were being destroyed. Almost singlehandedly he halted the destruction and pioneered conservation in North America.

In 1923, when Bernhard Fernow died in Toronto, newspapers across this continent carried the story of the man they called the 'masterbuilder' of every new forest in North America. In Europe, he had been called 'the First Forester' of the New World.

In 1876, when Fernow landed in New York as a young immigrant from Germany, few people had ever even heard of the word 'forester.' He arrived at the time of the opening of the West. Hundreds of thousands of square miles of forests were being burned to the ground by settlers to provide new land for farms, and in the 1880s Fernow was almost the only one who spoke out against this destruction.

Gradually, a few important people began to listen. In 1886, when he was still in his early thirties, Fernow was chosen by the president of the United States to establish the first forestry department within the government. In 1898, he opened the first forestry school on this continent. In 1907, he was invited by the University of Toronto to establish the first forestry school in Canada and Toronto became his home for the rest of his life.

Throughout his long career, Fernow was honoured as the founder of the conservation movement on this continent. The number of awards that he received began to embarrass him and he started reminding his audiences that he had become the first forester of the New World entirely by accident. 'I am a fatalist,' he told them, 'a believer in chance and accidents shaping our lives.'

The most publicized of all these 'accidents' was the chance encounter that brought him to North America. He had never had any intention of becoming an immigrant. His family was wealthy and he had a promising future in Germany, but in 1876 he left home and sailed for New York to follow an American girl he had met and vowed he would marry. His family was totally against the marriage. They were German aristocrats and believed the proposed marriage would end all their hope for their brilliant young son.

He was then 25 years old. He had been born at the family's home in Inowrazlaw in the province of Posen in Prussia on January 7, 1851, and as a young boy had always been happiest working on the family's land, particularly with the men who managed the large forest estates. In his teens he enrolled at the renowned forestry academy at Muenden in the province of Hanover, and it was there that he met and fell in love with a young American visitor to Germany.

In a full page tribute to Fernow in the *New York Times* on January 30, 1910, he was described as 'a large ungainly young man, sort of a St Bernard of a youth, with a rugged head and burning eyes ... Young women do not often take to men of that type at first sight, but they frequently end by marrying them.' When this young woman returned to her home in the United States, Fernow immediately made plans to follow her.

In Europe the science of forestry was well established as a profession, but when young Fernow landed in New York, the subject was little understood. When the young woman told her friends that a 'forester' had followed her to America and wanted to marry her, they asked if he was something 'like Robin Hood'!

Fernow vowed he would not ask for her hand until he had a job with a future, and the only job he could find in New York was as a junior clerk in a law office. He soon discovered that the most promising way of getting into the field he wanted would be

Bernhard Fernow, North America's first
forestry expert and conservationist

to find a job with the mining engineers who were building plants
and offices in the more remote parts of the Eastern seaboard. He
began attending their meetings and soon attracted considerable
attention with his talk about the advantages of using red charcoal
rather than black charcoal in blast furnaces. He was offered a job
with the Cooper Hewitt company as manager of its charcoal works
and could now finally propose to the young woman who had
patiently been waiting for him. They were married at once and
spent the next six years living happily in the middle of the forests
of Pennsylvania.

Here, Fernow could at last study the North American forests at
first hand and was horrified at the extent of unwarranted destruction that was taking place. He was repeatedly told there was no
need to worry about the future availability of lumber since there
were forests of white pine alone stretching all the way from Mich-

igan to Texas. To shake this complacency, Fernow started publishing articles that predicted a far different future. He urged the government to begin working with the lumber companies to ensure that forests were planted to replace those being lost. He also helped found the first forestry association in North America. When President Grover Cleveland asked for recommendations for the position of head of a new forestry department, Fernow was the unanimous choice.

Among other accomplishments, he almost single-handedly drew up the laws that established the first forest reserves on this continent. In 1898, when he believed his work in Washington was over, he accepted an offer from Cornell University to establish a faculty of forestry and spent the next five years training the first young foresters of North America.

When the school had to be disbanded owing to a misunderstanding over the college's right to use state lands, Fernow became a consultant. In 1907 an unexpected offer arrived from the University of Toronto asking if he would be interested in establishing the first forestry school in Canada. He accepted at once, moved to Toronto, and bought a large handsome house at 16 Admiral Road in the Annex.

Once again, he found himself a crusader. When he called on the minister of lands and forests and told him that the people of Ontario would one day hold him personally responsible for the massive destruction of the provinces' forest, he was 'shown to the door.' To enlist the support of the public he began speaking to every group that would invite him.

At a Canadian Club luncheon in Toronto on February 26, 1908, he startled his audience by telling them: 'If you want to study the effect of denudation, visit the Muskoka district and you will see how a rock desert is started.' He warned them that in Wisconsin, 'a desert of four million acres had been made by man in less than 50 years.' Gradually, and almost entirely because of him, the official view began to change. By 1915 so many of his proposals had been accepted that the Canadian government set aside 28 million acres as forest reserves.

During those years in Toronto, he wrote his major work, a huge volume that he titled *A Brief History of Forestry*, but his working days were almost entirely devoted to his new school. When he began his work in Toronto, it had been quartered in a house at 11 Queen's Park. By 1925 so many young students wanted to become foresters that a large and handsome Forestry Building was built at 45 St George Street in the same Georgian style as the faculty of forestry building at Oxford University. It was there, on March 28, 1982, on the 75th anniversary of the very day of Fernow's appointment, that hundreds of foresters of Ontario gathered in front of the main entrance and dedicated a memorial plaque to him.

By the 1990s, the number of forestry students had again grown so large that the faculty moved into an imposing new Earth Sciences Centre at 33 Willcocks Street. The plaque to Fernow was moved to the main entrance of this new building.

The former Forestry Building at the University of Toronto

Fernow died in his sleep at his home on Admiral Road on February 7, 1923. At his request, his body was cremated and the ashes taken to Point Breeze in New York. There they were cast into the waters of Lake Ontario, the lake that washed the shores of both the state where he had begun his teaching career and the province where that career had ended. To friends he had confided that this would also be the final and symbolic act of his belief that, at the end of life, 'man returns to energy in a state of nature.'

41

The mystery surrounding Prince George's death

The Princes' Gates were named after Prince George and his brother, the Prince of Wales, who officially opened them in 1927. Many books have been written about the future Duke of Windsor; no historian has explained the wartime death of his royal brother.

Few mysteries surrounding the royal family are more curious – or more unlikely to be solved – than that surrounding the death in 1942 of Prince George, an uncle of the present Queen. At the time he was perhaps the most popular member of the royal family. He was also one of the two princes after whom the Princes' Gates, the eastern entrance to the Canadian National Exhibition, were named.

On the day in 1927 when he and his oldest brother, Edward, Prince of Wales, arrived in this city for the official opening of the gates, they discovered that the original simple ceremony had escalated into one of the more spectacular military events in Toronto's past. The story of the opening of those gates has been told in many books about Toronto, but has always concentrated on Prince Edward, who was then heir to the throne and the future King Edward VIII. No biography of the younger Prince George was written until almost a half century after his death, and yet his life ended in a tragedy that shocked millions throughout the British Empire.

During World War II, when he was in his thirties and serving with the Royal Air Force, he died when his plane crashed in a remote corner of northern Scotland. Despite wartime security measures in effect at the time, his death was reported in surprising detail in the world's press. But there were a number of omissions, and they have continued to puzzle everyone who has ever tried to discover the true story behind that crash.

Prince George was the favourite son of his mother, Queen Mary. He was born on December 20, 1902, at York Cottage, on the grounds of his family's home at Sandringham, about 100 miles northeast of London. He was christened with an imposing list of kingly names – George Edward Alexander Edmund – but within the family was always known as 'Georgie.' (The Queen's father, King George VI, was known as Albert or 'Bertie' until his accession to the throne.)

Prince George grew to be the tallest, handsomest, and most charming of all the royal sons. It was said that if his oldest brother, Edward, was the 'Bohemian' member of the family, George had the brains. Despite the great differences between the two men, George hero-worshipped Edward, and throughout his life was always the Prince of Wales' closest friend. In 1927, when he was 25, George was allowed to make his first semi-official royal visit when the Prince of Wales persuaded the King to allow George to accompany him on a visit to Canada.

The Prince of Wales had become enormously popular with all Canada's troops during World War I by insisting, over family objections, that he be allowed to serve in France. As soon as the Canadian Legion learned of the Prince of Wales' plans to visit Canada, he was invited to review a parade of veterans who wanted to welcome him. When the Prince replied that he would review that band of men at any site the Canadian Legion might choose, officials scrambled to decide on an appropriate site.

The year was the 60th anniversary of the founding of Canada, and the unanimous choice for a site was on the Toronto waterfront, near the great gates that were then being built at the entrance to the exhibition grounds. In honour of the country's anniversary, those gates were to be called the 'Jubilee Gates.' Even their design was to symbolize Canada, with nine huge columns on either side of the centre gate representing each of the provinces that then constituted Canada.

Prince George, Duke of Kent, with the
Duchess of Kent, shortly before
his death in 1942

On August 30, when the two young princes arrived in Toronto
to review the veterans and officially open the gates, the event had
grown to a massive assembly of close to 10,000 ex-servicemen.
Once the ribbons were cut, these veterans were the first to march
through the gates. Afterwards, the two princes spoke to a cheering
crowd of veterans and their families who filled Exhibition Stadium.
The day was such a triumph that, after the departure of the two
young men, it was agreed by all officials in the city that the original
name for those gates must be changed to commemorate that royal
visit.

Within the royal family, it had always been expected that George
would follow his father, George V, by seeking an early career in
the navy, but he was constantly sick at sea. In 1929, the prince
finally persuaded his father to allow him to resign from the navy.

He soon found a position that could better use his particular talents. He joined the Foreign Office and became the first son of Britain's royal family to work as a civil servant. He regularly walked to his office in Whitehall in a black overcoat and pin-striped suit, rarely recognized by the public.

He was rapidly becoming a great favourite of the press world. At Westminster Abbey, in 1934, with the Prince of Wales as his best man, he married one of Europe's most beautiful and intelligent young princesses, the Princess Marina of Greece. The marriage, according to the *Dictionary of National Biography*, marked 'a turning-point in his life, strengthening his character and making his purpose in life more definite.' The king conferred a new title on him, and he and his wife became the Duke and Duchess of Kent.

When war broke out in 1939 he had been scheduled to become the new governor-general of Australia, but he asked to be allowed to remain in Britain. He was then 37 and volunteered at once. He was appointed to the Training Command of the Royal Air Force and began enthusiastically fulfilling his duties, supervising the welfare of the members of the RAF both in Britain and at bases overseas.

By 1941, he had flown more than 60,000 miles to work with RAF officials at bases throughout the Empire. In the late summer of 1942, he was given leave to return home. It was a particularly happy time for the duke and duchess. Their fourth child, a son christened Michael, was one month old and there was time for a new set of family photographs including one memorable, informal portrait of the duke and duchess together.

Late in August, he left his home to travel by train to Inverness to return to wartime duties. On August 25, he was scheduled to fly to an air base in Iceland, and shortly after 1 p.m. a Sunderland Flying Boat carrying him took off from a base in northern Scotland.

The plane turned north to follow the coast. Shortly afterwards people in the inland village of Berriedale heard a deafening explosion. The plane had crashed on a hillside. Two and a half thousand gallons of fuel had exploded, killing everyone instantly except the rear gunner whose turret had broken off at the moment of impact.

The tragedy stunned everyone. The duke had become one of Britain's royal heroes; it has always been surprising that for 40 years after his death no biography was published until the appearance in 1985 of Audrey Whiting's *The Kents* and in 1988 of Christopher Warwick's *George and Marina*. Despite their extensive investigations, neither author was ever able to solve the mystery that has continued to surround the crash.

The plane had been flown by a carefully selected crew of seasoned pilots and other officers but, Warwick wrote, 'for some unexplainable reason, in thick mist and over hazardous terrain, the plane had descended to an altitude of less than 700 feet and crashed into a hillside.' All the occupants of the aircraft were on duty at the time and all four engines were under power on impact, which indicates there was nothing wrong with the aircraft, but Whiting noted that 'there was unusual haste in clearing the wreckage after the crash.' The crash had caused the death of the fifth in line to the throne but 'all documentation pertaining to the official Court of Inquiry apparently vanished into thin air.'

The original model of the Princes' Gates, opened in 1927 by Prince George and the Prince of Wales

In 1978, the sole survivor, tail-gunner Sergeant Andrew Jack, died without leaving any record of what had happened.

In the final lines of his book *Great Mysteries of the Air*, Ralph Baker wrote: 'In that 32 minutes between take-off and oblivion, something went wrong ... something that confused or misled the crew, something that would have confused or misled any other crew at that particular moment in the history of the flight ... What it was will almost certainly remain a mystery.'

42

The sculptor who designed Canada's 'caribou' quarter and 'Bluenose' dime

Emanuel Hahn of York Mills was one of the most important North American sculptors of his time. He created Toronto landmarks and revolutionized the look of Canada's coins.

If you look very closely at a Canadian 10-cent coin, you'll discover a small 'H' in front of the ship on its reverse face. The same small 'H' appears directly below the throat of the caribou on the 25-cent piece.

Both letters are the signature of a man who lived in York Mills; and if you own both coins you own two signed works by the artist, Emanuel Hahn. In the early decades of this century he was probably the most famous sculptor in the country. Some of his greatest works are now among the important landmarks of Toronto.

He was eight years old when his parents came to Canada with their ten children. A few years earlier their father, Otto Hahn, had been hired by the Canadian government to work with officials in Germany to help advise German families who wanted to emigrate to Canada. The elder Hahn became so intrigued by what he learned about Canada that he decided to emigrate himself. In 1888, he brought his entire family to Canada and they settled in Toronto. Here Emanuel's older brother, Gustav, would become a highly successful painter.

As a small child, Emanuel showed a marked flair for drawing. In 1903, when his father returned to Germany to visit relatives, he took Emanuel with him. For the next three years Emanuel studied at an art school in Stuttgart. He won several scholarships and when he returned to Toronto he soon found a position as instructor of design and drawing. Shortly afterwards he became an instructor at the Ontario College of Art and, in 1922, was appointed head of the college's sculpture department.

The 1920s were one of the few great boom periods for Canadian sculptors. Almost every major city in the country was commissioning enormous works of art to decorate its parks and avenues with giant figures from Canada's past. In Toronto a competition was held in 1926 to select a sculptor to design a statue honouring the first great international sports figure in Canadian history. The winner of the competition was Emanuel Hahn. Today, his nine-foot-high bronze figure of Ned Hanlan, the Canadian oarsman who conquered the world, stands in Exhibition Place, in front of the main entrance to the Marine Museum.

The following year Hahn won the commission for a statue to honour the founder of Ontario Hydro, Sir Adam Beck. For the centre of University Avenue at Queen Street, he created an enormous figure of Beck standing above a waterway.

Like the Group of Seven painters, Hahn became fascinated by the rich, rugged beauty of the Ontario northland and spent most of his holidays canoeing through northern lakes and rivers. In 1936, when the Canadian government announced a commission for the design of a new one-dollar coin, Hahn submitted a startlingly original proposal. In place of the coats of arms and other regal symbols that decorated most coins at that time, Hahn's design showed a voyageur and an Indian travelling together by canoe through a northern Canadian landscape.

The government chose his design, and the following year commissioned him to design new 10-cent and 25-cent coins. Hahn filled the entire reverse side of the quarter with the solitary head of a magnificent Canadian caribou. For the reverse of the dime he chose the sleek lines of Canada's most famous sailing vessel, the *Bluenose* of Lunenburg, Nova Scotia, under full sail as in one of the many international competitions she won during a 20-year racing career.

His designs revolutionized the look of Canada's coins and won him a reputation as one of the major sculptors in Canada. At the same time, he was also winning a reputation as one of the most popular teachers in the art world of Toronto. He was a gregarious man who enjoyed hosting parties for his students. After hours of drinking wine and eating cheese and sausages they would all descend on Chinatown for dinners that would last long into the night.

The most talented of his students was Elizabeth Wyn Wood, from Orillia, an arrestingly attractive dark-haired woman who al-

Emanuel Hahn revolutionized the look of
Canadian coins and inconspicuously
placed his initial on the dime and quarter.

ways dressed in either white or gray. Hahn instantly fell in love with her and in 1926 they were married. Hahn was then 45; Elizabeth was 23. In later years, Hahn often joked that he had fallen in love with her simply because she was the first woman he ever met who knew how to hold a sculptor's knife properly.

Her parents probably knew that Elizabeth was going to be a sculptor long before she did, for as a very small child she would regularly mix water with her talcum powder and soda crackers to create 'clay.' As soon as she was old enough she was allowed to come to Toronto to study at the Ontario College of Art. Among her first lecturers were A.Y. Jackson, Arthur Lismer, and Emanuel Hahn.

Soon after their marriage, the Hahns became principal figures in the founding of the Sculptors' Society of Canada. Hahn was the unanimous choice as its first president. For close to 40 years, until his retirement in 1951, he continued to serve as head of the OCA department of sculpture; it was said that almost every major sculptor in the country came to study under him.

Among his many works, one has been hailed 'one of the finest examples of the sculptor's art in Canada' – a portrait of his wife that he carved in marble. It is one of the most prized Canadian works in the collection of the Art Gallery of Ontario; a second version is in the National Gallery in Ottawa.

Elizabeth Wood shared her husband's love of the Canadian northland and the finest of her works use the Canadian landscape as their subject. One critic said: 'She achieved for stone what the Group of Seven had achieved for painting.' Like her husband, she was a great teacher and taught at Central Tech for almost 30 years. Among her best loved works are figures of John Graves Simcoe and his wife at Niagara-on-the-Lake.

In the late 1940s she was chosen as one of the artists who would work with UNESCO in Paris to help rehabilitate the culture of the war-devastated countries of Europe. She insisted on retaining her own name, and was always known professionally as Elizabeth Wyn Wood. During her long career, she produced an impressive number of works but, in the words of Alan Jarvis, former director of the National Gallery of Canada, she remains 'shamefully un-recognized' in her own country.

After the death of Emanuel Hahn in 1957, she continued to live in the house they had shared at 51 Plymbridge Road in York Mills. She added a 20-foot-high studio where she worked almost until the day she died in 1966.

Emanuel Hahn made this bust of
his wife, the fellow sculptor
Elizabeth Wyn Wood, in 1926.

43

Dr Tupper, Sir John, and the 'picnics' that changed Canada's history

Dr Charles Tupper outlived all the other original Fathers of Confederation. In a distinguished public career after 1867, a few years he spent in Toronto proved some of the most decisive.

When Sir Charles Tupper died in 1915, he was the last of the men who in 1867 had created a new country called Canada. In his early career he was premier of Nova Scotia, and Nova Scotians have always claimed him as one of their most illustrious sons. But he was also a major figure in Toronto's past. In the mid-1870s all Toronto was aware that the celebrated Dr Tupper had moved to this city to start a new career.

He was a lifetime friend of Sir John A. Macdonald, Canada's first prime minister. Macdonald held that office for most of the country's first quarter-century, and during all the last years of his life it was Tupper he wanted as his successor. But, in the early 1870s, only a few years after Confederation, it seemed to everyone that Macdonald's political career was over. An affair known as the 'Pacific Scandal' had driven his Conservative party out of office. Macdonald left Ottawa and moved to Toronto and returned to his career as a lawyer. Shortly afterwards, Tupper also moved to Toronto and resumed his career as a doctor, with an office on Jarvis Street.

During the next few years Macdonald and Tupper joined forces to stage a celebrated series of 'political picnics' in towns and cities throughout Ontario. These they turned into one of the most colourful and successful political campaigns in the history of this country. In 1878, the voters overwhelmingly swept Macdonald back into power as prime minister. Tupper also returned to Ottawa and, the following year, was awarded a knighthood for his service to Canada. But to most Canadians and to the Fathers of Confederation, Sir Charles Tupper was always 'Dr Tupper.'

Many historians would rank Tupper as more important in the story of Canada than Macdonald himself. Few people ever knew anything about his personal life, but everyone knew the story of his extraordinary rise to power.

His family was originally from England. In the 17th century they were among the first settlers in the new British colonies in North America, and in the years following the American Revolutionary War part of the family moved north and settled in Nova Scotia. One of them, Charles Tupper, became a Baptist minister and it was his son, also named Charles Tupper, born in Amherst on July 2, 1821, who would become, in many ways, the decisive figure in the achievement of Confederation.

He attended Horton Academy (afterwards Acadia University) and at an early age decided on a career in medicine. His father arranged for him to study in Edinburgh. In 1843, after graduation, he returned to Nova Scotia and began his practice at Amherst.

Like his father, he was a staunch Conservative but had little interest in entering politics. When he was in his early thirties friends persuaded him to run as the Conservative candidate in the next election. No one thought he had a chance of winning, for his opponent was the powerful leader of Nova Scotia's Liberal party, Joseph Howe. But the popular young doctor from Amherst surprised everyone. He proved to be both a brilliant and forceful debater and swept the polls.

Tupper was now convinced he had found his true career and began to reorganize and revitalize his party. By 1864, when he was 43, he was premier of Nova Scotia. Politics had become his life and he had also become one of the strongest advocates of the idea of a union of all the maritime colonies in British North America. As soon as he was elected premier, he called for a conference in Charlottetown to discuss the idea of a confederation. It marked the first step in the confederation of all the colonies of British North America.

Macdonald was joint-premier of what was then called the province of Canada. As soon as he learned of Tupper's plans, he asked if he could attend, and arrived with a totally unexpected and large number of delegates from Canada East (later to be renamed Quebec) and Canada West (later to be renamed Ontario). Tupper and Macdonald found themselves totally in agreement on all principles for a confederation and the two men soon became friends.

A second and even more important conference was held in Quebec in 1864, and a third and final conference was held in London in 1866. There was now agreement for the proposed confederation of the British colonies in North America.

The men who attended those three crucial conferences would become known in history as Canada's 'Fathers of Confederation.' Early in this century, when the Confederation Life Insurance Company planned to mark its diamond jubilee, it commissioned a number of Canadian artists to recreate, in a series of large canvases, many of the important moments in Canada's history. One of the most frequently reproduced paintings from this Confederation Life Gallery of Canadian Art is a scene of the Fathers of Confederation meeting in London, painted by the Toronto artist J.D. Kelly. It is not a relatively minor point that Kelly portrayed Tupper seated at the head of the conference table at the right of Macdonald. By the time of that final conference, Tupper was constantly being referred to as Macdonald's right-hand man.

On July 1, 1867, a new nation called Canada formally came into being. John A. Macdonald, now Sir John, was chosen as the country's first prime minister.

Six years later, Macdonald and almost the entire Conservative party were forced out of office by disclosures in the House of Commons of the unsavoury affair known as the Pacific Scandal. Macdonald was accused of accepting money from the proposed builders of his 'national dream,' the Canadian Pacific Railway. The amount of money involved was so large it could only be seen, by his enemies, as a bribe.

Macdonald was defeated in the next election and was convinced his political career was over. The law firm he had established in his hometown of Kingston had recently moved to Toronto, and Macdonald decided to move his family there and return to practice. Shortly after his arrival he bought the large house that still stands at 63 St George Street.

Tupper soon joined him in Toronto, but for a different reason. Tupper had survived the scandal in Ottawa and had not lost his seat in the elections of 1874. A little-known and deeply personal tragedy made him decide to move.

His son, J. Stuart Tupper, had become a lawyer in Toronto. Charles Tupper received word that his son's young wife had died very suddenly, leaving him with an infant daughter. He immediately decided to come to Toronto to help look after the family. He moved into Stuart's home at 209 Jarvis Street, and in one of the corners of the house opened a doctor's office.

In this well known painting of the Fathers of Confederation at the London conference of 1886, J.D. Kelly placed Tupper at the head of the table, on the right hand of John A. Macdonald.

He and Macdonald were soon seeing each other regularly. It became obvious to everyone that Macdonald was not happy away from the political life of Ottawa, especially when he heard that the new Liberal prime minister, Alexander Mackenzie, was threatening to abandon all Macdonald's plans for a national railway. To Macdonald the railway was vital if the country was to expand successfully into the West. Its construction was in fact a condition of British Columbia's agreement to join Canada.

A series of meetings was held at Macdonald's home on St George Street. His supporters proposed that he appear as a surprise guest speaker at the many outdoor social gatherings held in towns throughout the province during the summer months. It was an ingenious plan, for Macdonald was always at his best speaking informally, among friends, in the open air. It would also supply him with the perfect setting to explain his own vision of Canada.

There was no question in Macdonald's mind that Tupper must be with him at all of these now highly 'political' picnics. Both shared the same dreams about the future of the country and, to Macdonald, Tupper had become his logical successor. Macdonald also realized that few people outside the Maritimes had ever had the opportunity of discovering Tupper's fighting qualities.

Tupper quickly became one of the principal reasons for the phenomenal success of these picnic-rallies that now swept across the province from Toronto. It was his fire and anger that the voters remembered.

Wherever Macdonald and Tupper spoke in advance of a by-election, the Conservative candidate was elected. In 1878, the Conservative party was swept back into office and Macdonald, once again, became the country's prime minister. Tupper was made a member of the cabinet and was later appointed Canadian high commissioner in London; but whenever Macdonald called another election, Tupper immediately returned to Canada to campaign on his behalf.

In 1891, ill and exhausted, Macdonald died in office at the age of 76. To the surprise of many of his friends, Tupper was not automatically chosen by his party to become the new prime minister. He had angered a number of highly influential men who considered his participation in election campaigns as an unpardonable breach of the duties of a high commissioner. A number of prominent men tried to fill Macdonald's place but none could hold the party together. In May 1896, with the sudden resignation of the latest aspirant, Sir Mackenzie Bowell, Tupper was finally chosen as the party's new leader and became prime minister. His term in office was brief – only 10 weeks after years of waiting.

In the election of June of that year, the Conservatives were defeated and Sir Wilfrid Laurier and the Liberal party came into power. Tupper served as leader of the opposition but was defeated in the general election of 1900. He could never forgive those who had abandoned him after Macdonald's death, and had no wish to spend his last years in Canada. He had enjoyed his life in England during his years as high commissioner and now bought a house in Kent where he lived quietly and in comfort until his

Charles Tupper, last original
Father of Confederation

death on October 30, 1915, at the age of 94, the last of the original Fathers of Confederation.

For years after his death he was seen as a principal figure in the story of this country and, in many ways, its most important. It was not until the 1950s, with the publication of Donald Creighton's two-volume biography of Sir John A. Macdonald, that the full and true story of Macdonald was finally revealed.

He had not been the wily politician he had often been portrayed. He had been a statesman in the fullest meaning of the word and had been beyond any question the founder of this country. But in the years following Confederation it was Tupper who was seen, by many, as the guiding force behind the Confederation movement.

In the *Dictionary of National Biography*, that massive work of many volumes that records the lives of every important figure in the history of the British Empire, it is not surprising that the following tribute would be paid to Sir Charles Tupper in 1920, shortly after his death.

'Tupper was perhaps the most fearless and constructive statesman whom Canada has produced. Without him, Sir John A. Macdonald would almost certainly not have pulled through the lean years of opposition from 1873 to 1878. Without him Canada would almost certainly have had neither a 'national policy' nor the Canadian Pacific Railway. Without him, the Canadian Dominion could not have been formed.'

In that list of achievements, the years in Toronto were decisive.

44

Miss Deeks' notorious lawsuit against H.G. Wells

Florence Deeks of Toronto sued one of Britain's most famous writers for half a million dollars. The case eventually led to the highest court in the British Empire.

In 1925, the English novelist and writer H.G. Wells read in a newspaper clipping that he was being sued by a woman in Toronto for $500,000. Florence Deeks of Farnham Avenue accused him of stealing an idea from her for one of his most famous books and was suing him for plagiarism. Wells called the charge 'fantastic' but within weeks the story was appearing in newspapers throughout the United States and Britain and the affair had escalated into an alleged international scandal.

Deeks was not only suing Wells, she was also suing the Macmillan Publishing Company. She claimed that its editors had taken her manuscript about the history of the world and, without her permission, had sent it to England and given it to Wells. Ten months later, the first chapters of Wells' book, *The Outline of History*, had started appearing in the English press. Deeks claimed it was so similar to her own book that Wells could not possibly have written it unless he had her manuscript in front of him. The lawsuit that followed became one of the strangest and most drawn-out court cases in the history of British jurisprudence. It lasted seven years and was fought not only in the courtroom of Toronto but in the Supreme Court of Ontario and in the highest court in England.

At the time it began, Wells was 59 years old and one of the best-known authors in the English-speaking world. At the age of 31 he had written *The Invisible Man*. During his long career he would write more than 100 books, radio dramas, and film scripts, including the script for one of the first science fiction films, *The Shape of Things to Come*.

Deeks was a 60-year-old wealthy but relatively obscure woman who had published virtually nothing. She had been born in Morrisburg, Ontario, in 1865 and her family later moved to Toronto. After graduating from Victoria College, she took a course in journalism and, largely as a hobby, began writing articles for newspapers and magazines. For a while, she worked as a clerk for the Toronto newspaper, the *World*.

In 1913, at the age of 48, she started work on a major book. It was to be a history of the world but with a special emphasis on the role women had played. She proposed to call it *The Web* and during the next seven years she was a familiar figure in the libraries of Toronto. Although literary experts would later testify she wrote an extremely dull book, there was never any question in their minds that it was based on an enormous amount of research.

On August 8, 1918, she submitted her manuscript to the editors of the Macmillan publishing branch in Toronto and was told it would require some time to evaluate it properly. Ten months passed. In the late spring of 1919, Macmillan returned her manuscript, saying it was not interested in publishing it. Deeks would later repeatedly state under oath that it had been returned 'in a very soiled condition.'

The following year, she read a review in *Saturday Night* about a new book by H.G. Wells called *The Outline of History* and bought a copy. As soon as she read it, she began consulting lawyers. During the next four years she spent most of her time searching for experts in the United States and Canada who would testify on her behalf. In 1925, when she believed she had the proof she needed, she announced to newspaper reporters in Toronto that she was suing both Wells and Macmillan.

Her charges against Macmillan were among her most serious legal mistakes. The copy of Wells' book she had bought in Toronto had been published by Macmillan in New York. Deeks was under the impression that all Macmillan branches acted on behalf of one central office. There were, in fact, three distinctly independent Macmillan companies involved – one in Toronto, one in New York, and one in England. The English company had actually rejected Wells' manuscript and he had taken it to another publisher, George Newnes. Newnes in turn had sold the North American rights to Macmillan in New York and the Toronto office of Macmillan had acted simply as the Canadian distributors of that edition.

Deeks was ignorant of all of this. She was convinced that someone in the Toronto office of Macmillan had sent her manuscript to the Macmillan editors in England, who had given it to Wells, who had then decided to write a similar book.

The truth was that Wells had been planning to write a book about the history of the world ever since the end of World War I. He was convinced that the appalling slaughter of millions of people during that war had been caused, to a large extent, by the bitterness and distrust that had existed for centuries between European nations. A book about the common origins of all people, he hoped, would promote a feeling of common citizenship among all nations of the world. He would call it *The Outline of History* and it would bear a subtitle, *The Whole Story of Man*.

When Deeks launched her suit, testimony had to be taken in England. During those preliminary interrogations Wells saw her for the first and only time. He later wrote, 'She impressed me as quite honest but vain and foolish.' There were a number of heated confrontations during those sessions but also many moments of unexpected humour. When Deeks' lawyers accused Wells of using the same words as she had used in quoting the ancient historian Plutarch, Wells turned in exasperation to the judge and asked: 'Am I to understand that Plutarch also pirated Miss Deeks' manuscript?'

When the case opened in Toronto, the court asked Wells to send the complete manuscript of his book to Toronto. Wells placed a value of $100,000 on it, so it was kept locked in one of the vaults at Osgoode Hall throughout the trial.

During the weeks of arguments in court, Deeks' lawyers constantly drew attention to the fact that Wells had used the same kind of phrases she had used to describe certain moments in history. Deeks had written, 'The Holy Roman Empire was broken into fragments.' Wells had written, 'The barbarians had broken it up into 14 little kingdoms.' The court was noticeably unimpressed.

Deeks' lawyers then attempted to discredit Wells by saying it was impossible for anyone to write a 600,000-word book in the space of ten months. Wells's lawyers informed the court that both Honoré de Balzac and Sir Walter Scott had frequently written at that speed. The presiding judge, Chief Justice W.E. Raney, drily added that chief justices were often expected to write their judgments at the same speed.

Florence Deeks during her lawsuit
against H.G. Wells. The photo first
appeared in the London *Evening Standard*
of November 1, 1932.

At the end of the Toronto trial, the court ruled that Deeks had failed in her action against Wells. She immediately announced that she was taking her case before the Supreme Court of Ontario. There it also failed. Her brother, a wealthy contractor, not only believed his sister was telling the truth, he was convinced she was a literary genius and offered to supply her with all the funds she would need to take her case before the highest court in the Empire, the Judicial Committee of the Privy Council in London. There on November 3, 1932, the now notorious case of Deeks vs Wells finally came to an end.

Three British law lords ruled unanimously that there was no evidence that Macmillan had ever sent a copy of Deeks' manuscript to England. Wells himself had testified under oath that he had never seen it and there was no reason to disbelieve him. As to the similarity between the two books, the court ruled that this had been inevitable, 'since neither Miss Deeks nor Mr Wells had been present, for example, at the beginning of the world' and would have had to rely 'on authors before them.' The case was dismissed with costs against the plaintiff. Deeks now had to confess that she was virtually penniless. Her brother had lost all his money and Wells would have to pay his own considerable court costs.

Deeks never attempted to write another book and lived the rest of her life in virtual seclusion with her relatives in the house at 140 Farnham Avenue until her death on June 27, 1959, at the age of 94. In the opinion of everyone involved in that famous trial she had been a truly tragic figure. No one ever doubted her sincerity. In her closing words in the courtroom in London, she had turned to the judges and said, 'My lords, even if you decide against me, there is a higher judge in Heaven who will know the truth.'

45

The man who raised Canada's first Red Cross flag

In 1885, at the height of the battle of Batoche, a Toronto doctor hastily tore strips of red and white cloth and made Canada's first Red Cross flag. Later he founded this country's Red Cross Society.

During one of the most decisive battles ever fought on Canadian soil, a young Toronto doctor cut two strips of red cloth and hastily sewed them onto a piece of white cotton. Then, on a hill above the Saskatchewan River at Batoche, he raised the first Red Cross flag to fly over Canada.

That battle is remembered as the final defeat of Louis Riel's forces and the end of the North West Rebellion. The story of the young doctor has been largely forgotten. Today, he is one of the least known members of one of the most celebrated families of old Toronto. Many were renowned Methodist ministers. His uncle, Egerton Ryerson, founded the public school system of Ontario and is remembered in the name of the Ryerson Polytechnical Institute.

The story of Egerton's nephew, George Ryerson, deserves to be equally remembered, for it was this Ryerson who became the champion and founder of the Red Cross Society in Canada. To those who know how the Red Cross began, it is not surprising that its flag flew for the first time in Canada over a battlefield. For although the society today is known for its work in many different humanitarian fields, it began on a battlefield in Italy during one of the bloodiest wars in modern history.

On June 25, 1859, 300,000 men fought on the outskirts of Solferino when Napoleon III and his French army made one of their final attempts to drive the Austrians out of Italy. At the end of that day, more than 40,000 men lay dead or wounded. The closing hours of that slaughter were witnessed by a 31-year-old Swiss banker, Henri Dunant, who was travelling in Italy. When he realized that thousands of wounded soldiers were dying before the army's few medical officers could reach them, he ran to the village and organized its citizens into relief parties. He turned the local churches into hospitals and commandeered every doctor in the surrounding towns. When he finally returned to his home in Switzerland, Dunant wrote a book to tell the world of the horror he had seen.

He called it *Souvenir de Solferino* (Memory of Solferino) and sent copies to every king, president, and leading statesman in Europe. In his book, he called for the creation of a new kind of international relief organization, staffed by neutrals, who would be allowed to enter all future battlefields to care for the wounded.

In the summer of 1864, almost every major country in Europe sent representatives to a convention in Geneva where Dunant's proposals were adopted internationally and a new organization born. In tribute to the young Swiss who had conceived the idea, the representatives agreed that its symbol would be the reverse of the Swiss flag. In place of Switzerland's white cross on a red background, it would be a red cross on a white background. The society was named the International Red Cross.

Throughout its first 50 years, its work was devoted solely to saving the lives of soldiers on the world's battlefields. The Canadian who became its principal crusader was George Sterling Ansel Ryerson, though he was more famous during his lifetime for his role in the military affairs of Canada than for his work as a practising doctor in Toronto.

He was born in this city on January 21, 1854. His father was a clergyman. From his earliest years, he was interested in a military life. At the age of 16 he joined the Queen's Own Rifles and served as an under-age private during the Fenian Raids. For his profession, he chose a career in medicine and after graduating from

Trinity College in Toronto he went to Europe to complete post-graduate studies.

He was in Vienna in 1878 when Austria occupied Bosnia and Herzegovina, and he immediately offered his services; his second experience on a battlefield was as a medical officer at an Austrian military post. When he returned to Canada, he was 25 and opened his first medical practice in an office at 317 Church Street. He established himself as an eye and ear specialist but still found himself drawn towards a career with the military and joined the Royal Grenadiers as an assistant surgeon.

His experience in two wars made him increasingly concerned about the lack of adequate staff to care for the wounded in battle. For his own regiment, he organized an ambulance corps and later wrote, 'To the best of my knowledge, this was the first stretcher section ever organized in Canada.' In 1885, when Riel led a rebellion against the government, Ryerson was with his regiment when it travelled west and was at the final battle on a hill above the South Saskatchewan River near the village of Batoche.

As soon as the battle began, he converted one of the army's wagons into a makeshift ambulance – but soon realized he would have to do something quickly to distinguish it from all other miliary wagons. The wartime organization that Dunant had founded in Europe had received worldwide publicity. To identify his medical post Ryerson ordered a piece of Turkish red cloth from one of the ammunition columns. He tore it into two strips and sewed them onto a square piece of white cotton and, above his small spring wagon, he raised Canada's first Red Cross flag.

In the years following the end of the rebellion, Ryerson campaigned for the creation of some kind of medical corps to work with Canadian troops. He wrote to every doctor he knew and dozens volunteered to serve with him. But within hours of the first jubilant inaugural meeting, Ryerson received word from irate government officials demanding that the group be disbanded. His idea was called 'subversive' and he was informed 'A medical officer's duty is to obey, not to protest.'

Furious over what he considered the stupidity of government officers, he began exploring the idea of creating a Canadian branch

Canada's first Red Cross flag was hastily created during the Battle of Batoche in Saskatchewan.

of an organization that had been founded recently in England. The slaughter of British troops during the Crimean War had led to the founding of The National Society for Aid to the Sick and Wounded. In tribute to Henri Dunant, the society was subtitled the British Red Cross. Ryerson began a steady stream of correspondence and, on October 15, 1896, he established a similar organization. This became the first branch of the Red Cross in Canada.

Three years later, in 1899, when war was declared in South Africa, the Canadian government ordered the formation of a contingent to fight alongside the British troops. A field hospital would be needed and Dr Ryerson, the fiery young agitator who had now become a middle-aged and respected crusader, was appointed to sail with the troops as the first Canadian Red Cross commissioner. After the war, in 1909, the Canadian Parliament passed an act that officially established the Red Cross Society in Canada.

By the early 1910s, in Ryerson's words, 'Things finally began to move.' A surgeon, Dr Frederick Borden, had been appointed minister of militia and defence and had immediately created the Canadian Army Medical Corps. In 1914, when war broke out in Europe, Ryerson could proudly boast that Canada's wartime medical service would be 'equal to that of any other country.' He was appointed head of the Canadian Medical Service and throughout the next four years of the war served as president of the Canadian Red Cross. When the war ended, in recognition of his years of service to the military, Dr George Ryerson was made honorary colonel-in-chief of the Canadian Army Medical Corps.

He lived to the age of 71. When he died in Toronto on May 20, 1925, there was a great public service at St James' Cathedral, with full military honours. As his coffin was borne through the streets to St James' cemetery, it was draped with a single large Red Cross flag.

46

The monument to Fort Rouillé, where the city of Toronto truly began

The language of the first 'Torontonians' was not English but French. The city was not born in the streets of the Town of York but in a French fort near the Humber River called Fort Toronto.

Long before the first British settlers arrived in this province, the most important landmark on the site of the future city of Toronto was a set of ruins at what is today's Exhibition Place. And for almost a century after Toronto was founded in 1793, this collection of fire-blackened ruins was one of the main sights shown to important visitors to the city.

In the early 1880s there were plans to level this land and turn it into a landscaped garden. Thousands of people in Toronto raised enough money to build a cairn on the site so that the exact location of the ruins would never be lost. In 1887, Torontonians raised an even larger sum of money so that a 32-foot-high column of Credit Valley stone could be built over the site. Bronze cannon were placed on either side of it to remind future generations of the last and most important of all the French forts that were built in this part of the New World in the days when Canada was known as New France.

It had been built in 1750 and was no minor outpost. It was to be part of a great chain of forts and trading posts that would stretch westward along the shores of the Great Lakes and southward through the French territories along the Mississippi River. The man who had ordered it to be built was the most powerful and most intriguing official in New France at that time, Jacques Pierre de Taffanel, Marquis de La Jonquière.

He was born into one of the noble families of France and, at the age of 12, had enlisted in the navy as a midshipman. In his teens he served on board one of the French warships that were attempting to capture English pirates who were plundering the French islands in the Caribbean. In 1711, as a young lieutenant, he was part of the French expedition that captured Rio de Janeiro. By the time he was in his forties he was a flag captain and, in 1746, a rear admiral. Later that same year, Louis XIV appointed him governor of New France.

Today, his name appears on the Ontario government blue-and-gold historical plaque at the base of the column in the exhibition grounds. The full story of his adventures is probably better known in Canada than it is in either France or England.

In the collection of the National Library at Paris there is no copy of the only complete biography of his life, written by a descendant, another Marquis de La Jonquière. Nor is there a copy in the collection of the British Museum. One of the few surviving copies is in the Baldwin Room in the history department of the Metropolitan Toronto Library. To write the definitive summary of his life, the editors of the *Dictionary of Canadian Biography* chose one of France's leading scholars, Etienne Taillemite of the National Archives in Paris.

At the time of La Jonquière's arrival in Quebec he was at the height of his career. But, as Taillemite recorded, all of La Jonquière's earliest attempts to reach Canada ended in colossal naval disasters.

In 1746, when he first sailed for Canada, he was part of an expedition of 54 ships that planned to recapture the French fort at Louisbourg, which had recently been seized by the British. When the French fleet arrived off the shores of Canada, it was hit by a fierce gale. A British fleet of warships attacked and almost the entire French fleet was lost. More than 2,800 of the French complement of 7,000 were killed or wounded. The leader of the expedition, the Duc d'Anville, died during the attack and La Jonquière had no choice but to order the expedition back to France.

On his second attempt to reach Canada, his fleet was overwhelmed by a superior number of British ships, and La Jonquière was captured and taken to England as prisoner. Two years later, France and England agreed to a peace treaty and La Jonquière was released. On August 14, 1749, three years after his appointment, he finally arrived at Quebec as governor of New France.

His primary orders were to establish a more secure and stronger colony, and he immediately began to strengthen its defences. Larger forts were to replace earlier ones. Among the new forts that he ordered built was one on the north shore of Lake Ontario at the site of the future city of Toronto.

Two smaller French trading posts had been built earlier along the banks of the Humber River. This new location on the lakefront would serve as both a garrison and a trading post. Here the French would attempt to intercept Indians on their way to trade furs with the English who were established along the south shore of the lake. The new fort would receive the rare honour of being named after Antoine Louis Rouillé, Count de Jouy, the French minister of marine, who was head of the French navy and who had full authority over all France's colonies. But from the time the fort was completed in 1750, it was always known as Fort Toronto after the Indian name for the area.

The mid-18th century was one of the most chaotic periods in the history of New France. It was a time when fortunes could be made, overnight, by officials speculating in the fur trade. In the words of Taillemite, despite La Jonquière's personal wealth, he 'turned out to be regrettably greedy.' Rumours of a scandal surrounding the office of the governor started reaching the court at Versailles, but in a letter to Rouillé, dated October 19, 1751, La Jonquière protested his innocence: 'There is not a drop of blood in my veins that does not thrill for the service of my King. I will not conceal from you that the slightest suspicions on your part against me would cut the thread of my days.'

Though he still appeared a commanding figure, La Jonquière was now 66 and his health had been broken by exhaustion and his constant quarrelling with officials. In 1751, he wrote to Rouillé begging to be recalled, but before an answer was returned he died at his quarters at Quebec on March 17, 1752. It was said, wrote Francis Parkman in *Wolfe and Montcalm*, that although La Jonquière was rich, 'his habits of thrift so possessed his last hours that, seeing wax candles burning in his chamber, he ordered others of tallow be brought instead, as being good enough to die by.'

Four years after his death, the first 'global war' erupted. It became known as the Seven Years' War, and during these years

The Fort Rouillé monument in Exhibition Place was built in 1887 to mark the location of the most important of the three French forts that once stood on the site of today's Toronto.

England and France fought their final battles for the possession of the lands that now are Canada. By 1757, the tide of war had turned against France, and two years later the French began abandoning their forts in the west. When British troops seized the French fort at Niagara and began advancing north around the lake, the French commandant at Fort Toronto ordered the buildings burned to the ground rather than let them fall into the hands of the British.

For almost 150 years, the ruins remained virtually untouched. They became the only surviving landmark of an era in the 17th and 18th centuries when the site of Toronto belonged to France, and had witnessed the arrival of many of France's greatest explorers and adventurers. By the late 19th century, the location of the French fort had become part of the city's new exhibition grounds. On September 6, 1887, a towering new monument was raised over the site. Lord Dufferin, the governor-general of Canada told the large crowd at the unveiling ceremonies that the monument had a unique importance among all the landmarks of Toronto: 'To preserve from obliteration the traces of the first beginnings of this city.'

47

Frederick Denison and the valiant effort to save 'Chinese' Gordon

In 1884, a young Toronto officer led hundreds of voyageurs up the Nile River in a race to rescue General Charles Gordon at Khartoum.

It was called 'the greatest adventure story of the 19th century Empire.' In the autumn of 1884, thousands of British soldiers raced up the valley of the Nile to rescue a British general who was being held under siege in the village of Khartoum. To guide the fleet of boats that would have to navigate the dangerous cataracts of the Nile, Britain called on Canada to send hundreds of voyageurs. The man chosen to lead this extraordinary band of adventurers was a young alderman from Toronto who belonged to one of the most noted families of old Toronto, Frederick Charles Denison.

The story began when the British government sent General Charles ('Chinese') Gordon to help Egypt in its southern province of the Sudan. For the past three years, there had been riots throughout Egypt. Followers of a mystical leader known as the Mahdi had been attempting to seize control, and Britain, as one of the major countries holding Egyptian bonds, believed it had a responsibility to itself and to the Egyptian government to restore peace. When it became clear that the Sudan could never be held against the growing number of rebels, Gordon was sent to evacuate the 21,000 Egyptian troops who were trapped there. Gordon was a hero of British actions in China and had served the Egyptian government previously as governor of the Sudan. He arrived in Khartoum in February 1884 but did not leave immediately. A month later the city was under rebel siege.

For months the British government of Prime Minister William Ewart Gladstone stalled over financing an expedition to rescue Gordon. *The Times* began to attack this inaction with editorials stating, 'We refuse to believe the government means to abandon Gordon.' Queen Victoria herself wrote to her prime minister, 'Gordon is in danger. You are bound to try and save him.' Finally the money was approved. The problem now was how to get a relief force safely and quickly to Khartoum.

One force was to proceed by the way of the Red Sea and then cross overland. A second force, possibly the critical one, was to sail directly up the Nile. To carry a force of 4,000 men, 400 boats 32 feet long would be built to carry 10 men each, plus their provisions, for 100 days. Experienced men would be needed to navigate these craft through the upper reaches of the Nile and its cataracts, and it was at this point that Canada became involved in the expedition.

In 1978, Roy MacLaren, a Canadian magazine publisher and politician, gave the first full account of the expedition in *Canadians on the Nile*. He argued that the story has rarely received the attention it deserves – that the Nile Expedition was, in fact, a major turning point in Canada's history. 'The fact that Canadians were involved in such an undertaking half-way around the world was an indication that Canada was at last coming of age in the imperial era of Victoria ... It was also Imperialism at its most romantic ... and there was something both natural and splendid in the way in which Canadians gathered to make a daring attempt to save a beleaguered brother officer.'

Canada became a part of the story because of the man who was chosen to head the British forces, Garnet Wolseley. He had only recently returned from serving in Canada. In 1870, he had led a force of 1200 men in an expedition into the Canadian West and had never forgotten the skill and ingenuity of the Canadian voyageurs who had guided his boats through the rapids of the northern rivers. As soon as he was appointed to head the British expedition, he sent word to Canada asking for hundreds of voyageurs to accompany his troops up the Nile. The prime minister, Sir John A. Macdonald, gave his approval and posters went up from Quebec west, calling for volunteers. Within a few weeks a company of 386 men was raised. The man Wolseley chose to lead them was the very same young officer who had served as his orderly officer in 1870 and who was then serving as an alderman in Toronto, Frederick Charles Denison.

Denison belonged to one of the oldest and most famous military families of Toronto. The family had originally settled here in 1796 and their estate had once surrounded the area that is now Kensington market.

In 1884, the 37-year-old Frederick Denison was an officer in the smartest militia unit in Toronto, the Governor General's Body Guard. He was a reserved and gentle man and, as MacLaren wrote, the expedition needed the tact and understanding of someone like Denison to win the affection and trust of the tough, obstinate voyageurs who were naturally suspicious of an English-speaking patrician from Toronto. In the fall of 1884, the voyageurs and a band of young Canadian militia officers arrived in Egypt to begin the long and hazardous journey up the Nile.

At every major cataract, tracking lines had to be put over the men's shoulders while they walked through the water or along the banks pulling the boats through the rapids. It was dangerous work, for there was always the risk, in the deeper waters, of being swept away and crushed to death against the rocks of the river.

Time was also running out. The land forces had been unable to reach Khartoum. On January 28, 1885, when the river expedition finally reached their goal, they found that the town had been captured. Four thousand corpses lay in the streets and the severed head of Gordon had been rammed into the fork of a tree.

The expedition began facing a barrage of rebel fire from the hills and had no alternative but to make its way back down river. The skill of the voyageurs was now even more important, for the boats had to be guided down a fast and rampaging river. There is no question that dozens of the boats would have been lost and hundreds of men drowned but for the Canadian presence.

Canadian voyageurs and British troops tow boats through the second cataract of the Nile in a vain attempt to relieve the siege of Khartoum. This sketch appeared in the *Illustrated London News* in November 1884.

Though the expedition had failed in its mission, the British commander paid his respect to the participation of the Canadians in a special farewell review before the men sailed for home. In Ottawa, cheering crowds filled the streets to welcome them back. In London, the young colonial officer, Denison, was in great demand as a speaker and became a social lion for a season before returning to Canada.

In Toronto, he resumed his law practice and entered politics as the member for West Toronto. But he never fulfilled the career that had once been so full of promise. In 1896, at the age of 49, he died of cancer at his home in Toronto.

In Britain, the British public never forgave Gladstone for his delay in sending the relief expedition. Gladstone once had been known affectionately as the 'GOM,' the Grand Old Man. He now became the 'MOG,' Murderer of Gordon.

48

The subject of one of history's most romantic utterances finds a home in Toronto

On the eve of the Battle of Quebec, General James Wolfe read a line from Thomas Gray's poem, 'Elegy Written in a Country Church Yard' and created one of the world's most romantic legends.

It is one of the world's most famous historical paintings and records an event that took place on the banks of the St Lawrence River on the morning of September 13, 1759. The scene is the death of the young British general James Wolfe, mortally wounded at the age of 32 on a field known as the Plains of Arbaham at the height of a battle that would alter the history of North America.

The picture was painted by Benjamin West, one of the celebrated artists of the 18th century, and it is known today to literally millions of people through reproductions in an untold number of history texts and art books. The painting itself is enormous and created a sensation when it was first exhibited and sold at a gallery in London. King George III immediately ordered the artist to make a replica, still in the Royal Collection. In the years that followed, West produced other replicas. The brother of Robert Monkton, one of the generals portrayed in the painting, acquired one of these, and in 1931 it was bought by the Friends of the Royal Ontario Museum. It is now one of the major treasures in the museum's Canadiana Collections.

Despite the fame that has always surrounded West's painting, there is growing controversy about it. In the words of Canada's foremost military historian, C.P. Stacey, 'As a representation of an historical event, it is among the worst ever produced.'

The scene as West depicted it could never have taken place. But there is no question about the value and authenticity of a personal possession of Wolfe's that is also in Toronto. It is even more celebrated than the painting and provoked 'one of the most romantic utterances of history.'

There is a legend, constantly retold over the past centuries, that on the night before the battle, as Wolfe secretly led his fleet up the St Lawrence River to attack the French forces, he read to some of his associates lines from his favourite poem, Thomas Gray's 'Elegy Written in a Country Church Yard.' When he reached the words, 'The paths of glory lead but to the grave,' it is said he whispered, 'Now, gentlemen, I would rather be the author of that poem than take Quebec tomorrow.'

The slim, leather-bound copy of Gray's 'Elegy,' owned by Wolfe and marked with his handwriting in the margins, now lies in the Thomas Fisher Rare Book Library of the University of Toronto.

There has always been more to the story of Wolfe's last days than is recorded in most history books. He had a presentiment of his death and, before the battle, gave his copy of the 'Elegy' and other personal items to a fellow officer. During the battle, he deliberately exposed himself to fire and, in Colonel Stacey's words, 'perhaps actually courted death.' After the British victory at Quebec, the fleet brought his body back to England. He was buried with full military honours and a monument to him was placed in Westminster Abbey. It was not until after his death that the legends began.

Wolfe, the son of a British officer, was born on January 2, 1727, at Westerham, Kent. At the age of 14 he joined the British army. In those war-filled years of the mid-18th century, promotions came quickly to any young officer who survived. At the age of 23 Wolfe was a lieutenant-colonel.

In 1758 he was at the siege at Louisbourg. Jeffrey Amherst, who was in charge of the British expedition, considered him one of his most efficient officers and in 1759 William Pitt, the British prime minister, recommended him to the king as the ideal commander of the British forces assigned to attack Quebec. This was to be one of the most decisive battles of that century, for, if victorious, Britain would gain permanent control of the vast lands known as New France that had been held by the French since the early 1600s.

Wolfe was given command of an exceptionally fine army, with a core of 10 battalions of regular infantry. The French force at Quebec, under the command of the Marquis de Montcalm, was twice as large but, according to Stacey, was far inferior. Wolfe knew if he could fight the French in an open field he could win the battle. He had never had any experience leading such a large force, and deliberated for weeks about the best plan of attack. Finally he chose what can only be described as a decidedly risky plan. He would attempt a surprise attack at night, sending his men to scale the great cliffs up-river from Quebec at a point that came to be known as 'Wolfe's Cove.'

Luck was with him. On the morning of September 13, when the startled French garrison attempted to drive the attackers from the heights, 'the British forces blew them into ruin and retreat.' During the battle, both Montcalm and Wolfe were mortally wounded.

Twelve years later, when Benjamin West exhibited his *Death of Wolfe* at the Royal Academy, it caused a sensation. It was bought by Lord Grosvenor whose descendant, the second Duke of Westminster, later presented it to Canada in tribute to the role Canadians played in World War I. That painting is now in the National Gallery in Ottawa.

But, in Stacey's view, the scene painted by West could never have taken place. As he commented in the *National Gallery of Canada Bulletin* in 1966: 'In the final stage of the battle, [Wolfe's] officers had other things to do besides grouping themselves picturesquely about the dying general.' The particular surgeon who is shown attending Wolfe was hundreds of miles away at the time, if he was in North America at all. Of far greater importance, many key figures are curiously missing if West meant to record all Wolfe's principal officers. According to one story, West demanded a fee for each officer included; many of the senior ones who disliked young Wolfe refused to subscribe, so West simply omitted them from the picture.

Benjamin West's famous painting of *The Death of Wolfe* shows a scene
that could not have happened.

'The painting is historically absurd,' concluded Stacey, but 'its
fame has become an integral part of that interesting phenomenon
of British history, the Wolfe legend.' All of Britain had celebrated
his victory. He had won Canada for the Empire, and a highly
romanticized view grew around the young indecisive soldier who
'was really no better than a second-rate commander.'

The legend that he had read Gray's 'Elegy' on the eve of the
battle simply added to the romance that surrounded him after his
death. In this case, however, there is documentary evidence that
the legend is true. By the early 1800s it was in print and recorded
by such writers as Sir Walter Scott. And the story of the survival
of Wolfe's copy of Gray's 'Elegy' through the centuries was fully
revealed in the *Colophon, New Series* in 1937.

Perhaps the most haunting part of the romance that surrounds
the book is that it was given to Wolfe, on the eve of his departure
from England for Canada on the *Neptune,* by the woman it is
believed he planned to marry, Katherine Lowther. On the title

page you can still clearly read two hand-written lines 'From K.L./ Neptune at Sea.'

After Wolfe's death, almost all his personal possessions were sent to his mother in England, and the book eventually found its way back into Katherine's hands. Many years later she married Lord Powlet, later Duke of Bolton. Shortly before her death, she gave the book to her faithful personal maid. Another note was added to the book by the maid's daughter, Mrs Day: 'Given to my mother, Mrs J. Ewing, by her mistress, the late Duchess Bolton, as having belonged to the celebrated General Wolfe. L.D.'

In 1913, when the book was offered for sale at a London auction, its sudden reappearance was reported in newspapers throughout Britain. Officials from the manuscript department of the British Museum and the Royal Colonial Institute verified that the annotations in the margins were unquestionably in Wolfe's hand. The book was bought by an American collector, Morris Wolf of Philadelphia. It was not until the 1980s that his family decided to sell it.

To many people in Canada, particularly members of the Cultural Properties Review Board and the Friends of the Thomas Fisher Rare Book Library at the University of Toronto, the book was seen as the ideal historical work from Canada's past to celebrate a major event in the life of this city: the university library's acquisition of its seven millionth volume. A fund-raising drive was launched and in 1988 the slim, calf-bound volume of Thomas Gray's melancholy meditations on death, marked with hand-written notes that have made the book a national treasure, was formally presented to the University of Toronto Library.

A N

E L E G Y

WRITTEN IN A

Country Church Yard.

THE NINTH EDITION.

L O N D O N:

Printed for R. and J. DODSLEY, in Pall-mall;

And sold by M. COOPER, in Pater-noster-Row. 1754.

[Price Six-pence.]

The title page of Thomas Gray's 'Elegy
Written in a Country Church Yard'
– the actual copy that General
James Wolfe carried with him on
the eve of the Battle of the Plains of
Abraham in 1759. This copy,
published five years earlier, now is a
treasure of the University of Toronto's
rare book library.

49

Toronto's first book of photographs reveals an almost unknown city

In the mid-19th century, the world's first book of photographs caused riots in the streets of Europe and started a world-wide craze for photography. Toronto's first such book was published a few years later.

It was the first book of photographs ever published about Toronto. When it appeared in the bookstores in 1868, no one realized how valuable it would be one day. Many people began tearing out their favourite pictures and framing them. Others sent pages of photographs to their families and friends outside Canada. Today, a copy of this book with all its original photographs has become one of Canada's rarest books.

Even its most important photographs have rarely been seen by most Torontonians. For, in spite of the scores of books about Toronto that have been published over the past century, no one has ever printed a second edition of this historic volume.

It is called *Toronto in the Camera*, and when it appeared in the 1860s the world was at the height of a photographic craze. The world's first photograph had appeared within the lifetime of most people and few inventions had ever captured the imagination of the public more. Millions of families in almost every country in the Western world had started their own collections of photographs. The timing of the book moreover was superb. For the first time in its history, Toronto had suddenly become a beautiful city.

Although it had been a major centre in Canada for more than half a century, Toronto remained a city of mainly wooden buildings until as late as 1850. Visitors during its early Victorian years wrote that it looked like any one of the second-rate provincial cities of England. But in the 1850s everything about Toronto changed.

With the coming of the first railways, the city entered one of the greatest boom periods in its history. Money poured into it. Enormous new buildings like Osgoode Hall, St James' Cathedral, and University College rivalled the splendour of buildings in the leading cities of Europe. When St James' Cathedral finally completed its spire, it became the tallest church ever built in Canada.

From *Toronto in the Camera*, published in 1868, the first book of photographs of this city, come four images of a rapidly growing and prosperous provincial capital. This is Yonge Street looking south at Colborne: the building at left was the head office of the Canadian Bank of Commerce.

An extraordinary 'Crystal Palace' appeared on the waterfront. In the streets of downtown Toronto, rows of office buildings were designed in the style of the classical age of Greece and Rome. By the time *Toronto in the Camera* appeared, the city was being described by a new generation of writers as 'rising like an Imperial city' above the shoreline of the lake.

Although this first book of photographs must have created a sensation, it was nothing compared with the virtual riots that surrounded the world's very first book of photographs, which arrived in the shops of London in June 1844. Only a very few people had ever seen a photograph before. When the book appeared, filled with black and white photos pasted on each page, most people called it a fake. They said the photographs were nothing more than the work of a skilful engraver. The arguments in the bookshops soon became so intense that the man who produced the book finally had to take back all the copies. A special insert was printed and the books were sent back to the stores.

On the insert, the author explained that the pictures in his book were not engravings. Each of them had been created solely by light. They were the work of nature herself. They were 'sun pictures.' That was why he had called his book *The Pencil of Nature.* When people finally began to accept that what they were seeing were true reproductions, his book became one of the most sensational works of that century. As would happen in Toronto many years later, no one realized its value. People began tearing out their favourite scenes and framing them. Today, there are only 24 known copies of *The Pencil of Nature* in the world – and only 13 have all the original photographs.

The man who produced that book was William Hay Fox Talbot, famous in history as 'the Father of Photography.' He was born in Chippenham, Wiltshire, England, on February 11, 1800, and was a brilliant student at college, winning a Chancellor's Prize during his final year at Cambridge. By the time he was in his thirties he had been elected a Fellow of the Royal Society and reports of his scientific work were regularly appearing in the papers of the society.

He was also an ardent amateur painter and, in 1833, while on holidays at Lake Como in Italy, he spent most of his mornings and afternoons painting scenes of the lake using an apparatus that was familiar to all artists of that time, a camera obscura. It was simply a dark portable box with a lens at one end that projected an exterior view onto an interior wall where an artist could trace it. Talbot found the use of the box frustrating and began wondering whether it might not be possible to use a similar lens to project a scene onto a piece of paper coated with chemicals and so produce a lasting impression. After his return to England, he spent most of the next five years searching for the right combination of chemicals and paper. In 1839, as soon as he had produced his first successful 'sun picture,' he published his work in the papers of the Royal Society and was hailed as the pioneer of a new science.

In Europe, notably in France, others had found a way of repro-

The home of William Cawthra, millionaire landowner, at the northeast corner of King and Bay Streets. It was built in 1854, demolished in 1946. The site now is part of the head office of the Bank of Nova Scotia.

The Queen's Hotel on Front Street was the most famous hotel of 19th century Toronto. The Royal York now stands on the site.

ducing a scene onto a glass plate, but only one copy could be made. The plate was also fragile and often expensive. What Talbot had discovered was a way of producing a paper negative from which countless relatively inexpensive prints could be made. Talbot's invention became the basis for modern photography.

In 1843 Talbot opened the world's first printing house for the mass production of photographic prints and the following year published *The Pencil of Nature*. He was proud of his invention and on the title page of his book he quoted a Latin verse from Virgil's *Georgics*: 'It is a joyous thing to be the first to cross a mountain.'

The craze to collect these new 'photographs' (Greek for 'light written') soon swept across the ocean to North America. Photographic studios sprang up in every major city. In 1868, one of Toronto's photographers decided to produce the first book of photographs of his city. His name was Octavius Thompson. The book he produced, with 48 4 x 3-inch black and white photographs pasted on its pages, was *Toronto in the Camera*. To add to its value, he included a brief history of the principal buildings in each picture.

Today, it is almost impossible to find a copy of this book for sale, even at rare book auctions. Only seven libraries in Canada are known to have a copy. In Toronto, copies may be found in the Rare Book Library of the University of Toronto, the City of Toronto Archives at City Hall, and the Baldwin Room of the Metropolitan Toronto Library.

It is an astonishing collection of photographs and is important not only because it is the first of its kind. It is the only known comprehensive pictorial record of Toronto as it looked at the end of its stagecoach era and at the beginning of its life as a metropolis.

The Post Office at 10 Toronto Street, built in 1853. When this photo was taken it had two main entrances, one for men, one for women; Toronto had five letter carriers. The building still stands, and now is headquarters of the Argus Corporation.

50

The maple tree that stands as a memorial to 5,000 heroes

A silver maple tree planted by the Prince of Wales in 1919 has become a memorial to the veterans who lie buried beside it.

1919 had been declared 'Victory Year' in Toronto – the first year of peace after World War I. That summer the young Prince of Wales was due to arrive in Toronto.

All the plans for his visit had been approved long before he had sailed from England. But on the very eve of his arrival in Toronto officials were informed he had ordered a change in his tour of the city. On the final day of his visit, he would drive to what was then the northern outskirts of the city, to a new military burial ground in Prospect Cemetery. That afternoon, August 27, he planted a small silver maple tree in memory of all the Canadian veterans of World War I buried there.

The tree still stands and more than 5,000 other veterans now lie buried in the grounds beside it. This plot of land has become Toronto's official burial ground for veterans of World War I. Every Remembrance Day at 8 a.m. a sunrise service is held in front of their graves. It has become the oldest and most honoured of all the sunrise ceremonies held by veterans across Canada.

At the outbreak of World War I, Canada had a population of barely 7.5 million, but more than 420,000 Canadians enlisted and served overseas. About 228,000 were killed or wounded; Canada lost as many men as the United States from a population less than one-tenth the size.

When the prince arrived in Toronto thousands of Canadian soldiers were still waiting in England for ships to bring them home. For many people the war was not over. When he stepped from his train he was wearing his uniform as a captain in the Grenadier Guards. 'It was,' wrote the Toronto *Star*, 'fitting and proper in a city that had been clad in khaki itself for five long years.'

Few Canadians had known anything about the Prince of Wales when war had broken out. In 1914 he was only 20. In 1919, he was 25 but looked more like an English schoolboy than a seasoned army captain. But Canadian soldiers told legends of his visits to the front, and took pride in the fact that he had been with Canadian troops on the day the war had ended.

In 1919, he was probably the most popular member of the royal family. Years later, in 1936, he would become its most notorious when he suddenly abdicated as Edward VIII to marry a divorced American woman, Wallis Simpson. The tragic events surrounding his later years have almost obscured the story of his early years as a gallant and courageous officer.

He was born at White Lodge in Richmond Park in June 23, 1894, the eldest of five sons of the Duke and Duchess of York, who later became King George V and Queen Mary. When war came in 1914, he was at Oxford. He immediately enlisted and received a commission in the Grenadier Guards. He asked to be allowed to serve alongside the troops at the front but his request was refused by both his father and the British government. Everyone in authority feared that he might be captured and used by the Germans as a hostage. Only after weeks of arguments was he finally permitted to go to France as a member of the staff of the commander of the British Expeditionary Force.

From the time he arrived, he was determined to visit the front lines. He was given a Daimler car but preferred to travel around the countryside on a green army bicycle. He soon found ways of eluding the aides who had been assigned to watch over him. By the time of the first great battles, messages regularly reached army headquarters that the Prince of Wales had been seen 'somewhere at the front.' Hundreds of stories were told of his sudden appearances, usually alone, at one of the trenches, sharing cigarettes and chatting with the men.

Towards the end of the war he was given the Military Cross, normally awarded only for great acts of courage. He was frankly and sincerely embarrassed.

The war proved a formative period in his career. When it was over and questions were raised as to where he could now most usefully serve, the British prime minister, Lloyd George, said: 'The appearance of the popular Prince of Wales in the far corners of the empire might do more good than half a dozen solemn Imperial conferences.'

And so it proved. His first official royal tour was to Canada and on the morning of his arrival in Toronto an enormous crowd had gathered at the railway station. The premier, in his welcoming address, spoke in glowing terms of the 'Soldier Prince' and his part in the war. The prince politely protested: 'You have spoken too kindly, Mr Premier, of the modest part I was able to play in active service ... but I come among you as one who has seen with his own eyes the patriotism and staying power of your men. That experience I can never forget.'

Every morning, afternoon, and evening of his three-day visit was filled with events, and it was said that half the city's population lined the streets to greet him. Two of the major events were visits to the military hospitals, where he presented medals and awards to many of the patients.

The last day had always been planned as the climax of his visit. 'Today,' wrote the Toronto *Star*, 'the CNE is in the hands of the veterans.' More than 40,000 veterans and their wives and children packed the exhibition grandstand and field for the greatest military spectacle that had ever been staged in this city. When the prince arrived on horseback in front of the grandstand, the entire audience stood and cheered. To many, the day was a reunion. There was thunderous applause when he told the crowd: 'I want to tell you just how greatly I appreciate your coming here this afternoon in such numbers ... and I am glad to say that it is not the first time some of us have met.'

During the ceremonies that afternoon, he presented medals to some 200 of Ontario's veterans who had displayed conspicuous gallantry and courage. The only moment when the crowd became silent was during a presentation to a group of women dressed in black, who had come forward to receive the medals awarded to their sons and husbands who had been killed in the final months of war.

It was late when all ceremonies were completed but the prince insisted that no part of his proposed tour be cancelled. A royal motorcade was now to drive him through Sunnyside and High Park, then across the northern part of the city to the Danforth and Riverdale, and, finally, back to his train.

When the motorcade reached the corner of Lansdowne and St Clair Avenues a detour took place that had been ordered by the prince and caught the officials by surprise. The ceremony that followed was particularly recorded in a number of Britain's newspapers, notably *The Times.*

Many Canadians knew Toronto had sent a greater proportion of its men to serve in France than any other city in Canada. But few people, even in Toronto, were aware that one district, Earlscourt, in the northwestern corner of the city, had sent a greater proportion of its men than any other in the entire country.

On the eve of his arrival in Toronto, when the Prince of Wales was being briefed by aides, he was told he had been invited by the Earlscourt Branch of the Great War Veterans Association and the people of Earlscourt to plant a maple tree in Prospect Cemetery where many of the veterans from Earlscourt had been buried. But, he was told, his schedule did not allow time for such a visit. Then he was told of the special role that the men of Earlscourt had played in the war. He demanded that the route of his tour be changed. He would most certainly visit this cemetery and would plant the maple tree as requested.

It was 6.22 p.m. by the time the royal motorcade drove through the gates of Prospect Cemetery. Men from the Earlscourt Branch of the GWVA were lining the driveway to the veterans' plot, and it seemed as if the entire population of Earlscourt had crowded into the cemetery to witness the ceremony.

Veterans line before the Cross of Sacrifice at a
Remembrance Day service in Prospect Ceremony.

As the prince stepped from his car, Private A. Stackable, a double
amputation patient from one of the military hospitals, came forward and presented him with a membership in the GWVA, Earlscourt Branch. Then, as the crowd stood still, the prince walked to
a site, just east of where the great Cross of Sacrifice now stands,
where he was handed a silver trowel. He began filling earth around
a small silver maple tree. When it was firmly set, he stepped back
and said, 'I declare this tree well and truly planted.'

With his official role now over, he looked for a place where he could stand and see everyone. His aides protested that he was already behind schedule, and that they should leave. He told them, 'But I must speak to these people.' He noticed the small platform that had been built to hold the presentation trowel and stepping up onto it began to address the crowd.

'First I want to thank all of you for your very kind welcome,' he said. During the next few moments he spoke of his feelings 'in being allowed to honour the memory of these valiant veterans.' Afterwards he stepped from the platform and spoke to as many as possible of the people who were now crowding around him. Finally, he made his way back to his car, and that night left the city.

The Prince of Wales, later Edward VIII,
in the uniform of the Scots Fusiliers

The cemetery where this unexpected ceremony had taken place remains unknown to many Torontonians. It was founded by the trustees of the Toronto General Burying Grounds, now known as the Commemorative Services of Ontario, in 1887, when the city first began expanding into the northern and western suburbs. After war broke out in Europe in 1914, the first wounded soldiers were brought back to Toronto to the new military hospitals where many would die. The trustees set aside five acres in Prospect Cemetery as a special, honoured place for them and for all other veterans who wished to be buried there. The Veterans' Burial Plot has since become the site of more than 5,000 graves. Originally each grave was to be marked with a small white wooden cross, but that would have soon been damaged by weather. Instead every grave is marked with a stone of Canadian granite 'as imperishable as the memory of the men who died.'

It is a place to be visited not only on Remembrance Day. The main gates of Prospect Cemetery are at 1450 St Clair Avenue West. Directly through them, at the top of a slight rise in the ground, stands a large white Cross of Sacrifice, placed there by the Imperial War Graves Commission as the central memorial to all who lie buried near it.

On its base, engraved in stone, are the words, 'To the memory of those who in the Great War died for King and Country.'

Credits

I am grateful to all the following institutions for providing the illustrations for this book, often at considerable effort. Special care has been taken to acknowledge the proper ownership of all photographs and works of art used as illustrations. The author and publisher would welcome any additional information that would allow them to rectify or enhance any references in future editions.

The first number in each entry refers to the page on which the illustration appears in this book. The information in parentheses identifies the particular illustration in the collection of the appropriate library, museum, or archive.

Art Gallery of Ontario   125 (N-6708-3), 126 (C-6892-1), 169 (Arch. N-234.2), 172 (Bequest of Frank P. Wood N. 1204-1), 223, 225 (Purchase 1929, Acc. no. 1338)

Canadian National Institute for the Blind   91

Canadian Red Cross Society   241

City of Toronto Archives   99 (Gilbert A. Milne Collection 306 44-2)

Confederation Life Gallery of Canadian Art   229

Index